My Mate

Vincent Hopper

Copyright © 2024 by Vincent Hopper

All rights reserved.

No portion of this book may be reproduced in any form without written permission from the publisher or author, except as permitted by U.S. copyright law.

Contents

Chapter One

✷ Edited Version*

Avery's POV

Hello. My name is Avery Brighter, I am sixteen years of age and I'm the daughter of an Alpha. My older brother, Daniel is next in line to be alpha, he's already begun his training, and father's even let him lead a few battles, he promised to make me his second in command when he finally claims the Alpha title within the next few weeks, although I think our younger brother, Finn will be better suited to being the Second, once he's old enough anyway.

The White Crescent Moon Pack is the pack in which my family and I belong to. There are twelve other major packs across the country, typically divided into three sides – each to their own beliefs and line of power. The Royal Pack is supposed to be in charge of all, they uphold our laws, keep us at peace, and they ensure that our existence is kept hidden from the humans. They aren't doing the greatest job at the moment... The Dark Shadow Pack is most powerful pack under the Royals, and they've been causing havoc around the country, demolishing many smaller, under developed packs, they've been getting away with it because these smaller packs aren't registered as a major pack like mine or the Royals or the other main Packs. I worry though that the menacing pack may make a move on one of the main packs soon, my father isn't too concerned though. He says we're still ranked the 4thmost powerful pack out of the major thirteen.

...

I stared blankly at the crème coloured ceiling. Small lines of sunlight slyly crept through the closed blinds, and the animals outside made certain to ensure that all sleeping people aware that the sun was up and so were they. The smell of bacon and eggs waffled through the air, and I felt the internal struggle of choosing between staying in my warm, cozy bed or getting up, dressed and food.

With a long sigh of defeat, I dragged myself out of the queen sized bed and headed straight for the bathroom that joint onto my bedroom. I shared this bathroom with Daniel, because his room was on the other side and also shared a door with the bathroom. I now stood in front of my sink and mirror, I looked ahead to see a pair of ocean blue eyes staring back at me. My baggy pyjama shirt had a large imprint of the Eiffel tower on it, it hung low, way past my shorts, and it hid my hourglass figure. My chocolate brown hair was in a messy pony tail and reached the middle of my back. I didn't consider myself to be tall, but I wasn't short either.

I hastily reefed a comb through my hair, many strands fell onto the tiled floor. I glanced at the tooth brush jar, but ignored the idea of brushing my teeth before eating. I then dug through the bottom draw under the sink countertop, and I pulled out mascara, foundation and an eye shadow pallet and applied a light amount of each. Once I was happy with my appearance, I skipped out of the bathroom and proceeded to get dressed into a pair of denim ripped jeans and a plain shirt.

My bedroom was decorated with a Paris Theme, ranging from the bed sheets to the curtains to the ornaments hung around. The furniture was all crème coloured, and the walls were contradicting a vibrant purple. I chose the colour when I was thirteen, I'm not bothered by the choice, I love the colour, but most people find it too bold for their liking.

I left my bedroom, slipping on a pair of socks as I walked. I passed Daniel's room, then Finn's bedroom, and then I reached the large stairwell. My hand trailed along the smooth wooden surface of the rail as I jogged down the carpeted steps. At the base of the stairs was the front of the house. I walked through the first doorway and into the kitchen. My mother and father were already seated at the table.

Finn also sat at the table in his special chair. There was nothing different about his chair that compared to the others, it was simply just his chair. Daniel was no where in sight. "Morning." I chirped as I walked over to the kitchen bench top where the cook stood beside the cooking bacon and scrambled eggs. I grabbed the tongs and began to move a couple pieces of the sizzling bacon onto my plate.

"Oh Miss Brighter, I was going to do that for you-"

"It's okay Stacey, I don't mind." I smiled. "Thanks for cooking." I said as I also placed some of the egg on my plate. I then walked back over to the dining table in the joint room and sat down opposite Finn. My father frowned disapprovingly.

"We have staff who bring the food to us. I don't understand why you insist on doing it yourself."

I shrugged and took a bite out of my food. A few minutes of awkward silence passed before my super hearing picked up on Daniel finally walking down the stairs. He entered the room and sat down beside me. He ran a hand through his hair, his eyes jumped around, his breathing was uneven and quick, his heart rate faster. I eyed him suspiciously, what had him so flustered?

The waiter brought his food out to him and he joined in the eating. We ate in silence as usual until finally we finished. After wiping a napkin around his mouth, my father looked directly at me, "Okay. Avery, today could you help your mother out in the Nursery?" He asked. I nodded and smiled,

"Of course Father."

In this house hold, you won't ever catch us calling our parents mum or dad or anything other than Mother and Father. My father is big on respect and adequacy, mainly because of his title.

My father then turned to my older brother, "Now my boy, you will help me with some pack work today. Finally see what it is like to be Alpha." He smiled proudly at his son. Daniel nodded,

"Yes sir."

"Mother, father, what do I do today?" Finn asked chirpily, he swung his legs back and forth quickly. My mother smiled at the giddy boy,

"You, my little Finn, can go outside and play with Chester all day."

Finn's smile turned into a large, teeth baring grin. "Yes! Thank you mother!" He exclaimed excitedly. The waiter entered the room to collect and take away the empty plates. My family and I stand up and exit the room, Finn and my father walking one way, My mother and I another. I thought Daniel would have gone off with my father, however he hadn't yet left my side. He nudged my shoulder,

"Any closer to finding your mate yet?"

When a wolf turns sixteen years old, their inner wolf comes to life inside them, and they are able to shift into this wolf at any given time. Along with this inherited trait, we also receive the ability (Through our wolves)

to sense out our soul mate. I'm not exactly sure how it works, I've just been told when I'm close to my mate, my wolf will let me know.

I shook my head. "Of course not, I've been too busy with other things."

"Other things? What could be more important than finding your mate!?" He exclaimed. Daniel had not yet found his either, but he had in fact spent every free minute away from Alpha training, searching. He had been to many birthday balls around other major packs, but he hadn't had any luck.

I shrugged, "I don't know, school maybe? Besides who even needs a mate. All the boys at school have proven themselves to be trash anyway. They only flirt with a girl to get in her pants."

Daniel grabbed my hand and stopped my from walking. I looked back at him to see concern in his eyes. He shook his head, "Werewolves are different once they find their mates. Your mate will cherish you, and he won't ever do anything to hurt you! I promise you." He spoke sincerely. I grimaced doubtfully. Daniel arched an eyebrow. "Have I ever broken my promise?" He asked. I shook my head.

"No."

"Do you think I'd really lie about this then?"

"I guess not."

"Avery."

"Alright fine. I'll keep my mind open. But I'm holding you to that promise," I pointed my index finger into his chest and narrowed my eyes jokingly.

"Good." He smiled. He then gave me a side on hug, "Love you."

"Love you too big bro." I patter his back. Daniel then walked off in the opposite direction, towards our father's office. I hurried down the hallway to catch up with my mother. I made my way outside. Our house was on a fifty acre property, the Pack house was situated somewhere along one of the sides, and the Nursery house wasn't far from it. I jogged most of the way there. When I reached the single story house I entered with a large smile.

Hay crates were scattered around the walls of the large room, each one contained one wolf pup, each different colours. These were called Warrior Wolves. Werewolves still, but they were born in the form of a wolf, and remain in their wolf form until they turn two-years-old. It's a tricky concept to understand, but when they turn two, they shift into a human for the first time, and that human will be sixteen years of age.

Warrior Wolves are essential to every pack, they are the backbone in our defense and attack force in any battle. One of the Major Packs are called the Warrior Wolves Pack, this is where all Warrior Wolves originally descended from. This pack is strictly made of Warrior Wolves and they spend most of their lives in their Wolf form.

I continued to walk around the room until I reached the main desk. Behind the desk sat one of our Carers, her name was Carla. She has brought in so many of the Warrior pups and raised them mostly by her self. She loved her job.

"Ah, Miss Brighter." She looked up at me through her small, red, rectangular glasses. "I had asked your mother that you be sent here today. I'm glad you could make it." She stood up and walked around the desk and over to me.

"And why's that Carla?" I smiled.

"Because today I want you to start learning how to mother a pup." She explained. I stared at her wide-eyed.

"B-but I'm only seventeen."

"I'm aware of that," She nodded. "But your our brightest student in this pack. I believe you will do well." She then walked off down an isle before I could respond. I watched, my mouth opened and shut a few times as I wondered why she wanted me to learn how to raise a Warrior wolf 3 years before most learnt.

Carla eyed each young wolf carefully. The ones in her sight were all under a week old, most were a brown or a white and brown colour, like most of the wolves in our pack. There are many different colours and mixes of colours wolves can be, but unless you're in the Dark Shadow pack or the Pure pack, the chances of your colour being pure white or pure black are extremely slim. I got lucky with that, I'm one of two wolves in my entire pack that is a pure white wolf. My mother is the other one.

I glanced to see in the ten pups Carla was looking over, one of them was pure black. I found myself walking towards it. All the other pups were wriggling around and yapping with excitement as Carla patted them. This one black pup lay curled in a ball, his eyes were open, and eyeing me with caution. I slowly reached a hand out towards him to pat him. He growled then shuffled back into the corner of his crate. I tilted my head to the side and eyed him with curiosity.

"What's wrong with this one?" I asked. Carla glanced down at him with pity,

"I'm not sure how that one even got here. And I don't know why he is the way he is. I found him on the door step a few days ago, there wasn't a note."

I pursed my lips as I thought. I glanced at him again, a lengthy scar ran along the side of his face. She squatted down beside me and extended her hand out. She made a kissing sound, "Come on boy." She cooed. The little wolf looked at me hesitantly then he crawled over to Carla and nuzzled his head under her hand.

He was so calm and open with her. He trusted her, that was clear. And I wanted him to trust me too. I wanted him to let me pat him and hold him. I couldn't really explain why I was so drawn to him.

"Carla, do you think..."

Carla looked at me whilst she still patted him.

"I don't really know why but it's like, this wolf is the only wolf in the room to me."

Carla thought for a moment. I tried to reach my hand out to him again. This time he looked at it tentatively, before he started to sniff it. He then allowed me to pat him, but I could sense the nervous state radiating from him.

"He'll be a handful Avery. This pup needs a lot of attention and love. You can't get angry at him, or raise your voice."

I nodded, "I'm willing to put the effort in."

Carla smiled warmly, "Okay. He's yours. What do you want to name him?"

I looked back down at him happily. He licked my hand and yapped. His floppy ears perk up as I thought.

"Hmm. How does Darren sound?" I heard a small growl. "No? Okay, how about Hamish?" Another growl. "Um... Dylan?" He happily yapped and jumped on the spot. "That name's the one huh?" I grinned. I picked him up underneath his legs and hugged him. Shortly after, I signed some paper work. I would get to look after Dylan for one year before he would need to go off to the training section.

I worked at the nursery for the rest of the day with Dylan by my side. He helped me carry things like packets of food. It was a little funny watching him struggle to drag it along the floor. By the end of the day, he had full confidence in me.

"Come on Dylan," I looked down at him. He wagged his tail. "Home time." He jumped into my arms and I carried him back to my house. I walked into the kitchen to find my mother, father and Daniel sitting at the table. "Hey guys, guess who's the newest family member of the Brighters?" I chirped.

All looked over at me smiling, however my father frowned when his eyes rested on Dylan who cuddled in my arms. "Avery... Do you have any idea how rare black Warrior Wolves are?" He asked slowly. I nodded.

"It's almost impossible to ever see one in any pack except-"

"If you are a part of the Pure Pack or the Dark Shadow Pack!" He raised his voice, cutting me off. "Both enemies of our pack! And their Black wolves are known for their aggression. And this wolf here, is a rogue!"

Dylan jumped, frightened by the yelling.

"What was this infestation even doing in our nursery?" He roared.

"C-Carla found him on the door step of the Nursery a couple days ago..."

"He needs to go. Back to where he came from," he hissed.

"But we don't know where he came from. And we can't just toss him into the wild... He's only a pup-"

My father stood up, "Give him to me."

I held Dylan closer in my arms and shook my head, "No! You can't take him away! I won't let you!"

"Look at this! You're already attached to this beast. How is this?"

"I don't know father, I just know that I need to protect him."

My father was silent for a moment. It was like he was having an argument inside his head. He finally waved his hands again, "Hand him over." Using his Alpha command tone. A tone no matter how hard some Werewolves tried to fight, they could never resist obeying. I felt my inner wolf struggle.

"Please no." I whispered and shook my head, keeping my feet firmly planted, although every inch of my body was trying to push me towards him.

"Bring. Him. To. Me." He commanded through clenched teeth. I looked at my mother, my eyes begged her for help. She looked down at the floor. Coward. I thought bitterly. I then looked at Daniel, he was my only hope.

"Please Daniel, don't let him do this." I cried. Daniel glanced up at my raging father then back at me apologetically. He didn't want to risk facing the wrath or losing his Alpha title.

"Avery now!" My father's voice boomed. "I will end it quick."

My heart rate quickened. My father was going to kill him. My body had already started walking towards him, I shouted at my wolf who was controlling my body,

What are you doing!?

I'm sorry! I can't resist his command...She whimpered.

My body shook with fear and I struggled to grasp control. But before I knew it, I was handing Dylan over to my father. "I'm so sorry." I choked out in a mere whisper. Tears cascaded down my cheeks. As soon as Dylan left my hands, he and my father disappeared from sight. I could hear Dylan's howls becoming distant. I dropped to my knees, feeling grief and pain. I didn't understand why this had such a huge effect on me, but it did. It felt as though a piece of my soul had been torn out of my chest.

A felt a large, warm hand being placed gently my back. I shrugged it off roughly and forced myself to stand. I eyed Daniel with a rage forming in the pit of my stomach. Bitter hate daggered at him from my eyes.

"Brother? What a joke. A coward is what you are and all you'll ever be to me from this day forward."

I saw a swirl of emotions mix in his facial expression, hurt, guilt, regret... I had no desire to care about how he felt by my words. Dylan was gone. I got him killed. He is dead because of me, why didn't I just choose another pup instead? Or why didn't I just not show him to my family at all?

I didn't bother to shoot any glares at my mother, she wasn't worth the effort. I stormed out of the room, fuming.

...

Dylan's POV

As soon as I left Avery's arms, I felt nothing but a sheer coldness. How could she do this to me? Betray me!

I was carried out of the room, I howled out in pain. "Shut up will you?" The Alpha hissed spitefully. I obeyed and bowed my head. I didn't want to give him a reason to make my death even more painful than it had to be.

I watched as the Alpha carried me through a series of narrow hallways. We reached a door at the end. Behind it was a set of stairs that led below ground. I held my breath as he carried me down them. After several minutes over going down the stairs, I squeezed my eyes shut, the suspense was killing me!

I felt myself being thrown onto the cold, hard ground. I looked up and around. Why was I in the dungeons? I eyed the Alpha with puzzlement. "Look here, uh whatever your name is..." He spoke hesitantly. Dylan. My name is Dylan.I thought my reply, knowing he wouldn't be able to hear it. He continued to speak, "My daughter Avery doesn't want you to die. I saw how attached she is to you... It's been less than a day. The connection seemed impossible to me... But I know there is a reason for it, something I'll have to look into. But for whatever the reason is, I have this feeling that if I kill you, something bad will happen to my daughter. So I will keep you alive, for now. But locked up, so you can't harm anyone."

He then locked the bar door and walked back the way he had came from. I whimpered quietly and backed myself up into a corner. I kept myself on high alert at all times that night. And eventually after what seemed like hours, I felt the need of sleep creeping it's way through me, and finally I allowed the darkness to take me.

Chapter Two

✱ Edited Version*

Avery's POV

Two Years Later...

It has been exactly two years and one week since my brother had claimed the Alpha title. Two years I have hated him. Two years I have screamed at my parents relentlessly, two years I've also ignored them. And two years I have kept myself locked up in my room. I didn't even go to the ceremony in which Daniel was titled Alpha.

The only person I actually talk to, is Finn. Ever since Dylan died, I had felt this emptiness, or more a burning rage. I have mourned him way too long, I know. I was devastated when he left my arms, and have felt a burden of guilt ever since.

If I had maybe fought for him harder, or not have even shown him to my parents, Dylan would have survived. He would still be here today. I hate myself for letting my father take him away. If Dylan were still alive, he would have been a human by now, but no. He never got to experience that, and he never will. He'll never get the chance to prove that he could have been a kind, decent Werewolf, not the monster my father portrayed him as before he even knew him.

I sighed and flopped backwards onto my bed. Today was going to be stressful.

Over the past two years, the Dark Shadow pack had continued on their vindictive spiral and hunt for power. Their alpha, Jayden Jedson, had murdered 18 Alphas from smaller, mostly unknown and underdeveloped packs. One could only imagine how much power and skill had been added to his from that. The Royal Pack still hadn't done a thing about it, my guess was because they have been allies for decades.

Anyway, it was today that the Dark Shadow pack wanted Daniel to sign a contract, giving his oath that our pack will form an allegiance to them. It wasn't a two way street though. If that pack were to be challenged by another pack, our pack would have to support them and fight with them, risking our lives. However if the role were reversed and we were the ones under attack, the Dark Shadow Pack wouldn't offer their support in return.

My brother wasn't happy about it. He didn't want to be signing our pack up for any more trouble. We were comfortably at peace with most packs, and the packs we didn't agree with, we had treaties with. But it appeared as though our battle free period was at its end, because if my brother signed this contract, we would be entering a number of battles, and if my brother refused to sign this agreement, we would be in for a big battle, one with lots of casualties on our behalf and one we might not walk away from.

My brother has hope that they won't attack and wipe us out for refusing, but it's obviously they will. The White Dawn pack declined their offer previously and the Dark Shadow Pack destroyed them, from what I heard anyway. That pack had about the same amount of strength as our pack, and the Dark Shadow pack has only grown stronger since. So the stress was really on my brother's shoulders at the moment.

"Avery!" I heard my eleven-year-old brother call. He was outside my closed bedroom door.

"Yes Finn? You can come in if you'd like."

The door opened and the first thing I saw was Finn's shiny, warm brown hair. I still think his fringe could use a bit of a trim. I mean, it isn't that long, but long enough to reach his eyebrows. Finn Just stood there in the doorway, not moving. I looked at him with perplexity.

"A-Alpha wants you in his office... Like right now." He said, his voice wobbled.

"No. I won't go there. I don't wish to see Daniel right now." I crossed my arms and scowled at the thought. How rude, Daniel had to resort to sending Finn to fetch me.

"I was afraid you'd say that..." He mumbled and dragged his feet away, leaving my door wide open. Would you at least close the freaking door?I agitatedly asked in my head. I sighed and got up off my bed and walked over to the door, only to collide into Daniel as he stormed into my bedroom.

"Daniel, my man. What's up?" I feigned a cheerful tone. Daniel glowered,

"My office. Now." He growled, using his Alpha command. That stupid, damned Alpha command. He then stormed back out of my room.

"Sour puss." I muttered under my breath. No wonder he hasn't found his mate yet. She's probably been running in the opposite direction, away from his foul short temper and hideous odour.

"I can read your thoughts Avery." He called out in a pointed tone. I rolled my eyes and reluctantly followed him to his office. I leant against the door frame, arms crossed over my chest, and I eyed him, irritated. He sat down behind his desk in the spinning chair and placed his hands on the desk with his fingers entwined. He then looked up at me, "Close the door please, and take a seat."

I rolled my eyes and did as told. With a frown, I sat down in the chair in front of his desk and I crossed my arms over my chest again. "What do you want?" I snapped. Even though we had gone through two years of this, whenever I was rude to Daniel, whenever I pushed him away, I could always spot the hurt and regret in his eyes. He shook his head and looked at me before sliding the contract across the table, towards me.

"Read." He spoke the single word and watched me as I picked it up to read through it. It said exactly as I thought it would. We'd basically become their minions whenever they need us.

"Well?" I asked, looking up at him with questioning eyes. I placed the contract back down in the middle of the desk and began to fidget with my fingers.

"Well – should I sign it? Or decline? I mean, if we signed this, we would be fighting up to three battles a week because of how many Werewolves, packs and rogues challenge them now and vice versa. I think I would be putting my pack in more danger agreeing to this contract." He spoke his mind. I shrugged,

"Why don't you just ask dad? You seemed to follow his every order and advise before you became Alpha." I countered.

Daniel's eyebrows furrowed. "I'm asking you. You were the one I wanted to make second before everything between us went to crap."

I didn't have the energy to start up an argument, so I sighed instead. "Do whatever you think is best for this pack. Youare the Alpha. Youmake the decisions. Whatever choice you make, I'm sure you'll make the right one." I answered, then stood up and I walked to the door.

"Avery?" He stopped me in my tracks. I turned my head over my shoulder to look back at him in question. "Thanks." He gave me a small smile. I nodded once then walked out.

Hours later, my stomach began to grumble. It was 7:30, also known as Dinner time in this house. I sat cross legged on my bed, and a couple minutes later Finn knocked on my wooden door. I jumped up and opened it and he walked in carrying his tray and a tray of food for me. I shut the door behind him and walked back over to my bed. "Yum. Chicken!" I beamed. Finn nodded with a grin and he sat down opposite me.

"So... What did the mighty Alpha choose?" I asked with the roll of my eye.

"To decline." Finn shrugged and took a bite out of his chicken leg. I nodded. Smart but dumb. It really was a lose, lose situation. Because now, "They're going to come after us." I accidently whispered then slapped a hand over my mouth. I didn't want Finn to get involved with this or stress about the situation. He was only a kid. But alas he had heard me, for his head shot up and his bright blue eyes locked with mine.

"What?" He asked, bewildered.

"Uh... Nothing." I answered quickly. He looked at me with suspicion. I sighed,

"Fine. But you asked for it. When the Dark Shadow pack gave the same contract to the White Dawn Pack, they declined also. The Dark Shadow pack was outraged and called war on them. The White Dawn pack lost. Now the Dark Shadow pack is going to challenge us to a battle, one that we probably aren't prepared for. I'd say they'll receive the declined contract back in a couple days, get they're act together then march right over to us.

We have no more than a week to prepare for a battle we are most likely going to lose." I ranted at a fast pace.

Finn stared at me wide-eyed before springing off the bed and sprinting out of the bedroom. I stared at the now empty doorway. "Oops." I shrugged and shoved the rest of the chicken into my mouth before hopping up to follow my little brother. I heard him crying down stairs in the lounge room.

I walked in to see Finn sitting on my mother's lap, his arms clung to her as he cried hysterically. I looked from Daniel to my father. They both looked at me angrily. Daniel stood up and walked over to me. He roughly grabbed my wrist, "Why did you tell him everything?" He growled. I winced,

"Ouch, Daniel. You're hurting me." I tried to pry his hand off my wrist but his grip only tightened. Panic flooded through me, I had never seen him this mad at me before, not even when I lost his football he had signed by some famous player back when he was ten. "I don't know why I told him! A couple words just slipped out of my mouth and he harassed me to tell him what they meant so I told him." My voice trembled. "He deserves to know!" I still struggled against his bone crushing grip.

"No! He doesn't need to know! Look at him! How scared he is!" Daniel shouted.

"Daniel! He's not a baby anymore! He's eleven for Christ's sake!" I yelled. Daniel's face goes red with fury. I hear a crack, fear coursed through me as pain surged through my arm. A look of realization flashed across Daniel's face and he immediately let go of my Wrist. I snatch it back and cradle it close by my chest. The pain... It hurt bad. I knew in a couple hours it would be fully healed due to Werewolves abilities, but it still hurt just as intensely. Tears escaped me.

"A-Avery," he went to check my wrist. I stepped away from him quickly,

"Don't!" I snapped.

"I'm sorry," he quickly apologised, his voice desperate and guilty. I shook my head,

"I hate you!" I screamed. My parents stared between us, shocked. My mother opened her mouth to say something, but she closed it again before she could. I growled loudly, my eyes slowly folded over to black. I quickly ran out of the room before I could shift in front of them and caused some real havoc.

When I reached my bedroom, I slammed the door shut then I sat down on the bed, looking at my swollen and dislodged wrist. I inhaled deeply and closed my eyes before snapping it back into place. I could already feel it starting to heal.

Minutes later, I heard a knock at my door. "Go away!" My voice cracked.

"Sissy?" Finn called hesitantly. I sighed,

"Come in Finn." Finn walked in with red and puffy eyes. He then dives into my arms and hugs me tightly. "Shh. It's alright," I cooed in his ear. I then pulled back the blanket covers and Finn crawled into bed. I too crawled in. Finn snuggled up to me and I hugged him for a while before eventually I rolled onto my side with my back facing him and I fell asleep.

...

The next few days I kept to myself, locked away in my room. Finn came in three times a day to bring me food. What a sweetheart that brother of mine is. Thankfully, Daniel hadn't tried to talk to me. Chances are I would have punched him is he had.

Presently, Fin and I were eating dinner. I took one last bite and placed my knife and fork down on the plate with a small clank. Finn looked up at me,

"Daniel said the Dark Shadow pack is attacking tomorrow." He whispered and looked down again. Well damn. That was quicker than I thought. Sensing Finn's distress, I pulled him in for a hug.

"It will be alright Finn. We'll be okay. I promise." I moved my hand up to the back of his head and held him close. This meant I would have to finally come out of my room. And I did, later that night. Daniel called everyone in for a pack meeting. I held Finn's hand in mine as we stood in the large seminar room with sixty Werewolves standing around. These were just the adults that would be fighting in the battle tomorrow, a few females and children would sit the battle out, and we had another hundred and forty Warrior Wolves that would join us and be briefed tomorrow.

Daniel's Beta (Second in Command), Mark, stood by Daniel's side. Brandon, the Third in Command, stood on Daniel's other side. My mother and father stood not far from them. Finn and I blended in with the crowd.

Once everyone had arrived, Daniel cleared his voice. He spoke loudly and clearly. "Alright. As you all know, the Dark Shadow Pack is planning an attack on us tomorrow! They will arrive around seven pm, right at the start of Dusk. By five thirty, we need all the sick, our doctors, all the woman that aren't participating and the children hidden in the dungeons. I will place ten Warrior Wolves on guard down there with them." He lectured.

I glanced down at Finn to see his skin starting to turn pale. I squeezed his hand and smiled at him reassuringly. It calmed him a little bit, but not by much. Daniel coughed and ran a hand through his hair before he continued.

"I will also place an additional 10 Warrior Wolves on guard on the outside of the house. The rest will be on the battle field. Brandon, Mark and myself will be looking out for the Dark Shadow pack's Alpha, Jayden Jedson." There were nods and 'Yes Alpha's.

Daniel went into detail about the battle strategies. I didn't have to ay too much attention as Daniel was forcing me to sit out. I wasn't too thrilled about it, as I have had many years of training and experience in combat and I knew how to look out for myself.

An hour passed and the meeting concluded. We left the pack house and walked back to our house. I walked by Finn's side up the stairs. Finn yawned loudly, and I looked down at him whilst arching a brow, "Tired, huh?"

He nodded and his eyes started to droop. I smiled and scooped him up in my arms. Finn was far shorter than the average eleven-year-old, and it helped having the additional strength from my Werewolf side. Finn put his arms around my neck loosely, and rested his cheek on my shoulder. His eyes were now closed and he was sound asleep. I walked into his room and over to his race-car bed, then I tucked him into bed. He looked so peaceful when he slept.

I kissed his forehead, "Love you Finn." I whispered then I exited his room. I made my way to my bedroom, and bounded straight into bed. It took a while to get to sleep, as I was continuously tossing and turning in bed, stressing about tomorrow. I woke up a couple times through out the night from night terrors, but eventually fell and stayed asleep until dawn.

Chapter Three

Avery's POV

The next day passed slowly. The suspension bit at me the entire day, hassling me to snap and have a mental break down. The Dark Shadow Pack was going to attack tonight. We needed to be prepared. We needed to be ready for anything. Hopefully it wouldn't come to our demise, but I fretted it might. Daniel had set the house and property well with many traps, and I had packed multiple bags full with water bottles and food to last us a couple days. A few pack members had carried bedding down into the dungeons. Now all that was left to be carried were the bags of supplies, which I had offered to carry.

It was now nearing on five pm. I glanced at Finn who was packing his own bag of stuffed toys. I nodded at him then at the bags, "Come on Finn, help me carry these to the dungeons." He nodded and grabbed two heavy bags. I carried two also. We walked down the hallway and stopped at the open doorway atop of the stairs. I glanced down them hesitantly. I had never been in the dungeons before. Daniel used to tell me scary stories as we grew up, to keep me from ever wanting to go in there. He'd tell me they were haunted from the prisoners who died down there. But my father told me he hadn't locked anyone down there in over ten years.

"Stay close to me, okay?" I told Finn. He nodded. He wasn't afraid of the dungeons though. We then proceeded to walk down the stairs and when we reached the bottom, I saw nothing but multiple, empty cells. I found the light switch and flicked it on. A couple hanging light bulbs dimly light up and glowed faintly in each cell. Finn and I walked slowly up past the first few cells, the floors were made from a rugged cement, and cobwebs hung around in every corner and they were woven between multiple rusty bars. "Let's put one bag in each cell." I told Finn. He nodded.

"H-h-hello?" I heard a faint, frail voice call out. I froze. Could I be a ghost?

"Who's there?" I called out, my eyes narrowed.

"Please help me," his weak voice pleaded. I turned to look down at Finn,

"Stay here." I whispered, he nodded and I put the bags down on the ground. I then began to walk forward, and came to a halt outside the only locked cell. I felt a strong connection pulling me towards it, it was a feeling I couldn't quite describe. It was dark inside this cell, the light bulb had obviously been blown out. "Hello?" I spoke. I heard a rustle. "Finn, could you please bring me a torch?" Finn nodded and ran back up the stairs.

"What is your name? A croaking male voice asked. I couldn't see him, for he hid in the back corner against the cobblestone walls.

"Avery Brighter. The Alpha is my brother, if you even try to threaten Finn or I to release you, there will be severe consequences." I warned.

"N-no, I would never hurt you. I've been locked down here my entire life Miss." He coughed. I heard Finn's small feet come running back down the stairs, and in a few seconds he stood beside me, baring the torch I had asked him to fetch. I took the torch from him and clicked it on. A bright light shone from it and I aimed it into the cell, in the direction of the young man's voice.

A small wooden bench sat along the back wall with a thin, worn-out mattress placed on top of it. In the far left corner, I saw a teenaged boy, curled up on the floor wearing just a pair of ripped shorts. His raven black hair was scraggy and unevenly cut at a short length. His wrists were bound by chains that had been drilled into the walls with a one metre allowance.

"Who are you?" I asked. He looked up at me, he was a poor, malnourished sight to see. So scrawny and pale. When was the last time he ate or saw the sun?

"I-I..." He coughed again. I turned to Finn again,

"Can you please go get me a sandwich and a water bottle?" I asked him. He nodded and rushed off to get them. I pulled out the set of keys I received from Daniel earlier, and I went to unlock the cell door.

"What are you doing?" The boy asked and looked at me and the cell door with concern. Finn rushed over to me and I took the food and water from his hands. "Why don't you go bring the rest of the bags down here?" I suggested to him. He nodded and fled back and up the stairs. I then turned back to face the cell and I walked in cautiously, the food and water in one hand, and the torch in the other. The boy sat up quickly, I looked at him with pity, there were far too many ribs showing.

I noticed him shivering also, but not from fear. He was cold. Which is extremely unusual for Werewolves, as our body temperature is naturally a lot higher than humans. "Finn! Can you also bring me a blanket please?" I called out.

"Yes Avery!"

I squatted down about a metre away from the unfamiliar boy. He looked at me with uncertainty, and he watched my every move. I held out the sandwich and water to him with a small smile. He looked at it then back at me.

"Why?" He asked quietly, confused by my kindness.

"Because you look like you haven't eaten in days." I almost chuckled, but didn't because of how serious the situation was. He stretched out his skinny, shaky arm and I gave him the sandwich. He slowly unwrapped the plastic wrap around it with difficulty, and then he took a bite out of it. He moaned as he stuffed the rest into his mouth quickly, afraid of it being taken away from him. I watched him, baffled. He looked back at me sheepishly.

"Uh s-sorry. I haven't eaten in over four days, and I was just... Famished." He looked down, his cheeks turned slightly pink. I then passed him the water bottle with a smile,

"Bet you haven't drank anything either," I stated with a half-hearted chuckle. He hesitantly took the water bottle from my hand and he took off the lid. Finn walked in seconds later with a folded blanket in his arms. I stood up and took the blanket from him, "Thanks." I smiled at him, he then walked back out to keep placing the bags in the different cells.

I walked back over to the boy sitting on the hard ground. He looked no older than sixteen years of age. I unfolded the blanket and bent down to wrap it around him. The boy had almost skulled the entire water bottle.

Why did I trust this boy so much already? Why did I just know that he wouldn't hurt me? He's probably so angry and ready for vengeance, after being locked down here for so long. What could he have possibly done wrong at such a young age?

He placed the water bottle down on the ground next to him and looked up at me with a small smile of gratitude. I can already see the colour starting to come back to his face and skin, and he already started to look less scrawny than he was before. "Thank you." He says in a more firmer, healthier tone. He didn't sound anywhere near as weak either.

I now sat cross legged on the ground, facing the boy. "So. Tell me. Why are you locked down here?"

"I don't know really, truth be told. I was locked down here when I was only a few weeks old. As a baby, I guess. They said it was for my safety and for theirs, that I remain down here alone, for the rest of my life."

My eyes widened. "You've been locked down here for fifteen, sixteen or so years?" I exclaimed. He looked at me with furrowed eyebrows.

"No... Two."

"You're a Warrior Wolf." I whispered as realisation dawned on me. He nodded. "How long ago did you first shift?" I asked.

He shrugged, "A couple weeks ago maybe?" Realisation hits me again, hard, as I put two and two together. I shook my head. That couldn't be right. No. This can't be. It's not.

"What's your name?" I forced myself to ask.

"Dylan."

I jumped to my feet. "No. This is impossible."

"No where near, sweetheart."

That tone. It was familiarisation. "You remember me?" I asked quietly and he nodded.

"Quite hard to forget a scent like yours." He answered. He watched me with a questioning gaze as I walked out of the cell. I entered a couple other cells and brought back four sandwiches and four water bottles to Dylan's cell. I placed the supplies down in front of him.

"I thought my father killed you." I murmured, confounded. I handed him another sandwich and he took it with a grateful smile.

"Thanks. And he didn't. He took me straight here. He said something about how you had this 'connection' or this 'bond' with me. Not a mate bond no... But like... I don't know, some sort of protection thing."

"Oh." I responded, trying to process all my thoughts and the new information. I was still dumbfounded by the fact that Dylan was still alive.

"Did they treat you okay down here? I mean, besides the starvation?" I asked quietly, praying that he hadn't been physically abused.

"Yeah they treated me fine I guess. No one really spoke to me or anything. Your father gave me these technology devices that talk me how to read and speak. They only started to starve me once I shifted into my human form for the first time, it was because they didn't want me to turn back into my wolf form."

I nodded and looked down at the ground, feeling a mass of guilt wave over me.

"What's wrong?" He asked. I heard his chains rustle and in a few seconds he was sitting right in front of me, he placed his hand on mine, and instantly I felt calmer. I didn't have a clue as to why he had this effect on me, there was just this aura he had. It made me feel as though I could trust and confide in him. I knew it wasn't a mate bond, but it felt like some kind of bond that could be just as strong.

"I feel so ashamed. I failed to protect you. I let my father do this." I admitted.

"No, no you didn't fail me. Your father used the Alpha command, there wasn't anything you could do. And he was only just doing what he thought was best for all of us." He spoke in a soothing tone. I nodded and sniffed, trying desperately to contain the tears that burned in the back of my eyes.

"I'm so sorry this happened to you Dylan." I whispered.

"It's okay. Really, it's okay. It wasn't your fault." He reassured me. I nodded again.

"Sissy, I got all of the bags and put them all in the cells!" Finn called out to me. "We need to start getting everyone down here and sorted into the cells now."

I nodded and looked back at Dylan and the chains that bound his wrists. I went flicking through the set of keys and took off the one that was for the chains. I placed it on the ground in front of him. Dylan looked at me surprised. I only smiled then hopped up and walked out of the cell. "Hold onto the sandwiches and water bottles. You might need them for later." I told him as I walked out. I glanced back to see he hand unlocked his chains and was now sitting on his bench/bed. His body had already started to fill itself out properly. "If you keep eating right for the next couple days, you'll be all good."

"Thank you Avery."

I nodded and walked away. All twenty other cells had been packed and set up, ready to be occupied. Dylan's cell was at the very back of the room, on the right hand side.

I looked down at Finn's watch. The time was twenty-five past five. "Dylan keep that door shut and the food hidden. I don't want father to know

I've helped you, he might make things worse for you." I called to him. He nodded.

I then heard the door from the top of the stairs open, I stood by Finn at the bottom of the stairs whilst Daniel leads people in. Daniel looked at me, I couldn't detect a single emotion on his face, but I knew he was just masking them. He was scared. Really scared.

Five pack doctors, and several mothers and their children had entered the large room and I set them up with seven in each cell, aside from Dylan's cell.

"Why does that cell have a prisoner in it?" A concerned mother asked. I glanced at Daniel, and he looked at me with a questioning gaze.

"It would appear that our father never killed said Warrior Wolf two years ago like he said he did." I told him. A look of shock crossed Daniel's face,

"W-what?" He choked out.

"He's alive." I smiled. "Dylan's alive."

"Dylan? Who's that?" My mother cut into the conversation. I scowled at her,

"Like you care." I muttered bitterly. I then turned back to face Daniel, he's still shocked and confused, he also looks relieved. I couldn't help myself. I hugged him. At first he was taken aback, because I hadn't hugged him in over two years. But after a few seconds, he wrapped his arms around me and rested his chin on the top of my head, sighing contently.

"I'm so sorry I never stood up to our father that day. I should have." His voice cracked.

Dylan wasn't dead, so my anger towards Daniel had disappeared. A part of me would probably still never trust him again, but I didn't want to be angry at him anymore. Especially if – God forbid – he might die in battle tonight. "I forgive you." I whispered. "I love you Daniel." The words finally left my lips after two years.

"I love you too little Sister." He then pulled back to look down at me, "I promise to come here right after the battle finishes."

"You seem confident." I stated. He smirked and straightened his posture.

"Of course I am. I have to be. If break down, if I even lack the confidence, so does the rest of the pack. There's nothing worse than a leader scared and doubtful of the battle he is leading his troops into."

"Come on Avery, it's time to go into the cell." My mother called from the very back of the room. I looked from her then back to Daniel, I smiled delighted.

"I'm proud of you Daniel. I'm sorry I said you weren't my brother. You are." I speak in a strong tone, I wanted to break down, I was scared this would be the last time I would see him. But I had to be strong for him. "I'll see you later."

"Thanks Avery." He then saluted me in a joking manner and he winked, "So long soldier." He then turned and walked back up the stairs.

"Be safe." I whispered, staring at his back that disappeared out the doorway at the top of the stairs.

"Come on Miss Brighter," one of the Warrior Wolves escorted me into the cell my mother, Finn, a pack doctor and two children were in. This cell is at the very back, right next to Dylan's cell. The guard looked the cell door after I entered, I was the only one in the room who had a set of keys that would unlock the cell doors once the war ended.

Minutes passed slowly, and every second I spent worrying about Daniel and the rest of the pack. I still held negative and resentful thoughts for my father, it was sad, but I didn't care at this moment if he made it out alive or not. He had never been much of a father to me, and after what he did to Dylan? I just didn't care what happened to him.

I had my wolf hearing tuned up to the max, ready to listen to the entire battle.

"Avery, everything will be okay," I heard Dylan whisper.

"Thanks." I whispered back, not caring that the others could hear the conversation. I looked down at Finn and used our mink link to talk to him,

Finn, you can't tell anyone about Dylan, okay? Not even Mum.

Alright Avery. I won't.He mind linked back.

More minutes ticked by at a agonisingly slow rate. I paced back and forth, a nervous wreck I was internally, but I had to put up a strong front for everyone else. An hour passed, of me pacing, sitting down then standing back up then sitting down again. Most other people down here were seated on the mattresses on the ground. The suspension was too much for me to be sitting still. I paced around the edge of the cell again until finally I heard it.

"ATTACK!" The voice of my brother Daniel, echoed through my ears.

...

Wow, listening to everything going on above the ground, is bloody exhausting! Wolves were snarling menacingly, growling ferociously, whimpering and yelping in pain. It didn't give me too much of an indication with what was really going on. It just wasn't enough. I didn't want to risk distracting Daniel by using the Mind Link to ask him what was going on.

Approximately thirty minutes into the battle, I heard the Warrior Wolves protecting the house above, starting to be attacked. That meant they had made their way past Daniel and the front line. I grimaced, then flinched when I heard one of their necks being snapped. They were already losing! Finn had tuned his hearing in too, and he instantly grew panicked. He jumped to his feet and raced to my side. I hugged him tightly as the minutes surprisingly started to tick by faster and faster.

My body starts to tremble with fear. Half of the Warrior Wolves guarding the house were dead, and two from what I could tell, were severely injured. They had only managed to take down two of the attackers. I sensed a strong aura of power, and I went rigid. He's near. The Alpha of the Dark Shadow pack was getting close.

I ran to the door of the cell and began to unlock it. The guards looked at me as thought I had grown a second head. "Miss, what are you thinking!?" He slammed the door shut again the moment I pushed it open.

"You have to let us out!" I yelled with panic. "The Dark Shadow pack has almost killed all of the Warrior Wolves protecting us from the outside. Once they die, the Dark Shadow pack will have access to coming in here, and then we all die! We won't have a chance at running!" I cried. The other Werewolves nodded, agreeing.

"She's right! We're trapped and defenseless down here!" A middle aged woman yelled.

"I'm sorry miss, but Alpha's orders-"

"Screw Alpha's orders! Let us out!" I yelled and went to force the cell door open. I froze in my tracks. The last Warrior Wolf outside the pack house died. The rest of our Pack's Warrior wolves for kilometers away, fighting off the other attackers. The doors bursted open. "They're inside." I spoke quietly and backed away from the cell door, holding Finn closer to my side. The other people gasped and children started to cry.

"Protect the children!" A mother cried. Screw it, I'm contacting my brother. I just hope he is within range to receive it.

Daniel! Daniel please! It's urgent!

Avery? What's wrong? Are you okay? What happened? He replied worriedly.

They've killed the Warrior Wolves outside the Pack house. There's now only the ten inside, we don't stand a chance... And the Alpha is here. I can sense him.

I'm on my way. He then disconnected from the mind link. I heard the door at the top of the stairs being smashed down, and several black wolves came bounding down the stairs.

"Dylan, stay hidden okay?" I whispered. I knew if he stayed back he would be hidden by the shadows in his cell.

"Okay." I heard him reply. He was too weak to fight anyway, and he knew it. Hopefully the invading Wolves would just assume that the cell was empty. Our Warrior Wolves down here shift into their wolf forms, and I see flashes of wolves running a muck and fighting one another, clawing, biting and blood. Lots of blood.

Mothers shielded their children's eyes and they shrieked, terrified by the sight. And minutes later, all ten of our Warrior Wolves were down and back in their human forms, covered in blood. Yup, that's the end of us. We're goners.

I stood in front of Finn defensively as the enemies shifted back into their human forms. There is about twenty of them down here, but I am catching scents of more from upstairs. One of the Werewolves step forward, power radiating from him. His hair is jet black and short, he's broad and well built, very muscly with a nice toned set of abs and V-line. Oh my God, am I really checking him out? No... Don't Avery, eyes up front, his monstrous face is higher. He is not eye candy for you to look at!

My inner wolf started to get antsy and I could hear her thoughts growing louder in my head, she started howling and I slammed my hands over my ears as an instant reaction, though it did nothing to drown the sound out.

What is it Daisy!?I yelled at her. I then looked back at the Alpha of the Dark Shadow pack to see him sniffing the air and his eyes turning black.

"Mate." He growls, looking straight at me.

"Oh crap." I muttered as he stepped closer to the door of the cell. Finn clenched onto my hand tightly, he was terrified and confused.

Let him in! I must go to him!Daisy barked at me. I frowned,

Are you insane? He's torn apart our pack! He's killed so many people. He's a monster!I snapped back at her.

He has good reasons for it, I'm sure.She huffed in defense.

"Unlock the door." The Alpha growled. I shook my head. His eyes were lustful and demanding.

"Never."

"Open. The. Door!" His voice roared. I glanced back at Finn and my mother and the two children hiding behind her. I looked back at the Alpha, he appeared hurt that I didn't want to obey, that I'd rather hide behind the barred cell.

"I won't let you hurt my family." I hissed.

"I promise I won't let any harm come to them," he said, he glanced down at Finn who hid behind me, then over at my mother and the two children that hid behind her and also at the pack doctor, he of course didn't realise the pack doctor and the two extra children weren't related to me. "Now please, open the door."

I wanted to reject him as my mate. How could fate be so cruel to me? How could I be mated to this vicious monster?

My hand trembled as it found its way into my pocket and pulling out a set of keys. I didn't want to give in to his command. I didn't want to go anywhere near him. But if it meant saving Finn's life, I was all for it. My mother gasped with horror as she watched me step away from Finn and unlock the cell door. Once it unlocked, the Alpha forcefully swung the door open and went to wrap his arms around me. I jumped back, startled. Hurt flashed through his eyes, but he quickly masked it.

He grabbed my arm and tugged me out of the cell, then he shut it and locked it. He then tossed the set of keys to another dark haired male. "Kill everyone in here except the people in that cell." He points at the cell my family hid in. I feel a burning rage simmer in the pit of my stomach and adrenalin coursed through my veins.

"No!" I shouted. My mate looked at me startled, then he glared.

"Yes. They have to die. Sorry love."

I clenched my fists and throw a hard punch at his stomach, feeling nothing but pure muscle. I looked up at him, he didn't even blink. How didn't that even cause a flinch?? I punch again, and again until he caught both my fists. "They're just children! You monster! You monster! How could you murder children?" I screamed.

My mate spun me around so my back was in his chest. I kicked and struggled against him as he attempted to hug me. The crazy asshole. "Shh, you're okay love." He cooed in my ear.

"Don't kill them." I sobbed. "Please." So many of the people in here I held close to my heart. I've been tutoring Little Jimmy for three years, Bethany and Caitlyn of my cousins, their mother is my aunt. Stacy our family cook, and Carla!

"Sorry love, but I have to. I can't have this pack reforming and plotting any revenge strategies. I have to tie up loose ends."

"Stop calling me love!" I yelled. The Alpha sighed then hoisted me up and over his shoulder. I screamed and pounded my fists on his back. "Put me down! Put me down!" I wept and began to choke on my tears as he walked us up the stairs. I heard a series of screams, and I struggled even more. The adrenalin was running over drive, my heart pounded in my throat and my head was spinning like crazy. I could feel myself starting to lose consciousness. No, no, no. Don't pass out. Don't-

I couldn't fight the urge any longer.

Chapter Four

✱ Edited Version*

Avery's POV

Darkness still invaded my vision. My head throbbed. Had I had a late night with alcohol?

I snuggled further under the blankets, cuddling to one of the pillows. Wait, my bed feels so much more comfortable than usual. I rolled onto my back and stretched out. I yawned and opened my eyes, instantly frightened. The roof was a dark brown and the walls a blood red colour. Drapes hung from the bed frame, and the carpeted floor was a dark colour also.

I shot up, now sitting and rubbing my sore head. Faint screams rang through my head, like a memory. And then tears brimmed my eyes. I looked around the huge room again. It was twice the size of my own. There was a painting of a forest on the wall, a set of dark wooden draws and a mirror along the same wall. A large walk in closet was to my left and further along the wall was a door that led into a large bathroom. The door was open so I could see through it, the bath tub looked more like a spa and the there was a shower too, with multiple heads. To my right was a set of double glass doors that led onto a balcony. Who's room was this?

I groaned as I kicked the heavy blankets off, I then swung my legs over the side of the bed and stood up. On the end of the bed, I could see a pile of clothes, old shirts and pants and undergarments. Everything was neat and orderly. I changed into the clean clothes then I walked over to the glass double doors. I opened them and stepped onto the dark stone tiled floor. I walked over to the rail along the edge and looked over, at the view of this mansion's backyard. There was a large pool, hundreds of square metres of luscious green lawns, flower garden beds, and at the back was a forest.

"Where the hell am I?" I asked with bewilderment and amazement from the view.

"At the Dark Shadow Pack house." A husky voice replied. I spun around to see the Alpha standing in the doorway of the balcony, his arms crossed over his chest and side leant into the doorframe. His white shirt clung to his body, showing off his build, and his denim shorts cut off at the knees.

I frowned, "The Alpha." I said with the roll of my eyes. "Of course."

"The Alpha." He repeated, shaking his head. "Don't you know my name?"

I nodded, my frown deepened. "Jayden Jedson." I answered.

"Correct. And, you are...?"

Great. He didn't even know who I was. "Avery." I muttered.

"Avery." His voice echoed and he smiled. "I like that. What's your last name, Avery?"

I gave him a clearly fake smile, "Brighter." I answered then walked past him, roughly bumping his shoulder as I went.

"Shit." I heard him whisper. I sat down, cross legged on the bed, and I stared blankly at the wall. Minutes later, he stood behind me, "I'm sorry I had to kill your pack." Silence followed his apology. I could tell there was some sincerity to it, but I knew he still wouldn't change the fact that he had to kill them. My inner wolf snarled at me for being so bitter and resentful towards our mate. She wanted to be in his arms, for Christ's sake, she already wanted to claim his mark and complete the mating process.

I heard him sigh again. "I should have known who you were. The courage that radiates from you, definitely comes from the Alpha line." He chuckled humorlessly. "Please stop ignoring me."

I felt my throat tighten and a sharp pain in my chest, but I refused to cry. "Is my brother dead?" I turned my head over my shoulder and looked up at him, "Is the Alpha of the White Crescent pack.. dead?"

He grimaced, "I'm not actually sure."

I frowned, "How can you not be?"

"Well I was sort of pre occupied to follow up on that. I know several of your pack members ran off, but I'm not sure if Daniel was one of them." He explained. I started to laugh. Yes. I laughed. The Alpha looked at me perplexed. My laughing continued until it slowly turned into sobs and then tears began to roll down my cheeks. The Alpha's facial expression turned to sorrow and pity and even a little guilt. He stepped forward and crawled onto the bed, then attempted to wrap his arms around me. I shoved his chest hard with both hands,

"Get away from me!" I screamed at him. The Alpha jumped back, startled. He scratched the back of his neck, not sure how to react. My thoughts drifted over to Dylan, how I would give anything to hear his comforting tone again, or to be in the arms of my big brother. "Why do you hate me?" The Alpha asked quietly. "Why won't you let me comfort you?"

"You're joking right?" I scoffed and wiped my tears away with haste. "You destroyed my home, and you murderedseveral members of my pack. And to top it off, you kidnapped me."

Now he was silent. He scratched the back of his neck whilst scrambling for any words. He then walked out of the room without another word. Thank God. I was surprised to see him walk back into the room moments later. He held a small phone out to me. "If this will help at all... Call your family."

I eyed him with suspicion. He spoke again, "I wouldn't ask them to come get you though if I were you." He threatened. I scowled. What was with this douchebag? He brought me the phone hoping a phone call to my family would comfort me, but then he threatens me? He has a funny way of making his matefeel loved and secure...

I took the phone regardless and dialed the home phone number of my family, praying they would answer. It rang seven times, and the hope began to fade, until someone answered it on the other end.

"Hello?" Finn's tiny voice answered. A wave of relief washed over me. It was so good to hear his voice.

"F-Finn?" I croaked. I heard a small gasp,

"Sissy!" He then yelled for joy.

"Yes Finn, it's me." I felt tears brim my eyes again. I frowned when the Alpha sat on the edge of the bed beside me. He placed a comforting hand on my thigh. I shuffled away from him.

"Avery, father wants to talk to you."

"No Finn, wait, I want to talk to you though. Don't go." I pleaded quickly. My eyes then widened a little. My father survived, maybe there was hope for Daniel after all.

"Love you Avery." He said ruefully and handed the phone over to my father.

"AVERY MICHELLE BRIGHTER! WHERE ARE YOU?" I flinched as my father's voice roared down the phone. Wow, since when did he care about my whereabouts and safety anyway?

"Father calm down, I'm okay." I glanced at the Alpha, he was surprised too, but I think the surprise was aimed at the fact that my father was still alive.

"You're okay?!When I returned home this morning, your mother told me you were taken away by the Dark Shadow pack!" He yelled, furious.

"Father-"

"Where are you? Where did he take you!? Whydid he take you?"

"Dad where's Daniel? Is he okay?"

"Don't change the subject young lady. Where are you? And why did he take you?" He demanded. I glanced at the Alpha beside me and he nodded.

"I'm Jayden Jedson's mate..."

"YOU'RE WHAT??!"

I flinched again. I then gritted my teeth nervously. "Seriously though dad, where is Daniel? Is he okay? Is he alive?"

"I can't believe this. You're mated to that disgusting, vile brute."

"Dad!"

He sighed. "I don't know Avery. "I haven't seen him since the middle of the battle."

"Wh-what? How could you not have seen him?"

"We haven't had a chance to collect all our dead yet, I'm not sure if he is with them, or if he took off with the other missing pack members." He explained. "Brandon and Mark are also missing."

"Put Finn back on the phone," I spoke nonchalantly.

"A-Avery?" Finn's voice cracked seconds later.

"Finn, I just need you to know that I love you, okay? I have to hang up the phone now, but I'll see you soon. I promise. If you see Daniel, tell him I love him too and I'll be home soon."

"Avery wait! There's something I got to tell you."

"What? What's wrong?"

"It's uh... That guy you were talking to before in the cells."

"Finn, be reallycareful about what you say next please." I didn't want the Alpha to know about Dylan.

"Okay. I just want to tell you he's missing."

"What?" I feel the blood drain from me.

"They took him." Finn said. And by 'they', he meant the Dark Shadow pack.

"Okay... Thanks Finn. I love you, don't forget that."

"Okay sissy, love you too." He said and then I hung up the phone and passed it back to Jayden.

"Thank you." I muttered and closed my eyes. I inhaled deeply as I thought about Daniel and Dylan. I glanced at Jayden to see both his hands were pressing against his thighs and he bent forward slightly and stared at the floor. He frowned.

"I'm really sorry Avery. About your brother, and everything I've put you through."

I looked at him a little confused. I couldn't forgive him now. And I never would if Daniel turned out to be dead. I stood up and looked down at him as he looked up at me with pleading, desperate and guilty eyes.

"Because of you, my brother is missing. My friends, my aunt, my cousins, my pack are dead. My brother might be dead." I paused. I could feel the next line of words struggling to come out of my mouth as Daisy begged me not to say them. Tears threatened to escape me again but I forced them back and instead I pointed my index finger at his chest. "If he is actually dead... I willreject you." I said calmly in a nonchalant tone, then I calmly walked out of the bedroom and down the corridor.

How could you?!Daisy shrieked at me.

You do realise that he killed most of our pack and possibly our brother, don't you? I yelled back at her.

But you hurt him...She whispered.

Only after he hurt me.I countered. And I meant every word that I said. I will reject him if Daniel turns out to be dead. Regardless of what you want.

Doubt it. There's a part of you that's already drawn to him. She spoke in a mocking tone. I frowned,

Yeah. You're that part.I rolled my eyes. I reached a set of stairs that led to the first floor. I walked down them whilst tuning Daisy out of my head. I entered the kitchen, it was bright and white, large and super clean. It reminded me a little of mine. I then flinched surprised when I spotted four tall and broad males seated at the bench, chatting amongst themselves. I walk past and straight to the fridge, what sweet and unhealthy food did they have in stock?

The men fell silent and they eyed me curiously.

"Why don't you take a photo? It'll last longer." I snapped, not sparing them a glance.

"Sorry Luna." One said quickly. I almost cringed at the name, but my wolf yapped with glee. I found a bar of chocolate and finally I felt a small smile creep onto my lips.

"Good morning Luna, did you sleep well?" Another one of the men said.

"Don't see what's so good about it." I muttered to myself as I pulled the chocolate out of the fridge and ate a few squares. I glanced at the blonde haired male and frowned. "Can you stop calling me that?"

"But aren't you our Luna?" He looked at me perplexed. My frown deepened,

"Not for long." I grouched and ate more chocolate. Blondie was silent, he then looked at me a sadly,

"You're going to reject out Alpha?" He asked faintly. I ignored him and walked over to the table. "Please Luna, don't reject him. I know he has done many awful things in his life, but you're his mate. He already is in love with you. He would never do anything to hurt you."

I suddenly felt a pang in my heart.

"Werewolves are different once they find their mates. Your mate will cherish you, and he won't ever do anything to hurt you! I promise you." The word Daniel spoke three years ago, replayed in my mind. Well you broke your promise Daniel. Tears swelled in my eyes but I forced them back, refusing to let anyone see them. Blondie continued to speak,

"Luna, whether you realise this, you have the power to change his awful ways. You can make him a better person. We all really want that." He said quietly then walked out of the room. The other three at the bench continued to eye me. I furrowed my brows,

"What?" I snapped. Instantly they looked away. "That's what I thought." I muttered. I then too, walked out of the room whilst carrying the chocolate bar. I wondered around the mansion, and into a large room that contained a huge flat screen television and a few couches. On the couches were of course, more Werewolves.

My mind wondered over to Dylan. How could I forget?! Finn said that these guys had taken him, did they kill him? Did they lock him away? I had to find out, but I didn't want them knowing I would be looking for him, they couldn't know that I know him.

I spotted Blondie on one of the couches, his head turns and he looked at me. I waved him over with a small, forced smile. He hopped up off the couch in a heart beat and walked directly over to me.

"Yes Luna?"

"Seeing how I have to stay here a while, I need to find things to do that will stop me from dying of boredom. It'd be helpful if I knew my surroundings better and what there was to do around here. Would you maybe, perhaps give me a tour?" I asked with hopeful eyes.

"Uh... Sure Luna. But would you rather Alpha Jayden to show you around?" He asked a little confused and hesitant. I then found my thoughts wondering over to Jayden, and found myself feeling guilty and drawn to the idea of him being the one to show me around. Maybe there was a good, interesting side to get to know-

WHOA. No Avery. Stop right there. Do not go down that path again. Your brother might be dead because of him. You pack isdead because of him.

"Um. No. I'd rather not go near him for now."

"Oh... Okay Luna. Right this way then."

"Please call me Avery."

"A-are you sure?"

"Yes," I half heartedly chuckled.

"Alright then, Avery." He gave me a small smile then led the way around the mansion.

"What about you? What's your name Blondie?" I asked. He raised an eyebrow at me. I shrugged, "I could just keep calling you Blondie?"

"Tyson. It's Tyson." He answered quickly. "Beta of the Dark Shadow Pack." Wow, I really didn't catch that Beta scent before...

"Okay Blondie, that's cool." I smirked. He playfully nudged my shoulder and we continued to walk around. Tyson opened a door, to reveal a few long and comfy looking couches along dark walls, and a large projector screen against the wall.

"This is our theatre room."

"Wow."

The next room shown was the gym, and then a games room filled with foosball and pool tables, and Xboxes and other electronics. Tyson then led me up the stairs and down a hallway. "Behind those closed doors are the Warrior Wolves bedrooms." He waved a hand at the doors. "That one's my room. And that one's the Third in Command's room... His name is Kyron."

"Have you found your mate yet?" I asked suddenly. He nodded with a smile,

"Yeah. Her name is Katy." He sighs contently and his eyes light up at the thought of her. "She's beautiful, and the most loving and caring and genuine person you will ever meet." I smile at his reaction.

"Where is she?"

"Shopping with Kyron's mate. Her name is Sasha." He muttered with distaste.

"It sounds like you don't like her very much." I commented as we continued to walk again.

"Not many people do," he answered bluntly, he paused and pointed at a familiar door. "That's Jayden's room. Let's go back down, the girls will be back soon."

I nodded, "Okay. So I'll get to meet them soon then." Thank god. I thought this was like a Guys only house or something!

"Yes. Katy's thrilled to meet you."

I smiled at the thought.

"So down there is the laundry and down those stairs is the basement." Tyson states as we reach the hallway at the base of the stairs. "And the kitchen, games room, theatre, gym and lounge room are that way as you already know."

"Hm, what about the dungeons?"

"Oh they're this way." He says and leads me to the door of the basement. We entre and walk down the stairs. I frown seeing nothing but boxes on shelves with storage items.

"They're not here Blondie..."

Tyson playfully glares. He then smirked and walked to the back of the room and proceeded to pull a shelf off of the wall to reveal a hidden door. He opened it and I watched with amusement. I then followed him through the hidden doorway. The dungeon was the same shape as mine, only more spooky, gory and medieval styled. The walls were tainted by blood, and several groans and painful cries could be heard. Instantly I regretted wanted to check in here. What if Dylan was experiencing the same pain as these poor other Werewolves?

"Don't worry, each of these wolves deserve what they're getting in here. Some have betrayed our Alpha, others are rapists..." He explained. "Just mind your step Avery, don't get to close to the cells, some prisoners will try to grab you." I nodded a response of understanding. We then walked along the centre. "Do you want to leave yet?"

I shook my head, I had to see if Dylan was in here first. I glanced in each cell. And finally I caught his scent. I followed it hastily to the back, Tyson followed me, confused and surprised. Dylan was chained to the wall, but he sat in stood as he trying to pry his chains off.

"This one is new. We rescued him, actually from your pack's dungeons. We realised he was one of us, not that any of us have ever seen him before."

"If he belongs to you, why chain him down here like a criminal?"

"Because he was aggressive when we brought him here. We're not sure we can trust him not to hurt anyone. We keep trying to calm him down and getting him to talk to us but he refuses. Avery, do you know why he was a prisoner in your dungeons?"

I glanced at Tyson hesitantly, unsure of whether or not I could tell him. I watched Dylan sniff the air, and his head snapped our way. We locked eyes, and I immediately say him relax just the slightest.

'You okay?' I heard his voice in my head. My eyes widened,

'Yeah... How can I hear you in my head?'I asked him with perplexity. You have to be in the same pack to mind link- oh... 'But I haven't completed the Luna transition yet... I don't wear the mark and I haven't mated fully-'

'I don't think that really matters. If you reject him then maybe it'll change and you won't hear me. But technically you are apart of this pack.'Dylan answered. I turned to look at Tyson,

"I met him the morning, a some hours before the attack started. I don't know much about him."

Tyson nodded, and I watched as his eyes turn lighter than normal. I looked at him in question but then realised he was mind linking with someone, just as I had been with Dylan seconds ago. After a minute, his eyes returned to normal. He then smiled at me, "Alpha Jayden wants to speak with you... Just don't tell him we came down here, okay?" I nodded and he then led me out of the dungeon and up the stairs of the basement. I hesitantly trailed behind him, a strong scowl on my face.

We walked to Jayden's office and we stopped outside the closed door. "This is where we part ways for now." Tyson stated with a grin. I waved him goodbye then I faced the door. I sucked in a sharp breath and knocked.

"Come in." Jayden's husky voice rang through my ears. Spine tingling shivers ran down my back at the sexy tone of his voice.

'Daisy really?'I hissed.

'Hey, I'm not the only one who likes the sound of his voice, and you know it.'She huffed defensively. I sighed and opened the door. Jayden was sitting at his desk, his face hidden in his hands and elbows rested on the glass desktop. His hair was messy, sticking up in certain places, and his shirt was all torn, a few cuts grazed his arm and neck. I looked at him concerned,

"Jayden?" I called his name softly. His eyes snapped up to meet mine. His eyes were red and puffy, he looked distraught and upset.

"I'm sorry." He whispered. "I'm so furious with myself for putting you through this pain, I need to be more considerate of your feelings and how my actions have and can affect you." He said and stood up. I felt my heart beginning to crumble, and I felt guilty for snapping at him earlier.

'Look at the stress and pain you've put our mate through!'Daisy yelled at me. I then frowned. I'm not at fault here! He damn well should be sorry.

I felt the anger quickly subside as my eyes locked with his again. I could see the sincerity and regret radiating form him. I tentatively walk over to his side. Agitated with myself, I found myself hugging him to comfort him. He hugged my back and buried his face in the crook of my neck. He inhaled deeply and pulled back to look at my face. I spot a couple tears sliding down his cheek. I wiped it away and he bent down a bit so he was more level with me. His eyes dropped to the floor,

"I'm sorry I'm such a disappointment to you. I should be a better mate, I shouldn't have forced you to come here against your will, and I shouldn't have done what I did to your pack. The truth is, I've done many horrible things in my life, and I don't deserve someone... as kind hearted and as perfect as you. I don't deserve to have you in my life as my mate. And I understand if you want to reject me. I can have Tyson take you back to your family-"

I cut him off by standing on my tip toes and kissing him. Instantly I retreated and brought my fingers to my lips. That darn inner wolf of mine, giving me these stupid urges.

Jayden looked down at me, baffled. "D-Does this mean you want to be my mate?"

I looked at him, unable to reject him. I sighed, "I'll give you one chance." I held up a finger. "One. But if you continue to be cruel, to murder, to torture, to take over any more packs, thisis over."

Jayden beamed with joy and relief. He hugged me tightly and breathed in my scent. "I won't let you down." There was a knock at the door seconds later. "What is it?" Jayden asked and let go of me. The door opened and I turned my head over my shoulder to see a young man, about the same age as Tyson, peak through the door. "Kyron, what is it?" Jayden asked the man in his early twenties.

"Alpha, I just wanted to let you and Luna know that the girls have returned and they want to meet you Luna." Kyron said, his back straight and stiff.

"Katy and Sasha?" I clarify with a small smile. Kyron's cheeks blushed at the mention of Sasha's name. He nodded.

"They'll be waiting in the kitchen... I'm going to go now..." He muttered and shut the door. I looked back up at Jayden. He arched an eyebrow,

"How do you know their names?" He asked, curious.

"I was talking to Blondie- I mean Tyson, earlier and he happened to mention them once or twice." I explained with a smile. Jayden's dark brown questioning eyes softened, and he nodded.

"Well come on then, let's go say hi." He returned the smile and led us out of the office. I glanced down to see his hand lingered behind him, as though he were waiting for me to take hold of it. Hesitantly, I took hold of it, and noticed his smile widening. I have to say, this feels very natural.

I glanced down at our entwined fingers then back up at the side of Jayden's head. We then continued on, in the direction of the kitchen, to meet Katy and Sasha.

Chapter Five

✱ Edited Version*

Avery's POV

We walked into the kitchen to spot Tyson sitting on a stool with a twenty-ish year old looking blonde, sitting on his lap. Naturally I assumed her name was Katy, and she was beautiful. She had an olive toned skin, her blonde hair reached her mid back and her eyes were a sky blue. Have you heard of the couples that could pass for siblings? Yeah this was one of those cases.

I then glanced over at Kyron who sat on another stool, a couple over from Tyson and Katy. On Kyron's lap, I assume was his mate, Sasha. Her hair was dark and short, it cut off at the shoulders. Her skin tone was much darker than Katy's, and her cheek bones were far more predominant.

I found myself beginning to grow nervous, as the four on the stools eyed Jayden and I with curiosity. I gave an awkward wave, "Hi." I squeaked, then frowned at myself. Katy grinned and stood up, she walked over to me and pulled me straight in for a hug. Startled, I found myself hugging her back, I could only imagine how confused my facial expression must have looked.

"I'm so sorry!" Katy exclaimed. "What you must have gone through, must have been just awful!" She hugged me tighter, making it slightly difficult to breathe. I manage to smile. Although I felt mildly claustrophobic, I also felt far more comfortable, and at ease. This hug was exactly what I needed. It felt like a major relief to have someone sympathising and understanding of my situation.

"Thank you." I whispered, and she then pulled back to look at me with a cheeky smile,

"We are going to have so much fun! I can just tell we are going to get along fantastically!" She squealed with delight. I laughed and nodded, I liked her already. I felt Jayden's arm slither around my waist. My instant reflexes were telling my to pull away from his side hug, but Daisy urged me to stay in his gentle hold.

I looked over at Kyron and Sasha to see them sucking faces. I almost cringed at the sight, but I didn't want to appear rude.

"I'll be in my office if you need me." Jayden murmured in my ear then placed a quick, gentle kiss on my temple. "Come on boys, let's let the girls get to know each other." He called to Tyson and Kyron, eyeing Kyron particularly. Tyson nodded with a grin, walked over to Katy and he spun her around to face him. She giggled and wrapped her arms around his neck and kissed him.

"Love you babe."

"Love you too darling. Have fun," he said as he poked her nose, then followed Jayden off down the hallway. That was just a little cute...

"By babe. See you later." Sasha winked at Kyron, I regretted looking over as I saw her hand hover over his crotch. I looked away from them.

"Love you sweet heart." I heard Kyron say before he disappeared. I then looked back at Sasha and forced a smile,

"Hey, you must be Sasha."

Sasha looked over at me and scowled. "Yeah that's me. And you must be that pathetic cry baby, Ashlee. Who came from the world's weakest pack." She sneered and hopped up off the stool. My eyebrows furrowed and my hands clenched into fists.Wow. She didn't even get my name right.

"Sasha! You bitch! She's your Luna!" Katy yelled. Sasha rolled her eyes,

"Luna my ass." She muttered bitterly then she stormed out of the room. I turned to look at Katy, and quickly calmed my thumping heart.

"What's her problem?" I asked, astonished.

"Oh that? Uh that's this mental disease she's been stuck with, for like, her whole life." She then lowered her voice, "It's called jealousy." She grinned, mockingly.

"I CAN HEAR YOU, YOU KNOW!?" Sasha screeched so loudly that I was forced to slam my palms over my ears. I then laughed,

"What has she got to be jealous of? My pack being murdered? Me being abducted by an asshole mate?"

Katy bit her bottom lip, "Don't tell Kyron I said this please... But, Sasha has had the biggest crush on Jayden since the eighth grade." Katy whispered ever so quietly. My eyes widened,

"Seriously?"

Katy nodded. Wow, it looks like I've already made an enemy. "Hey, do you want to go for a swim? It's boiling hot and the pool is just waiting for us outside the back." Katy asked with a grin. I smiled with delight, only to frown,

"I'd love to, but I kinda didn't have the time to grab my bathers before I was taken here..." I trailed off, looking at the ground.

"Oh, don't you worry girl. I have heapsof bathers, especially bikinis!" She grabbed my hand and dragged me out into the hallway, and straight up the stairs.

"Oh, I'm not sure..."

"Nonsense. You'll look sexy in them. You've got the perfect figure." She then opened the door to Tyson's and her bedroom. We entered and I watched as Katy started to dig through a draw in the chest of draws. She threw several pairs of bikinis onto the bed. One was aqua and sparkly, another was bold red, a third was white and Greek like material. I took the white ones and looked at Katy questioningly. She grinned and nodded, "Those will look great. There's a bathroom at the end of the hallway if you want to change in there."

"There's also one in Jayden's room." I stated with a grin. Katy winked and nodded,

"Yes, go get changed in your mate's room." She hustled me out of the bedroom. My Mate. The thought was still bizarre to me.

I walked into Jayden's room and then into the bathroom. I shut the door and locked it behind me. I glanced at my mirror, feeling horrified by my yucky appearance. My hair was a bird's nest. My eyes had dark bags under them and my mascara had been smeared around. I sighed, shook my head and stripped out of my clothes, then slipped on the bikinis. I had to admit, Katy was right about how well these bikinis would flaunt my slender figure.

I quickly ran my hands through my hair and tied it up into a neater pony tail, then I ran the taps with lukewarm water and splashed it over my face. There was a knock at the door. "Come in." I said and twisted the taps off. Katy walked in, her eyes widened and she grinned,

"You. Look. Hot." She nodded in approval. "I knew those bikinis would suit you! O-M-G you have the perfect figure."

"Thanks." I smiled bashfully. "Back at you." I winked at the bold red bikinis she had on, her figure too an hourglass and her stomach way more toned than mine. Katy grinned and grabbed my hand,

"Come on, let's go!" She squeaked cheerfully and she dragged me out of the room and down the stairs again. "Shall we invite the boys to join us?" She asked as we reached the back, glass sliding door. I shrugged,

"I'm not fussed. If you want to, we can." I smiled. I guess it wouldn't be totally horrible having Jayden swimming with us, shirtless...

"BOYS!" Katy suddenly yelled, "Avery and I are going for a swim! Come join us!"

The next thing I hear are feet pounding heavily against the floor as the guys ran out into the kitchen and to the back door. Jayden froze, his eyes stopped on me. They started to darken, and they became cloaked by lust. My heart beat a little faster, and my palms grew a little sweaty. How did he have this ability to over me? How could I allow myself to be consumed by nerves.

'Could you be anymore awkward?' Daisy sarcastically asked.

'Could your impious thoughts be screamed any louder in my head?' I retorted. I then turned my back to Jayden Tyson and I made a dash for the unfenced pool area. I dived straight in and sighed contently as the cool water washed over me, making me feel refreshed. When my head bobbed back above the water, I saw Katy, Tyson and Jayden walking across the luscious green lawn and over to the paved bricks that surrounded the pool. Jayden tugged off his shirt, and I couldn't stop my eyes from roaming his entire body. Wow, is it getting hot out here or what?

Katy was second to jump into the pool, unlike my neat dive, she bombied, sending water flying metres into the air. I splashed her and she splashed back with a giggle. We then looked back at the boys. Kyron and Sasha had joined them. I almost couldn't hide the frown, when I noticed Sasha's bikinis. They were two tiny triangles that barely covered her nipples, they and the bottoms were decorated by light blue sparkles.

Kyron reached for her hand, Sasha moved her hand away. She glanced at Jayden and smiled. She then pranced towards the pool and dived cleanly in. I couldn't help but roll my eyes. Show off. I then looked at Jayden to see him smirking at me, I guessed her could sense the bitterness radiating from me. Tyson was next to jump into the pool. I watched as he swan under the water, behind Katy, he wrapped his arms around her waist and pulled her in for a tight hug.

Jayden and Kyron jumped in finally. And not minutes later, Sasha had climbed back out of the pool to sunbathe on one of the white pool chairs. Meanwhile, the rest of us had started up a splash war. Soon it turned into piggy back wars, with Katy and I on top of Jayden and Tyson's shoulders. I successfully won the first round, only to lose the next two rounds.

Kyron glanced over at Sasha, "Baby, come join the fun!" He called to her. He was the only boy not able to join in the piggy back wars as his partner preferred to tan. Sasha took her sun glasses off to look at Katy and I with full judgment. She scoffed,

"I'm twenty, not ten."

"Now that's funny, cause you often act like your thirteen, hitting puberty and becoming a sassy bitch, pretending to be far more mature than what you actually are." I said then shrieked as Katy successfully pushed me off Jayden's shoulders again. She laughed, at the fact she had won again, and also at my comment. The boys chuckled too, Sasha didn't find it so funny though.

"Why you bitch!" Sasha sat up and growled at me as I resurfaced the water. Jayden snarled at her,

"Watch your tone when you're talking to my mate."

Sasha rolled her eyes, "She won't be your mate for long." She stood up with her towel and sunnies in her hands, "Besides, she doesn't even wear your mark yet." She then walked off with a huff. I felt my face growing red with anger, my fists clenched and I went to lung out of the pool, however Jayden stopped me by wrapping his arms around my waist. "Whoa, chill love." He laughed and he turned me to face him. On instinct I wrapped my arms around his neck, this time the voice inside my head that usually screamed at me to resist every urge, was far more silent, and I felt myself leaning closer and closer towards his soft, plump lips.

I glanced up at him to see his eyes closed, and his lips slightly pursed. I then felt my eyes flutter close, and then our lips connected. Tyson cleared his throat, "Hey guys, I think the pool is starting to heat up." He whistled and winked. I blushed and quickly pulled away from Jayden's touch. My wolf growled at me for leaving his comforting and warm embrace, I could tell he too was a little disappointed.

The awkwardness quickly faded and we went back to our splash and piggyback wars. A couple hours later, still in the pool, I felt Jayden's presence behind me. He leant to whisper in my ear, his warm breath fanned against my ear as he spoke, "You are an amazing person, you know that?" He then spun me around to face him. I blushed at the way he looked at me, with awe and amusement. "See? We can have fun together, it doesn't have to be bad."

And that's when reality hit me full forced. I backed away slowly, towards the steps. Jayden looked at me confused and hurt crossed his face when he noticed the fear and woe that crossed my face. I ran up the steps and hastily wrapped a towel around me. I then began to run, to where? I wasn't really sure.

I couldn't believe that for the past several hours, I had been enjoying myself, while my family had been suffering! I had been happy while my brother could be dead! I have felt freedom and passion, even though they had been the ones to kidnap me! And Dylan is locked up, away in their dungeon! What kind of person am I?

I heard a wolf howl, and from the tingling shivers that ran down my spine, I knew it was Jayden. I ran into the forest, dropped my towel and began to sprint. My feet snapped twigs and I felt pine sticks pierce into my flesh. I winced but ran faster. I then heard his paws pounding against the ground in the near distance, and I knew he wasn't far from finding me. I ran faster, debating on whether or not to shift into my wolf. I stopped however, when a thought crossed my mind and a tall, thick tree came into my view. I stopped by it and began to climb it.

Once I reached a safe height, I waited, leant into the trunk and puffing immensely. I looked over the edge to see a midnight black wolf, walking around and looking about with a worried expression. There were two wolves behind him, one a sandy blonde, the other a dark brown. I didn't have to be a detective to know they were Tyson and Kyron. The wolves continued to sniff the air and walk around the surrounding area, knowing that they were close. I slumped further into the trunk's side, in an attempt to stay hidden.

About twenty minutes later, they moved on and walked off in another direction. I sighed in relief and slowly I began to climb down the tree. Once I reached the ground, I began to jog back to the pack house. I didn't know why. I should have been running the other way, I should have been heading towards my home. Not back to my kidnappers. But I knew they would just find me again, and maybe they wouldn't spare my family the next time... I couldn't risk that. I also couldn't leave Dylan behind.

Eventually, I walked through the sliding door and straight into the kitchen. I saw many people in there, chatting with sincere fret. As soon as I entered, all of their heads snap up and their eyes looked directly at me. They all looked relieved, but some also annoyed. "Luna! We thought you left us!" A woman in her mid thirties cried.

"Jayden's been worried sick!" Another yelled, irritated.

"We thought you ran away..." I heard a child say quietly, making my heart melt a little. I then held my hands up in surrender, as the other twenty people started on me also.

"Everyone please calm down," I clearly and loudly spoke. Their chatter ceased. "I only went for a walk to clear my mind. That's all." I said with a forced, reassuring smile. Everyone sighed with relief ad dispersed.

"Someone call Jayden through mind link and tell him that his mate is here and is okay." A male ordered.

"Yes sir," another said. I grimaced at the thought of Jayden returning. How angry was he going to be with me? Would he yell at me? Would I receive the unbearable silent treatment? You know what? It doesn't matter. I'm not the one in the wrong.

I sighed and carried my feet up the stairs and to Jayden's bedroom. I closed the door behind me once I entered the room, I then walked over to his bed and pulled back the covers. I glanced down to see I was still wearing the damp bathers. I shrugged and got into the bed and pulled the covers back up and over me. I then rolled onto my side and brought my hands up to rest them under the side of my head. I found myself quite comfortable, and then I began to doze off into a long sleep.

Chapter Six

 Edited Version*

Avery's POV

As I opened my eyes, I rubbed the sleep from them. I then began to sit up, and look around the room, pleading desperately to the Moon Goddess that this had all just have been one long, nasty nightmare. I was disappointed again, as I was still in Jayden's bedroom. I was definitely not in a dream, and I needed to stop hoping that I was, and face reality. I have been kidnapped by my mate, Dylan is locked up underneath the house, and my brother could very well possibly be dead.

"Morning princess." I heard Jayden's husky voice. Stunned a little bit, I looked around for him but could see him anywhere. I did however, notice the bathroom door creeping open, and I then saw Jayden walking out of the bathroom and into this bedroom, wearing a pair of knee length, denim shorts. Jeeze, why does he have to make this so difficult for me? Why cant he just put a shirt on?

Wait a minute."Morning? But I fell asleep in the mid afternoon." Surely I couldn't have been asleep for that long. "What time is it?" I asked as

I rubbed the back of my neck and rolled it around to stretch it. Jayden chuckled and looked down at the burgundy band watch on his wrist,

"Seven-Thirty." He smiled, "I uh, got Katy to get some more clothes out for you. She left them on the end of the bed." Jayden smiled sheepishly. I then looked at the foot of the bed to see some light, denim shorts, that probably reach mid thigh, a black, loose shirt and some undergarments. I hopped out of the bed, and as I walked over to them, I pulled the bather bottoms out of my cheeks, what a wedgy these have given me!

I picked the clothes up and walked into the bathroom, locked the door behind me and began to change. I heard Jayden chuckle again and flop his back onto the bed. I rolled my eyes and shook my head as I slipped on the shorts and threw the bathers into the basket. I then unlocked the bathroom door and re-entered the bedroom. Jayden's face lit up, he then appeared as though he had a question to ask.

"About yesterday-" he began, I cut him off,

"I'd rather not talk about it. I just needed to clear my head. That's all."

"Okay..." He then forced a smile. "I uh... I got Katy to go to the shops yesterday afternoon to buy you... Whatever it is that girls need, you know, makeup, hair brush, toothbrush, shampoo... Other bathroom things... She put them in the cabinet under the sink." He explained nervously. I smiled at his nervousness, he was so cute.

"Thanks. I'm gonna go take a shower," I then stated. Oh God how good it will be to finally wash my hair!I then walked back into the bathroom and locked the door behind me. I then began to strip again, and I turned the taps on to a hot temperature. I walked over to the cabinet and opened it to find a toothbrush, paste, hairbrush and tampons on the top shelf. On the shelf underneath them was hair products, a shaver, and a bar of Dove Soap.

I picked up the conditioner, shampoo, soap and razor, then made my way back to the shower. I hopped into the steamy, large, glass shower.

The steam slowly began to fog up the bathroom, staining the mirror starting from the top an working its way down, as I did the same with soap on my body. I gave myself a good scrub, then shaved my legs and underarms. I then proceeded to wash my long hair thoroughly. After I rinsed all the soapy suds off, I twisted the taps off again and I hopped out of the shower. In the cabinet I also found a setoff clean towels, I grabbed the top one and wrapped it around the body. I then grabbed a second towel to wrap around my hair.

I walked back over to the shower to tidy up after myself, by taking the hair products, shaver and soap out and I placed them back in the cabinet. I then grabbed out the toothbrush and paste and gave my teeth a good, couple minute long brush. Once finished, I changed back into my new clothes, rubbed the towel over my hair to give it a quick dry and while it was still a little wet, I ran the hard plastic, oval-shaped brush through it forcefully. A few, short minutes later, my hair was knot free and the brush was cleaned and put back into the cabinet. I found a bundle of hair ties. Wow Katy went all out for me, I should really give her a big thanks later, when I see her. She has no idea how much better she has made my stay here.

I French braided my hair to the right, and looked at my reflection. I had small bags under my eyes, and my skin was slightly red due to the hot water that had been hitting it the past ten minutes. I looked back in the cabinet to find a small, purple and sparkly bag, inside it carried mascara, lip sticks, blush shades, eye shadows, foundations and powders. After applying a really natural and basic look of makeup, I zipped the bag up and put it back away.

Finally, I unlocked the bathroom and walked back into the bedroom, again. Jayden was curled up on top of the made bed, sound asleep. Aww, he looked so peaceful when he slept. I looked at the bedside table to see the alarm clock, the time now read eight-thirty. Wow! Did it really take an hour for me to do all that??

I walked over to the edge of the bed, on the side Jayden slept on. I could just stand here for hours, watching him sleep... Did I really just think that? How creepy and corny have I gotten? Suddenly, his hand shot to the side and latched gently onto my wrist, and he pulled me down on top of him. I now lay flat on top of his stomach, my chest squished against his, and his arms were wrapped tightly around my waist. My nose was mere centimeters away from his.

"Hi." I whispered. He grinned and pecked my lips. I thought for a moment. "I am sorry about yesterday, if I stressed you out or upset you."

"Don't be, I understand, that with all the things going on right now, that you would be so upset." He said calmly. "I can only imagine what you're going through, although I did go through similar things when I was younger." He explained quietly, his warm breath fanned my face. Guilt washed over me and I instantly felt bad for him. I ran my hand up his arm slowly and gently.

"What did you go through?" I asked softly.

"You don't want to know. Believe me," Jayden chuckled half-heartedly.

"I do. I'm your mate, I want to know. I want to be there for you." And surprisingly, I meant every word I just said. Jayden looked at me shocked for a moment, he then sighed.

"When I was younger, about five years old I guess I was... My parents were murdered, and I was kidnapped." He answered quietly. I looked at him, bewildered.

"What? Then how... So I'm guessing your pack rescued you, otherwise you wouldn't be here, right?"

"No. My pack did not rescue me. Avery... Have you ever heard the old Wolf Tale, called The Midnight Warriors?" He asked and looked into my eyes. I nodded,

"Yeah, my brother Daniel used to read it to me when I was little. Why?"

Images of my brother flashed before my mind and I bit my lip.

"Well, you know how it says that The Midnight Warriors were a pack of wolves, all of the male Werewolves had pure black fur, and all the females had pure white?"

"Yes, but Jayden, it's just a Wolf Tale." I looked down at him to see him shaking his head,

"No. It's not just a story. The Midnight Warriors were a real pack, that thrived throughout Europe. The were the only pack in the world that consisted of White and Black wolves. No other pack had them, and that's how rare those wolves are. But just under four hundred years ago, the Midnight Warriors were the most powerful pack and the most feared." He sucked in a deep breath.

"Wait, so this pack was real? And the ONLY pack with Black or White wolves... Then how... In the book it says that all the other packs joined together as one and took out the Midnight Warriors. That they wiped that pack out ad there were no more..."

"What's your question then?" Jayden looked at her puzzled.

"Well my question is, how are there pure black and pure white wolves today is the only pack that contains them was completely demolished hundreds of years ago?"

"Love, that's what I was going to tell you." He said. I smiled and blushed. I love it when he calls me love. Ugh I sound like such a girly girl right now. I rolled my eyes at myself.

"Okay..."

"So yeah, as you already know, and as the book states, all of the other Werewolf packs joined together to destroy the Midnight Warriors. And they succeeded. But what the book didn't mention, is that there were survivors. The Alpha sent his daughter away along with all the other children and a few of the well trained warriors. He sent them away into hiding, to protect them, to make sure they would live their lives full, happy and they were to keep the bloodline going. Which they did, obviously." Jayden explained.

"So what you're telling me, is that when this pack was taken down, right before they were attacked, all the children went away into hiding, and when they had children of their own, their children had children, and their children had children and you are the generation after those?" I asked. Jayden nodded.

"And I wasn't just from any blood line. I was from the Alpha and his daughter's bloodline. She is my great, great, great, great, great grandmother.

"Jayden, what were we talking about before all of this story stuff about the Midnight Warrior Wolves?" I asked, noticing we had definitely gone off topic.

"What I went through as a kid."

"Oh yeah." I bit my bottom lip.

"Well, because I came from that 'special' pack, there were people after me, and my parents. We were living out in hiding until we were spotted. My parents knew what was coming, so the next morning, they hid me in the bushes, while they stood outside the front of the house... Waiting for what was to come. Werewolves showed up, not too long after that, and my parents were slaughtered, right in front of me." He said tonelessly, although I could tell there was a great sadness hiding behind his words.

"Jayden... You shouldn't of had to go through that. No one should." I rubbed his arm gently. He smiled down at me.

"Yeah, I guess it was just a bad turn of events... Anyway... One of the Werewolves that killed my parents, an Alpha actually, sniffed me out. And he... He took me in, well against my will. I refused to go with the monsters who killed my parents, so they kidnapped me, raised me as their own and when the Alpha retired, I took his position." Jayden shrugged.

"Jayden, that's awful." I said woefully and I looked down. And I thought that I had it rough,

"Yeah, well at least he taught me how to be strong, how to defend myself and whatnot." He said with a half smile. "But now you know everything there is to know about me." I smiled up at him. Then I started to think about my family and what their wolves looked like. I gasped in realisation.

"Um Jayden... There is something I need to tell you." I whispered. He looked at me, and he sat up with me still on his lap.

"You can tell me anything." He whispered in my ear, sending good chills down my spine.

"I-I am a pure white wolf."

Jayden looked at me surprised. "Really?" He grinned. I nodded.

"But I don't know who's bloodline I'm from. I have the Alpha gene in my blood because of my father, but he has a different coloured wolf, so he is not from the Midnight Warriors. My mum though, her wolf is a pure white one. Daniel's is black. But of course we don't know Finn's yet, because he's way too young to shift." I rambled on. Jayden chuckled,

"That's awesome. Show me."

"What?" I looked at him perplexed.

"Show me your wolf." He said simply. I laughed,

"Oh right. Okay." I said and stood up, grabbed his hand and I led him out of the room, down the stairs and outside. I then let go of his hand, and ran into the forest, behind a tree to strip. I heard a groan, so I popped my head out from behind the thick tree to look at Jayden weirdly. He was lying on the ground, his stomach faced up. His hands were underneath his head, but his eyes were closed. He had his famous smirk written all over his face.

"Avery Jedson, are you going to shift into your beautiful wolf or are you just going to stand there all day and look at me while your naked?" he asked and opened his eyes to look my way. I blushed and ducked back behind the tree. I took a deep breath and jumped into the air. My bones cracked and snapped, what used to be an immense, unbearable amount of pain, was now almost painless.

I landed on the ground, on all four paws. I forced myself to shift again and again until the pain became almost undetectable. However, it had been quite some time since my last shift, so this time it was a little uncomfortable.

I let out a deep breath, and trotted out of the forest and back onto the back lawn to see Jayden, still lying down, his eyes still closed. I crept up to him slowly, hoping to surprise him. I reached his feet, then pounced on top of him, both front paws on either side of his head. Jayden's eyes snapped open, and he stared up at me, a smile formed on his pink lips.

"Hey beautiful." He murmured, slowly he raised his hand to my head and he stroked my white fur tenderly. I barked playfully and licked his cheek, then I pushed myself up and ran off into the forest. I heard Jayden jump to his feet. "Hey!" he yelled playfully and I could hear him shift into his handsome black wolf.

And the chase was on. I always loved to play chasey when I was younger, Daniel and I used to play it all the time, even though he was a great deal faster than I was.

I ran through the forest, barely skidding around each tree. I found myself starting to slow within minutes. I hadn't shifted in so long, in over a year I might say, and my fitness levels are no where near as high as they used to be. Within five minutes, I could hear the pounding of Jayden's paws against the hard forest ground, and I knew he was gaining on me. He was close. As I skidded around a very large tree, I tripped over a large root in the ground, and I instantly tumbled over, my side hit the ground with a loud thump. Ouch, that hurt like a bitch.

I quickly tried to regain myself, I pushed myself up only to slip again and land on my face. I whimpered as I felt pain surging through my left hind leg. Ugh, I just had to trip over and hurt myself, didn't I?

Within seconds I heard Jayden running around the corner, and he stopped over me. He tilted his head in confusion, as to why I wasn't getting back up. I looked down at my sprained leg which I could feel was already starting to heal. Thank God it wasn't broken, because that would have taken a couple days to heal!I looked back up at Jayden again to see his eyes had softened.

'Shift'I heard his voice in my head. I looked at him as though he were crazy.

'No way! Are you serious? I'll just walk-' I said trying to get back up, but the pressure was still too much on my sore leg. I stood now, but had to hold my paw off the ground. Jayden looked at me in all seriousness.

'I can carry you back, but not if you are in wolf form. And not to mention, you can't walk like this.' I could just hear the pain in his voice. He didn't like to see me hurt, that much I could tell. I tried to place my paw back on the ground but winced and lifted it the second I felt the slightest bit of pressure in it. I must have snapped a ligament or something. I puffed in defeat and shifted back into my human form, instantly I turned my back to him and covered my breasts with my arms.

'You don't need to hide from me,' I heard Jayden's voice in my head again, this time it held a little humor in it. Was this guy for real? I barely know him! Why the hell would I let him see me nude?Jayden then let out a frustrated sigh, 'Get on,' he looked at his back, indicating he wanted me to hop on. I grunted but reluctantly turned to face him, still keeping my body covered up. Respectively, Jayden had turned his head away from me, to give me privacy.

"Thank you." I mumbled and climbed onto his lowered back. My leg stung but I knew the pain would be gone by tomorrow morning, maybe even by tonight. I crouched so my front was closer to his body, so it wasn't in the air on full display to the world. Jayden chuckled, but then started to run back to the house. The ride was so smooth and I started to feel myself dozing out.

Flash Back

I laughed, "Faster Daniel! Faster!" My seven-year-old self giggled. I currently sat on the back of my older brother's wolf, he had only shifted for the first time a few weeks ago, and every single day he gave Finn and I rides on his back.

Daniel ran out of the forest and into the open grassy field. He slowed down to a walk, and we then made our way over to the large Oak tree in the middle of the yard, where mother, father and my baby brother Finn waited.

We stopped a few metres in front of them, grinning from ear to ear. I felt Daniel shake his thick, black fur underneath me. "Whoa." I laughed as I felt myself being swayed from side to side. I looked up to see mother walking over to us. She placed her hand on Daniel's cheek and she smiled slightly.

"Daniel, I need you to promise me something, okay?" She asked him softly. He looked at her and nodded firmly. I slid off of Daniel's back and walked over to my mother's side, I looked up at Daniel with a smile on my face. My mother continued, "No matter what, no matter how hard your friends bed, never, and I mean neverlet them see your wolf, well unless our pack comes to a fight where we need every wolf to be in battle. Do you understand me?" She asked in a demanding tone of voice. With a eyes full of perplexity but with full intention of obeying, Daniel nodded. "I'm doing this for your own safety baby. I never let anyone see my wolf, and neither will you, or your sister, or even Finn."

"But why mother?" I asked confused.

"Because sweetheart. Our wolves are special. Others wouldn't understand us, we are different to them, and they fear us because of it. They would think we are evil, so we must hide ourselves." She answered and I nodded, still not really understanding,

"But why can Father show everyone his wolf?" I asked, glancing over at him. My one-year-old brother sat on his lap, giggling.

"Because he is like normal Werewolves. He isn't like us. He isn't... He isn't supposed to be apart of our lives but he is anyway." She answered dryly. Now that made me even more confused. What did she mean?

"Why isn't he supposed to be apart of our lives?" I asked, quoting her. She looked away from Daniel and down at me.

"One day, when you are older, you will understand everything, about who you are, about our kind, where you are truly from, why you are to keep yourself hidden, and even about love. I know it is confusing now, but later you will understand it all, when the timing is right, you will know everything." She explained with such a sympathetic tone. I nodded, still puzzled, but one day maybe I would know exactly what she was talking about. I doubt it though.

End of Flash Back

"Avery? Wake up baby girl."

My eyes slowly opened, I was lying on the ground, behind a tree in the forest. I sat up, blinking myself awake. I was in my clothes, behind me was the house. I looked up at Jayden with puzzlement. "What happened?" I asked, as I rubbed the back of my head. I went to stand up but winced as the pressure attacked my leg

"I don't know, you tell me." Jayden chuckled.

"I remember running, tripping, pain and falling asleep. Did you...?"

"Yes, I dressed you." Jayden smirked. I hit his arm. "Ouch!" he feigned hurt. I rolled my eyes,

"Thanks." I mumbled, and walked off inside. As soon as I walked in through the laundry and into the kitchen, the smell of meatloaf flowed through my nostrils. I looked around to spot Tyson, standing in front of the oven, with a pair of tongs in his hands. Then I actually realised how hungry I was.

I looked down at the table in the dining room, across from the kitchen, and I saw Katy, Sasha, Kyron and a few other familiar faces and four spare seats. Two at the same head, one beside Katy, and one beside Kyron. I walked into the dining room, but stopped about a metre away from the table, not having a clue where to sit or if I was even welcome to sit.

"Good evening Luna," One of the Wolves stood up. I smiled,

"Please, call me Avery." I answered politely. He nodded and Katy smiled up at me,

"You sit at the head with Jayden."

I nodded and limped over to the two seats at the back. I took a seat on the left one and waited patiently for dinner. A few minutes later, Jayden walked in with a smirk on his face. He took a seat beside me, still he smiled like an idiot. I looked at him in question, but before I could ask, Tyson walked in carrying a large plate that had a huge pile of steak on it, and another very large plate containing pumpkin, broccoli, corn cobs, and other disgusting healthy vegetables.

All dug in straight away, and I too found myself piling on many things on my plate, especially the steak. I made sure to steer clear of the Cauliflower and Brussels sprouts though! Jayden arched a brow at the massive pile of food on my plate. I grinned and started to eat.

Dinner passed by quickly, with small chit chat, mainly between Katy and Tyson, and then Jayden and Kyron. I finally finished and patted my full stomach. I then stood up as did the rest of the table, we picked up all the plates and cutlery and carried them out to the kitchen. I washed a few plates as did Kyron, Tyson and Katy. I spun around when I felt a hand placed gently on my back. Jayden smiled down at me,

"How's your leg?" He asked concerned, and he looked down at it. I smiled,

"Doesn't hurt at all now." I said honestly.

"That's good." He smiled, then washed his plate. "I'll meet you upstairs?" He asked. I nodded and made my way for the stairs. I walked up them, dragging my feet as I went, and I went straight into Jayden's room, whilst debating on whether to have a shower. Katy then walked in, carrying a set of pyjamas and undergarments. She hands them over to me and I take with gratitude.

"Thank you so much for helping me out." I smiled at her. I honestly don't know what I would have done with out her. She smiled back at me,

"Sure, no problem. Of course I would help you, one, because you're our Luna, and two, you seem like a really nice person, and I can tell we will be great friends."

I nodded, agreeing with her on that last part especially. "That may be true, but I can't just keep borrowing your clothes!" I laughed. She nodded,

"That's why we are going shopping tomorrow!" She beamed excitedly. I grinned,

"Sounds like fun! I can't wait... Only... I feel bad for not being able to pay for myself." I admit sheepishly. Well to be fair, it's Jayden's fault for taking me and not bringing my wardrobe with me. Katy laughed and patted my arm,

"That's fine, really. I'm sure Jayden won't mind paying for you at all." She answered sincerely. She then winked, "Besides, it's the least he can do after everything he's put you through."

I smiled and thanked her again, and then she departed the room. I made my way for the shower, grabbed out my towel and the soap. I tied my hair up in a pony tail and turned the water on. I stripped and hopped in, allowing the hot water to hit my skin. I sighed in relief as I felt my muscles beginning to relax.

Dylan crossed my mind. Was he okay down there in those dungeons? Was he at least being fed? I worried for him. What if they were hurting him, torturing him? Maybe I should tell Jayden about him. I know how much Jayden cares for the Warrior Wolves, how he considers them family to him even though he doesn't even know them. I know that Dylan descends from that pack because of his fur... Maybe Jayden will let Dylan live here like a normal person, treat him like family too? I don't know, but I hope so.

Another question popped into my mind as I washed my arms and legs. In my 'dream' I had earlier, I know it wasn't a dream, but more a memory. Remembering that speech my mother gave me, about understanding things, like who I am, where I come from, love... I understand most of it, but I don't get the 'love' part. I don't understand what she meant by that at all. I shrugged, and twisted the taps off. I guess I could just ask Jayden later. I then hopped out of the shower and dried myself off.

Chapter Seven

Avery's POV

Once I had hung my wet towel on the rail on the back of the wooden door, and changed into Katy's pyjamas, I unlocked the door and walked into Jayden's room to find him laying on his bed, stomach facing up. I speedily walked over to him, feeling the sudden need to be closer. I lay down beside him, and he wrapped his arms underneath me and around me. I snuggled closer to his chest. We laid there in silence but my thoughts loudly attacked my brain. I exhaled deeply and looked at Jayden, he looked back at me, questioning my questioning eyes.

"Jayden, there are a few things I want to ask you."

"Anything Love," he smiled sweetly and nodded for me to continue.

"Well today, when I fell asleep-"

"When you were lying naked on my back?" Jayden interrupted with a smirk and waggle of his eyebrows. So that is what he was so happy about earlier... Wait, ew!I shook my head, trying to get the thought out.

"Yeah, whatever. Look, when I was asleep, I had this flashback, memory thing. My brother and my mum was there, and I was riding around on Daniel's back when he was in wolf form. I was much younger then, and Daniel was new to being a shifted Werewolf." I explained, my voice gradually becoming quieter and quieter, and tears blurred at the back of my eyes. Just thinking about Daniel made me sick to the stomach. What if he was dead? The horrifying thought never seemed to leave my mind, it stuck there like gum on the bottom of a shoe.

"Sh Baby girl, don't cry." He stroked my cheek tenderly. I sniffed and brushed his hand away, I didn't want his sympathy. Not for that.

I continued, "A-anyway... My mum came over to us, and she told Daniel that he could never ever let anyone see him in his wolf form, because it was dangerous or something like that. And I wanted to know why so I asked her and she answered with, 'One day, when you are older, you will understand everything, about who you are, about our kind, where you are truly from, why you are to keep yourself hidden and even about love'... well something like that. I understand almost everything she meant now, but what I don't understand is, the 'love' part. She told me that day, that our father wasn't supposed to be apart of our lives, and then she mentioned I will understand about love. I haven't got a clue what she was on about there, and I was wondering if maybe, you had any ideas?"

I looked at Jayden with questioning eyes. He looked deep in thought. "I don't know if I'm right on this one Avery, but I believe I know what she meant by that." He muttered. I looked at him with pleading eyes,

"Please tell me your thoughts." I begged. He sighed and rolled over so he was on his side, facing me. He looked me in the eyes and he answered,

"Well, legend has it, that the Midnight Warriors' mates were always in their pack. That was why every single wolf in their pack was either black or white. No other colours. A black Werewolf's mate will be a pure white wolf and vice versa. So when your mother said your father wasn't supposed to be apart of your life, I believe she meant-"

"They weren't mates." I answered in a mere whisper, finally I realised the big secret my parents hid from me. "Then why were they together?" I asked confused. Why did they never tell us? Why did I not know of this!?

"I don't know, love." He cupped my cheek. "But I want to know as much as you do. But at least now, you know everything you need to." He said, drowsily. I nodded, I was quite sleepy myself, so I snuggled closer with my head on his chest and left arm across his chest. I buried my face into the crook of his neck and shoulder.

"Thank you Jayden," I mumbled before I fell asleep, still with unanswered questions swirling actively inside my mind. Wow. Who knew my parents weren't mates? Why did they lie about it? Why are they even together? Maybe they loved each other regardless? So Jayden and I are mates only because we originated from the same pack?

Then the more normal questions were, Is Dylan okay? He's from my original pack, so will Jayden except him? Should I tell Jayden about him tomorrow? And my brother Daniel, is he alive? Is he safe? Will I ever see him again?

I shut off my thoughts and allowed the darkness to take over me, to swallow me whole.

...

The next morning moved very sluggishly. I had decided to tell Jayden about Dylan after my little shopping spree with Katy, and boy was I nervous about it!

"What about this?" Katy queried as she pulled out a blue, loose shirt, that had yellow lined patterns all over it. Right now, we were in one of Katy's favourite clothes shops. I shook my head at her with a disapproving stare.

"No. Too bright for me." I muttered and flicked through the set of shirts that had buttons up the middle. I came upon a red and black checkered shirt, the collar was long, the sleeves stopped at elbow length, and they split at the end, I smiled and pulled out a size eight. I had a shirt like this at home that I used to wear all the time. It was baggy and I loved it.

I continued to walk around the shop, I had picked out several t-shirts, mainly black or blue and white with different patterns in them. I had also found several pairs of shorts, high waist and low, few went as long as just above the knee, but must stopped at mid thigh, I also picked out a couple skirts that had a length a little longer than the shorts– although skirts weren't really my style.

"OMG I love that shirt, maybe I should get me one." Katy grinned down at my plain green, fitted and sleeveless shirt. I smiled and pointed to where I found it. We then walked over to the counter to pay for everything. Katy pulled out two credit cards, "One's Jayden's," she said with a smile. I nodded with a grin and then we left the store, several bags in each hand.

So far, we had been to at least ten different shops, and I was starting to get tired. We had already had lunch over an hour ago, and it was getting close to three o'clock. I sighed heavily, "Do you think we should get going back now?" I yawned. Katy pouted,

"Naw, but we only just started shopping!" She whined. I blinked at her several times with both my eyebrows raised.

"Katy, we have been shopping for six hours!" I laughed. She frowned,

"Whatever," she mumbled but cracked a small smile. We made our way to the car and drove back to the house. After driving up the long driveway,

Katy parked the convertible car in the garage, that contained another seven cars. I grabbed my nine shopping bags and I walked over to Katy to give her a bone-crushing hug.

"Thank you again, for everything. Especially for today. I really needed a girls day out. I haven't had one in... ever." I laughed and released her from my death grip. She grinned,

"It's all G sister." She laughed and we walked inside. I saw Jayden and Tyson in the lounge room, sitting on the double couch, watching football. Jayden's head instantly turned to look at us, and a large smile washed over his gorgeous face. He stood up and walked over to me, he then engulfed me in for a hug, causing me to drop my bags in the process. He buried his face in the crook of my neck and inhaled my scent.

I laughed, "Miss me much?" He nodded and inhaled deeply. "Where do I put my things?" I asked, as I snapped out of my little day dream and glanced down at the several bags on the carpet. Jayden let go and smiled, he took some of the bags off of the floor and held them in one hand, then he took my hand with his other hand. I picked up the remaining four bags and followed him to his bedroom. He let go of my hand once we walked in, and he then walked over to his large, walk-in wardrobe and opened it.

"I cleaned it out today, got most of my clothes out and put them in the draws, and got rid of all the junk and crap. You can keep your clothes in here, is this enough space?" He asked and stepped back. I stepped closer to see a completely clean, near on empty give or take a couple suits and super nice shirts, hanging in the corner.

"Thank you." I exhaled with relief and awe. He nodded,

"Anything for you." He chuckled and walked over to the bed and plopped himself down on it. I opened my bags and started to hang up all my new clothes. Jayden watched me, every minute I could feel eyes at the back of my head, although I'm sure he wasn't staring the whole time, that would be kind of creepy.

After I had hung up the last piece of clothing, I placed all the bags inside the biggest bag and left it by the door. I then walked over to Jayden and jumped on the bed beside him. He pulled me in for a hug, "Avery, there are some people I would really like you to meet." He smiled down at me. I looked up into his eyes and nodded,

"Let's go then." I gave him a toothy grin. He nodded,

"Hang on, let me call them down to the meeting room." He said. I watched as he zoned out for a minute, he must have been using his mind link to talk to them. A couple moments later, he came back out of his little trance, and then he stood up and smiled down at me. I jumped off the bed and he took my hand in his and entwined our fingers.

We then walked out of the bedroom and down the stairs, through the kitchen and into the hallway. The end of the hallway, on the right was the lounge room, but on the left was the meeting room, from what I could remember. And I happened to be right. As we walked into the large room, I saw a very long, rectangular, glass table. Sitting around it, was about thirty other Werewolves. I hadn't seen these guys and women here before so I assumed they were extra pack members.

"Thank you for coming everyone. I would like to introduce you to my lovely mate, Avery Brighter, Sister of Daniel Brighter, the Alpha of the White Crescent Moon Pack."

They all nodded, and 'Ohh'ed. I smiled sheepishly and looked away, to avoid making eye contact. "She is also a pure white wolf," Jayden announced. I then heard a series of gasps, and I glanced around briefly to see several shocked faces. Jayden looked down at me and wrapped an arm around my waist, bringing me close into his side. "Avery, these Werewolves, in this very room, aren't any ordinary Werewolves. They too originate from the Midnight Warriors, and they were apart of the Warrior Wolves Pack." He grinned proudly. Now it was my turn to stare with astonishment.

"B-but how are they all here together? How did they all know to come here-"

"Avery, I've travelled far and wide, around the whole world, looking for fellow Werewolves, ones of pure white or black fur. A couple, the previous alpha had brought together. And from each pack that we have battled, the survivors of the black or white furred are spared and brought into this pack. So far there are twenty-eight of us." He waved his hand around the room. "Ten of these guys are mates, those five guys there, and their mates over there." He pointed at the small group. I nodded and Jayden continued, "The others are still searching for their mates." He muttered. "Oh, and there are now also a few children."

I nodded again, letting the information sink in. I spotted one of the mated females and her mate, standing beside one another, holding hands. But the female in her other hand/arm holds a baby, cuddled close up to her chest. I looked at it with awe, then my eyes averted to Jayden and I smiled.

"So, all of us, we are like our own pack?" I indicated with a grin. Jayden nodded,

"But a secret pack. No one can know about this, well except the rest of my pack, and your family, because Daniel, Finn and your mother, as they are like us too," He explained.

"Yeah, except for, Daniel might not be anymore..." I muttered under my breath. Jayden squeezed my hand lightly,

"Don't think like that. There's always hope." He said reassuringly. I nodded and looked up at him again. The part of me that hated him to much, had shrunk so quickly over such little time. My stupid wolf and the mate bond had been victorious into swaying me into liking my mate.

"So, what you're telling me here, is that every black of white pure wolf you come across, you take in to this pack, and treat them as family, no matter what pack they come from?" He nodded and I grinned, "Good, because I know another black wolf, and he's actually living really close by at the moment-"

"What? Who? Where is he?" Jayden became exceptionally alert. I smiled,

"His name is Dylan, and he's a good friend of mine," I answered and Jayden nodded, carefully listening to the details. "And you rescued him from my dungeon."

Jayden locked eyes with me, stunned. "That guy down in my dungeons right now, he is from our pack?" He hesitantly asked. I nodded. "Why was he locked away in the first place though?" He asked, dazed by the thought.

"My father locked him away, as soon as he discovered Dylan was a black wolf. Dylan was only a few weeks old. He's uh, what you call an actual Warrior Wolf, you know, the ones that are born wolf-"

"Yeah, I know. That's where they get their name from. The Warrior Wolf pack, originally every male wolf born from that pack was born a Warrior, all born in their wolf forms. But it has changed over time, and not as many are born in wolf form anymore." Jayden explained. I nodded.

"Look, anyway, my father thought he was a real threat, and thought he was protecting both Dylan and out pack, by locking Dylan away... So for the past two years, Dylan was locked away with out my knowing. I thought my father had killed him, but I was wrong... Had I known though, I would have busted him out a long time ago." I said, maddened. Jayden smiled,

"Well, let's go get Dylan out of that cell, and bring him up here." Jayden grinned and let go of my hand. "Wait here," he told me and then he jogged out of the room. I looked around the now very silent room. It had appeared they had heard our conversation.

"Um... Hey...?" I shyly greeted. They all smiled welcomingly and bowed their heads with respect.

"Hi Luna," they all returned, "Nice to meet you." Or "Welcome to the pack." They all seemed very friendly.

"Please, call me Avery," I laughed. I walked around the room, getting to know everyone. There were three children and a baby, then there were twenty-four adults. About ten or so minutes later, Jayden came rushing back into the room, with a boy behind him. The boy wore denim ripped jeans, a black, fitted t-shirt and black sneakers. I'm guessing that Jayden leant him the clothes. The boy looked up at me, his jet black hair swished upwards, it was wet, so I'm also guessing that he had just quickly washed it. His piercing eyes locked with mine.

"Dylan." I breathed with relief. He smiled,

"It's nice to see you again Avery."

Chapter Eight

✱ Edited Version*

Avery's POV

I couldn't believe my eyes. This was the first time I could get a good look at Dylan, well the other day when I first saw him locked away, I couldn't see his face clearly ad he looked awful, because of the malnourished, dirt ridden and beaten appearance. So of course he did not look like his natural self. But now... Whoa, I have to admit, he's definitely very attractive.

I mean, not as attractive as Jayden, Jayden's just.... Indescribably good looking. And Dylan... Dylan's just hot. Any who, I shouldn't be thinking about this right now. I shook the thoughts out of my head, and I stepped forward so I was only inches in front of Dylan. Then I did something I had been dying to do, from the moment my father snatched him out of my arms and took him away from me.

I hugged him.

Now I know he wasn't expecting it because straight away, his body went rigid. He hadn't been held like this before, that much was clearly evident. After a minute, Dylan was still as still as a plank, so I whispered in his ear,

"It's okay Dylan. Don't be afraid. It's just a hug." I reminded him. He relaxed a little, as though just my voice had a calming effect on him, and he then wrapped his arms around me and hugged me back.

"Thank you Avery," He murmured. I nodded and pulled away. I smiled at him,

"Look at you, all grown up." I faked a tear. "My baby's all grown up." I cracked a grin, but behind the forced smile, I was sad thinking about how I wasn't there for him, all the time he spent in those dungeons. How as he grew up, I didn't even know he was alive. I was supposed to raise and protect him. But I failed him.

"And you look much older too, Luna," he mocked. I frowned and tapped his arm. I heard someone clearing their throat, and I looked over my shoulder to see Jayden standing there, his arms firmly folded over his chest. I rolled my eyes and turned back to Dylan. "Well, anyway, I best be getting back to Jayden. Feel free to meet our... Uh, actual pack?" I laughed but Dylan however looked quite puzzled. My face turned serious, I walked over to Jayden, grabbed his wrist and dragged him over to Dylan. "Explain everything to him. And I mean everything." I demanded and looked between the two.

Jayden nodded, "Will do, Love." I rolled my eyes at his giddy tone and then I went to leave the rom, but before I left, I turned to face everyone,

"It was lovey to meet you all," I said, really articulating my words. I then exited the room and entered the eminent lounge room. Kyron sat on a single sized chair with Sasha sated on his lap, Tyson sat on the left side of the double sized couch with Katy straddling him, and of course they were making out. Super lovey dovey this atmosphere is...

I cleared my throat and both their heads snapped up and looked in my direction, Katy's cheeks flushed a bright red, where as Tyson only chuckled humorously. And just when I was about to politely ask Katy if she would help me make dinner, - "What do you want?" Sasha snapped venomously. I turned to look at her with an arched eyebrow.

"Have you got a problem?" I asked, my tone not so friendly, and I placed my right hand on my hip, giving me a sassy look. I watched, a little intrigued as Sasha stood up and she placed both hands on her hips,

"Well actually..."

Kyron frowned, "Baby, don't do this please," he pleaded her and went to lightly grab her wrist. Sasha roughly shrugged him off and took several steps closer to me, so she was right in my face.

"I do have a problem." She smirked. What a tough girl. I wanted to laugh. Instead, I pretended to think,

"Want to tell me what that is?" I asked, then I looked from Kyron, then to the meeting room where my mate was busy interacting. "Actually, I think I know quite well what your problem is." I sneered bitterly, feeling solely defensive.

"Oh you don't know shit. You're a crappy Luna, you aren't strong, or at all intelligent, let alone beautiful enough to lead this pack." She hissed attackingly. Now I laughed,

"And you are? Oh wait, Hun, please don't tell me you actually thought you were stronger, and prettierthan I. Because if you had at all looked in the mirror lately, you'd see a skinny stick, cake faced Barbie, who doesn't even know the answer to 'who's your mate?'. And FYI, it's not Jayden." I smirked and crossed my arms firmly over my chest. I heard a low growl coming from Kyron, so I turned to look at him,

"Great, now you've got a problem too. Go on," I nodded for him to spill it.

"Don't talk to my mate like that, you ugly bitch." He snarled and stood up to look at me menacingly. He stepped beside Sasha and wrapped his arm around her waist. I glanced over my shoulder to peer at Tyson and Katy, both had amused and interested expressions mixed across their faces. Well then, I'm glad they're enjoying the show.

I spun back around to face Kyron and Sasha, fairly unimpressed with Kyron's expressed opinion. "Kyron, you don't believe it, do you? You really have no idea." A small smile played upon my lips. I glanced back at the meeting room, then back at the Barbie and her Prince Charming. Sasha glared at me ominously as she caught on rather quickly.

"Believe what? What don't I know?" Kyron asked confused.

"It's nothing babe. The Whore is just trying to get in-between us." I could tell Sasha was trying her best not to falter or stutter her words. I laughed sharply,

"That was the most crappiest defense line I've ever heard! And I've heard some pretty stupid things in my lifetime." I laughed harder.

"Sasha, what is this crazy Bitch going on about?" He demanded and turned to look at her.

"Ouch, that hurt," I evidently feigned hurt, gasped and placed a hand over my heart. I mean, seriously? You think calling me a Crazy Bitch is going to effect me the slightest? You'll have to try harder pal... Oh how much rage would explode from Jayden if he heard this conversation. I'd take joy in watching Sasha snap in half, like the breakable twig she is.

"Ugh, just shut up already!" Sasha yelled, "No one cares about you! Not even your mate!" She screeched at me and threw both her hands up in the air. Now that hurt, just a little. Of course I know that's not at all true though, but the feeling that if it were... Nah it's not true.

"And you honestly think he cares for you?" I spat with a mocking laugh.
She looked taken aback. I turn to look at Kyron,

"Your mate is a snarky, stuck up bitch with no self dignity or morals. She is
the pack's slut who would gladly sleep around with other guys if it meant
she could climb her way to the top of the ranks. She's only using you
Kyron. And I pity you for being too naïve to see through her glass act."
I said sympathetically, and I placed a hand on his shoulder for just a couple
seconds. I then continued with my little speech, "Anyone can see that she
doesn't love you, and she never has. She is in love with the Alpha – well I
think maybe more lusting after the Alpha is a more accurate way of putting
it. But don't take my word for it, go ahead, ask her." I waved a hand at Sasha.
"But all you are going to get from her, is words coming out of her ass." I
shrugged.

I then walked out of the room without another word. I was mad at Kyron,
the way he spoke to me was down right disrespectful. But it really was Sasha
who was pulling his strings. I felt sorry for him, and for any other guy on
the planet who was stupid enough to see right through their partners like
that, and let them manipulate them blindly.

I walked into the kitchen, placed both my palms on the island bench, and
pushed myself back and forth lightly, as I desperately tried to control the
boiling fury that continued to grow in the pit of my stomach. I shook my
head, irritated. I then heard quiet footsteps enter the room and I spun
around to see Katy and Tyson walking in with pained facial expressions.
I looked at them with bafflement.

"We're sorry Luna. We should have stepped in- we didn't think it would get
that far-"

Instantly I cut Tyson off by waving a dismissive hand, "Tyson I'm okay.
Really." I smiled. I then frowned, "And please for the love of God. Call me

Avery! Or do I have to start calling you Blondie again?" I raise an eyebrow. His facial expression hardens.

"No Avery." He glared at me playfully. Katy then arched an eyebrow and looks at me questioningly. I laughed,

"When I first met Tyson, I didn't know his name, so I called him Blondie and it just became a funny habit... Well it was funny for me anyway." I explained, causing Katy to erupt into a fit of giggles.

Tyson pouted, "Gee thanks Avery. There goes my masculinity."

"Oh honey, that was lost a long time ago," Katy joked. I just winked,

"Anytime Blondie."

After the laughter died down, I spoke again, "So... Would anyone like to help me make dinner?" I smiled. Katy beamed and Tyson groaned.

"But I made it last night," he whined. I laughed,

"Tough luck Princess Blondie," I teased. Katy and I began to giggle again.

"You really aren't going to let that go, are you?" Tyson groaned. I grinned,

"Nope! Now. Help me with dinner!"

...

I flopped down on the bed, my hair was wet from the shower I had a few minutes ago. I heard the taps from the bathroom twist off, indicating that Jayden had finally finished in the shower. I pulled back the covers and crept into bed. I snuggled under the blankets and minutes later, the bathroom door creaked open, and the bed dipped beside me. I was then pulled into a firm but warm chest. Oh the warmth that radiated from his skin.

"Jayden?" I asked, my eyes were closed comfortably.

"Mmm?"

"Can I please call Finn tomorrow? I need to know how he is." I say quietly.

"And you want to know if there is any news of Daniel." He muttered, I nodded. He sighed, "Okay. But there is something else I want you to do."

I looked up at him in question, "And what's that?" I run my hand up his rock hard set of abs and up his chest.

"Invite your family to come live up here? I'm sure they were the only survivors after that battle, and we are trying to get the Warrior wolf pack back together."

I grimaced, "My father might try to kill you..." I mumbled. Jayden chuckled,

"Oh, I'm sure I can handle him." He smirked and held me closer to him. I nodded,

"I'll ask them. I can't guarantee a yes."

Jayden nodded, "Good night Avery."

"Good night Jay." I mumbled before dozing off into a deep, peaceful slumber.

...

I grinned as I pulled out Jayden's iPhone and pressed the 'on' button. I skipped down the stairs and into the kitchen, and I then took a seat at the island bench on a stool, beside Katy. The phone screen automatically lit up and the background of the sea shone through it. I swiped my finger across the screen and a passcode then showed up. It was a pattern password. Katy looked just as disappointed as I was.

"Don't look at me, I don't know any of his passwords." She muttered bitterly. Just as she said that, Jayden walked in, whilst running a hand through his messy bed hair. He walked over to the fridge and swung the silver door wide open with a yawn.

"Speak of the devil," I mumbled. I see Jayden lift an eyebrow with a questioning gaze.

"What are you two on about?" He asked in a cautious tone.

"What's your phone password?" I asked simply. Jayden spun around to face me, and he snatched his mobile phone out of my hand.

"Nooo, no, no, no, a thousand times no." He laughed and I pouted.

"But you said I could call my brother Finn, today." I looked down at the bench top surface.

"And you can," he handed me back the iPhone which was now unlocked, and switched onto Logs with the number pad up on the screen. "You just can't know the password." He poked his tongue out at me. I rolled my eyes and dialed my old home phone number. It rang a few times before someone answered it, it wasn't a recognisable voice I heard.

"Hello?" A gruff, male voice replied.

"H-hello? Who's this?" I asked, my voice quavered a little. Katy looked at me muddled and alert.

"Who's this? Lady, have you got the wrong number or something?"

No. I definitely had the right number. "No. This is the White Crescent Moon pack, is it not?" I spoke louder and more confidently. The guy was silent.

"Who is this?" He asked again. Realisation then hit and the voice became slightly more recognisable. No... It couldn't be him!

"Mark?" I asked, my voice softened. If our beta was back, did that mean Daniel was alive? Was he back too?

"A-Avery?" He whispered, shocked, but relieved.

"Yes Mark. It's me." A said as a couple tears rolled down my cheeks. Why am I crying at the sound of his voice?? I never got along with him!

"Avery, where are you? Are you safe?"

"Mark, calm down. I uh... I'm at the Dark Shadow Pack's place. I'm safe here, don't worry about me. Where's Daniel? Is he with you? Can I speak to him please?" I blurted out in a rush.

"Avery... Daniel's not... he's not here. The last time I heard from him, was two days ago, a couple days after the battle. We were out in hiding together, but we were separated when we were attacked by rogues. I'm not sure what happened to him, but I found myself wondering around, and somehow I made my way back home with out being detected." He explained.

"Wait... Are you saying that my brother is alive or dead? Mark! What's really going on?" I was so beyond worried now.

"Calm down Avery, it's okay. I'm sure he's alright. I'm not sure where he is, but I'm positive that he is alive. He's the strongest guy I know."

I nodded, taking all the new information in. After snapping out of those thoughts, I quickly asked, "May I speak with Finn?" A short silence was followed by,

"Yeah, sure. Here he is... Avery? Be careful okay?" Mark asked. I nodded,

"I will. By Mark." Then there was a muffled sound on the other end of the line. My younger brother received the phone. "Finn?" I called.

"Yes Avery. I'm here."

He sounds... different. Calmer. Sadder. Matured. "Finn, are you okay? You sound... different."

"I'm fine Avery. I've changed through out the past week. I've uh, been through a lot but I'm all good. I'm stronger now." He voice was stern and assured, almost emotionless.

"Look, um... I really want to see you. And there is something big you should know about... W-what I'm trying to say is... would you and mother come down here? Jayden and I have things to explain. A lot of things..." I trailed off.

"I don't know Avery. It doesn't sound like the smart thing to do. Not many pack members survived here, and we need to be here for them."

"Finn, it's not like I'm asking you all to come. Just you and mother. The pack will have Mark, and father." I reasoned.

"Look, you'll have to talk to mother about this." Finn said. He sounded agitated. Since when was he so stubborn and... not wanting to be my brother?Just last week he was so innocent, scared, loving and not to mention, excited just to hear my voice through the voice... But now... "You there Avery?" Boredom was evident in his tone. I sighed and rubbed my forehead.

"Yes Finn. Put mother on the phone please." I muttered, unhappy.

"Mother! Avery wans to talk to you!" Finn yelled. "Bye Avery."

"Finn, wait-" I was too late, he had already handed the phone away.

"Avery?" My mother's worried voice rang through my ear.

"Mother? Mum it's me."

"Avery! Are you okay? Are they treating you well?"

"Yes mother. I'm fine. Look... I need you and Finn to come here. I need to talk to you about certain things..." I trailed off again.

"Okay... Your father, Finn and I will be up there in a few days tops. You'll need to let us know where you are though."

"No mother. Father can't come. Him and Mark need to stay and watch the pack." I used as an excuse. In reality, I really just didn't want to see my mate and my father have a brawl.

"No sweetie. Mark can do that alone. There aren't that many pack members left-"

"Mum, there are other reasons that I can't talk to you about it now. It will just be you and Finn that can come. And we will come to pick you up. Jayden doesn't want the location of his pack to be known." I explained.

"Hmm, okay. At least I will see you, that's what I'm happy about, that's all that matters." I smiled, this was the side of her that I loved. She sounds so caring and loving, and I've missed that.

"Okay, we will pick you up in a couple days, maybe three or four?" I double checked.

"Yes darling, look I have to go, Finn needs me-"

"Oh wait. Speaking of Finn... What's got his nose out of joint?"

There was a silent pause. "Honey, I don't know what you're referring to."

"You know damn well what I am talking about." I snapped at her, suddenly getting very cross.

"Look, I have to go. I'll explain everything to you when I see you. Goodbye Avery, I love you." She spoke sincerely. I sighed,

"Love you too." I mumbled and hung up the phone. I frowned and looked over at Jayden, who sat across from me, happily munching away at his cereal. I slid his iPhone across the island bench to him. He grabbed it and stuffed it back into the back pocket of his black, denim jeans. He then raised his eyebrow at me.

"So...? Details?" Katy chimed in with excitement. I sighed again,

"We are going to pick them up in four days. Mum is all worried and everything for once, and Finn is a little, emotionless brad." I spat and rested my chin in my palm, and my elbow on the bench. Why is life so difficult?

"Oh." She said sadly.

"You okay Love?" Jayden asked, and he reached his hand across the bench to gently grab hold of my arm.

"Yeah. I'll live." I sighed. I then got up and walked over to the cupboards, and I dragged out my favourite cereal. I ate breakfast in silence, having Katy and Jayden watch my every move, both quite concerned.

Once I had finished eating, I dumped my bowl in the sink, and spun around, "Why are you two so quiet?" I asked, suspicious. Katy shrugged with a smile, and she then skipped out of the room. Strange girl. I meant that in a good way of course. I shook my head and chuckled. Jayden walked over to me, wrapped his arm around my waist. He looked down at me and grinned.

"What are we doing today?" I asked with a smile, and I wrapped my arms around his neck.

"That's a secret." He whispered, "But I'll need you to get changed into comfy, outdoor clothes." He smirked down at me.

"So these skinny jeans won't be any good for today?" I asked and glanced down at the white jeans I had on. I quite liked these skinny jeans.

"Nope, they won't be any good at all. But they are good at making your ass look great." He winked and pecked my lips. I laughed and kissed him back, then I made my way for the stairs and to Jayden's bedroom to change into comfortable leggings, and sneakers.

Twelve

A /N

Here's chapter twelve :) don't forget to vote and comment! :)Sorry for any spelling/grammar errors

Avery

I grinned as I pulled out Jayden iPhone and press the on button. Skipping down the stairs a d into the kitchen, I take a seat at the is,and bench beside Katy. The phone screen lights up and the back ground of a sea shines through. I swipe my finger across the screen and a pass code screen shows up. It's a pattern password. Katy looks as disappointed as I was.

"Don't look at me. I don't know any of hid passwords" she mumbled. Just as the said that Jayden walked in running a hand through his messy bed hair. He walked straight over to the fridge and swung the silver door open.

"Speak of the devil" I mutter. I see Jayden raise his eye brow questioningly. "What are you two on about?" He asked cautiously."What's your phone password?" I ask simply. Jayden spins around to face me and snatches his mobile out of my hand.

"Nooo, no, no, no a thousand times no!" He laughed. I pouted"But you said I could call my brother Finn today" I look down at the table."And you can" he handed me back the iphone which was now unlocked, and on logs with the number pad up. "You just can't know my password" he stick his tongue out at me.

I rolled my eyes and dialled my old home phone number. It rang a few times before someone picked up. It wasn't a recognisable voice."Hello?" A gruff male voice rang. "H-hello? Who's this?" I ask my voice quavered a little. Katy looked at me confused and alert.

"Who's this? Lady have you got the wrong number or something?" No I knew I had the right number."No this is The White Moon Crescent pack house is it not?" I speak up. The guy was silent."Who's this?" He finally asked. Realisation hit. No it couldn't be m! But where-

"Mark?" I ask my voice softening. If our beta was back did that mean Daniel was alive? Was he back too?

"A-Avery?" He whispered shocked yet relieved. "Yes Mark it's me" I say a tear runs down my cheek. Why am I crying at the sound of his voice? I never got along with him.

"Avery, where are you? Are you safe?""Mark calm down. I uh.. I'm at The Dark Shadow pack, I'm safe here don't worry. Where's Daniel? Is he with you? May I speak to him please?" I rush out.

"Avery.. Daniels not here. The last time I heard from him was two days ago, a couple days after the battle. We were out in hiding together but we were separated when we were attacked by rogues, I'm not sure what happened to him but I found myself wondering and here I am." He stated the obvious. Wait what!?

"So your telling me he's still alive? Or is he dead or Mark! What's really going on!?" I was so worried now.

"Avery calm down, it's ok. I'm sure he's alright. I'm not sure where he is but I'm positive he's alive." I nod taking it all in. Snapping out of my thoughts I quickly ask"May I speak to Finn?" There was silence for a moment.

"Yeah sure. Here he is. Avery.. Be careful ok?" Mark asks quietly I nod."I will. Good bye Mark" then there is a muffled sound and my younger brother received the phone. "Finn?" I call

"Yes Avery, I'm here" he sounds different. Calmer, sadder, older."Finn are you alright? You sound.. Different""I'm fine Avery. I've changed through out the past week. I've uh.. Been through a lot but I'm all good. I'm stronger now" his voice was stern, almost emotionless.

"Look um.. I really want to see you and there is something big you should know about.. W-what I'm trying to say is, would you and mum come down here? Jayden and I have things to explain" I trailed off.

"I don't know Avery. It doesnt sound like the smart thing to do. Not many pack members survived here and we need to be here for them-""Finn it's not like I'm asking you all to come, just you and mum. The pack will have Mark and Dad" I reason.

"Look you'll have to talk to mother about this" Finn said annoyed. Since when was he so stubborn and.. Not wanting to be my brother? Just last week he was so innocent, scared, loving and not to mention excited to hear my voice through the phone but now... "You there Avery?" Boredom showed in his tone. I sighed and rubbed my forehead.

"Yes Finn. Put mum on" I mutter distastefully."Mother! Avery wants to talk to you!" Finn yelled, "bye Avery""Finn wait-" I was to late, he left the phone."Avery?" My mothers worried voice rang through my ears.

"Mum? Mum its me""Avery! Are you ok? Are they treating you well?""Yes mother. I'm fine. Look.. I need you and Finn to come up. I need to talk to you about certain things" I trail off.

"Ok.. Your Father, Finn and I will be up there in a few days tops. You'll need to let us know where you are though-""No mum. Father can't come. Him and Mark need to stay and watch the pack-" I used an excuse"No sweetie, mark can do that alone, there aren't that many pack members left-"

"Mum there are other reasons that I can't talk to you about now. It will just be you and Finn. And we will come to pick you up. Jayden doesn't want the location of his back getting out" I explain.

"Hmm ok. At least I will see you, that's what I'm happy about" I smile. I love this side of her, she sounds so caring and loving. I've missed that."Ok, we'll pick you up in a few days, maybe four or five?" I double check.

"Yes darling. Look I have to go Finn needs me-""Oh wait. Speaking of Finn... What's got his nose out of joint?" There was silence."Honey I don't know what you're talking about-" I cut her off"You know damn well what I am talking about" I snap

"Look, I have to go. I'll explain everything when I see you. Goodbye Avery, I live you" she said in all honesty. I sigh"Love you too" I say and hang up the phone. With a frown I look over at Jayden, who sits across from me, happily munching on his cereal. I slid his iPhone across the island bench to him. He grabs it and stuffs it into his back pocket. Looking over at me he raises an eyebrow,

"So..? Details?" Katy chimes with excitement. I sigh"We are going to pick them up in four days, mums all worried and everything for once and Finns a little emotionless brat" I spit and rest my chin in my palm. Why is life so difficult?

"Oh" she says sadly. "You ok love?" Jayden asks reaching his hand across the bench and gently grabs hold of my arm. I sigh "Yeah I'll live" I then get up and walk over to the cupboards dragging out my favourite cereal. I eat breakfast in silence, having Katy and Jayden watch my every move. Once I had finished eating I dump my bowl in the sink and spin around.

"Why are you two so quiet?" I ask suspicious. Katy shrugged with a smile and skipped out of the room. Strange girl. I shake my head and chuckle. Jayden walks over to me, wrapping his arms around my waist. Looking down at me he grins.

"What are we doing today?" I ask smiling up at him. I wrap my arms around his neck."That's a secret" he whispers. "But I'll need you to get changed into comfy outdoor clothes" he smirks down at me.

"So these skinny jeans won't be any good for today?" I like these black jeans I have on right now."Nope they won't be any good at all" he mumbles and pecks my lips. I smile against his lips and kiss him back a little more passionately but pull back after a minute before it got to heated. I then ran for the stairs and ran straight to Jayden's room, locking myself in there.

"Avery open the door" Jayden knocks on the door, twisting the knob every so often. I laugh and dig through the wardrobe pulling out some black baggy shorts and a blue t-shirt. I chuck them on and skip over to the door unlocking it. Jayden walks in a frown on his face.

"Naw poor baby I locked you out of your room for two minutes and you're already crying" I used my baby tone. He glared at me but started to laugh."I wasn't crying" he defended."What ever" I stick my tongue out at him and walk into the bathroom. I brush my teeth and comb my hair. After braiding it to the side I walk back out.

Jayden stands up from the bed and walks over to me pulling me in for a hug. I find my self smudged up against his chest. "Can't. Breath!" I wheeze out. Jayden instantly let's go and looks down at the ground smiling sheepishly."Sorry" he mumbled. I laugh

"Come on, let's go" I chirp. He nods and holds my hand in his. Entwining he leads me out the room and down the stairs. "Where are we going?" I ask curiously, he ignores me with a grin and walks out the back door.

As soon as we step outside I am led into the forest. Boy am I glad I chose to wear sneakers today. Walking through the trees we come to a wide river, it's water so clear you can see the bottom. It was about two metres deep, three metres wide and it's length was I don't know, it went through the whole forest I'm guessing because I could see no end. I look at Jayden who just smiled back down at me.

"Is this it?" I ask smiling. It was beautiful. He shakes his head and picks me up bridal stile. I squeal "put me down Jayden!" He laughs and walks a few metres backwards, then looks at the stream. I shake my head, "no! No, no, you can't jump that far! Jayden I'll get soaked!" I screech. He laughs

"You seem to forget some of the werewolf perks and advantages" he says with a chuckle then runs towards the river. I scream as his feet lift off the ground and we sail through the air. I cling to Jayden's neck, and before I know it, his feet have safely landed on the ground. I look up at him startled.

"Wow" I breath. I then smack his chest "put me down!" I order, he laughs and places me on my feet and we start walking through the forest again."It's nice isn't it? Quiet, peaceful" he sighs in content, I nod agreeing with him."It's beautiful" I smile. I've always loved the woods. Coming across a wooden bridge over another river we walk over it. I run my hand over the smooth rails.

"So how's Dylan fitting in?" I ask breaking the silence."He's going good actually, the others seem to like him and are happily welcoming him into the pack" he smiled looking down."Something wrong?" I chuckle, he was silent. I stop and grab his arm "what aren't you telling me?" I ask seriously.

"Oh it's nothing really-""Jayden" I growl. He sighed"Do you have feelings for Dylan?" I blink at him."Yes I do. But not the way your thinking. Jayden. I don't love him that way, he's like family to me. You, are my mate Jayden" I rub his arm gently. He relaxed a little. "Why? How could you think that?" I ask a little hurt.

"I- I don't know I guess I'm just a little..." "Insecure?" I suggested. He playfully glared at me but sighed"Yeah" he admitted. I smiled and continued to walk, Jayden wailing beside me. "You're not mad?" He asked surprised. I chuckled

"Of course I'm not mad. I think it's.. Cute" I smile he scoffs "you know, how you would get jealous and insecure so easily" I tease. He growls and pulls me into his chest, spinning me around to face him. He wraps his arms around my waist and I place my two hands firmly on his chest. He breaths heavily.

"I don't get jealous" he whispers, I laugh and wrap my arms around his neck. "Well I haven't seen you jealous yet, but I beg to differ" I say laughing. I push him away and run off giggling like a school girl. Jayden catches up with me and I go back to walking. Before I know it bright light beams through my eyes and the trees disappear. There in front of me was a large patch of green grass, red, yellow and green flowers everywhere. A lake in the middle, and trees surrounded both the grass and the clear lake. I gape at it.

"It's beautiful" I breath."It is isn't it?" He smiled and walked to the only thick oak tree in the centre of the grass. I followed him and sat down next to him.

"Was this the place you wanted to take me to?" I ask looking around again. He nodded."Yeah" he looked down. I stand up and walk over to a patch of flower. I lye down on my back and look up at the sky.

Jayden walks over and joins me. I rest my head on his chest and we lay there in silence. I look up at Jayden, his features are soft and relaxed. "So tell me more about our legends, tell me stories of our pack" I say with a smile. He looks down at me with a grin.

"Well.. It all started when..." We lay there for hours on end, Jayden told me many stories and legends of our pack, but my favourite was of the battle that wiped most of them out. No I didn't like how they died, but the events in it, like acts of love. And before I knew it, the sun had disappeared and the moon had risen. Jayden stood up and dusted himself off.

I yawned and held my hands up. "Help me up" I demand childishly. Jayden chuckled and took my hands, hoisting me to my feet. We start walking back hand in hand, and before I know it my eyes start to droop. I feel my feet stumble beneath me and I head straight to the ground. Expecting to face plant, I wait for the pain, but it never comes. To firm arms wrap around me and pick me up.

Jayden holds me bridal style, up close to his chest. I yawn quietly and snuggle my head further against his warm chest. After a few minutes I find myself dozing off.

....

I wake up as I feel myself being placed down on the bed. My eyes slowly open and I stare up at Jayden who smiles back down at me. "Morning gorgeous" he smirks. "Haha funny, but it's not morning, I've been asleep for like half an hour?" I question

"Yeah yeah what ever, I'm gonna go down and get you your dinner" he smirks and leaves the room. I curl up under the blankets trying to get warm, why must they have the air-con on? I shrug and roll over onto my back looking up at the ceiling. A smile creeps onto my face as I think about today, it was so peaceful yet fun and entertaining. I loved talking to Jayden like that, and I lived listening to him.

Rolling over I look at the clock on the bedside table. It read 9:30pm. No wonder why I'm not 'that' tired.

Minutes later, Jayden returns carrying two plates of food. He placed a plate on top of the covers on my lap, then got into bed himself setting the plate on his lap. I dug in straight away, realising how starving I was. "So what do you think we should do tomorrow?" I ask taking a bite of mashed potatoes.

"Well sorry to break it to you sweet heart but I've got to do some pack stuff. You're welcome to join me but I think you would prefer to spend the day with Katy and Sasha" he smiled. I shivered remembering the fight I had with Sasha.

"What exactly would we be doing? The girls and I""They said they were going to the cinema to see some new movie.. 'the other woman' or something like that. They invited you to tag along so the offer is there. I'm sure it would be more entertaining than watching me talk about battle plans and patrolling." he answered shoving a spoon full of peas in his mouth. I frown. I'd love to go.. But only with Katy, not that bitch Sasha.

"Well.. I don't know. I don't think I really want to go to the movies with Sasha so I think I'll just watch you at your meeting" I smile sadly."Why? What's Sasha done to you? Has she hurt you? I swear if she touched you I'll rip her head off-" I cut him off

"No, no it's all good, I just got in a bit of a cat fight with her yesterday and I've got to say, I'm not too fond of her..." I answered simply. Jayden nodded in understanding. "And I may have ruined her and Kyron's relationship" I quickly stated in a whisper. Jayden raised an eye brow.

"You may have what? I don't think that's possible" Jayden chuckled. "Kyron loves her to pieces, what ever it is, I'm sure they'll get over it" he shrugs with a smile. I shake my head.

"No it wasn't some argument they had. I did a lot more than stir up tension between them.. I may have told a really big secret of Sasha and now Kyron probably thinks it's so unquestionably outrageous that he probably thinks I'm lying, and Sasha hates me even more than before!" I spit out. I don't care about Sasha but I feel so awful for Kyron, he must be so crushed and he must hate me so much.

"What exactly was this big secret?" Jayden asks placing his now empty plate on the bedside table. I look down at my hands."Sasha doesn't love him. I know They're mates an all but she doesn't love him" Jayden stares at me in shock.

"I'm sure that's just a rumour- they're in love with each other Avery-" I cut him off."No Jayden. It's true. She doesn't love him, she is in love with you" I slap a hand over my mouth. Oops. Jayden blinks a few times but looks like he doesn't give a crap. I shrug. Oh well, it slipped.

"Well I shall kick her out of the pack-""No! You can't do that-""Avery, she pretended to love Kyron when really she just wanted to get closer to me, she broke Kyron's heart and now Kyron is hurting. Shes probably called you god knows what, with a mouth like hers.. She insults people every five seconds. She is a bitch and deserves to be punished" he concluded.

"Look, I know she's done wrong things but no one deserves to be kicked out of their own pack!" I reason "she'll have no where to turn to-""I don't care what you say Avery. I'm kicking her out" he made up his mind.

"Ugh! I wish I never told you anything" I hit his shoulder. "Ouch!" He faked hurt. I rolled my eyes and rolled over on my side, my back to him, only to have him pull me close, into his chest. He rested his chin on my head and sighed. "You're not going to let this go are you?

"Nope" I say popping the p."Fine, I'll make you a deal. I won't kick Sasha out of the pack-" I start to smile. "IF-" my smile drops "if Kyron doesn't hate her. I mean, Kyron will be upset, angry, but if he wants her gone as much as I- then she shall be gone" he vowels. I sigh and roll over to face him.

"It's a deal" I say with a nod.

Thirteen

A /N

Here's chapter thirteen :) enjoy! Please don't forget to vote and comment (:

Sorry for any spelling/grammar errors

Waking up to the sun in my eyes, was not pleasant. I scold Jayden for forgetting to close the blinds last night but all he does is moan an 'I'm Soory' and rolls over and falls back asleep. Sighing I get out of bed and change into a pair of jeans and a blue shirt with small frills down the edges. I then walk into the bathroom to take a cool shower and wash my hair. After drying off I comb my hair, brush my teeth. I then leave the bathroom and head outside the room.

"Where are you going?" Jayden groans and rolled over to face me. I smile

"To go find Katy.." I answer

"Now, now Avery. Don't lie to me. You're going to find Kyron aren't you?" He smirked. I roll my eyes

"Yes I going to find Kyron. Now, good bye!" I run out the room and down the stairs, ignoring all of Jayden's protests. When I reach the kitchen I see Sasha and Katy sitting on the stools talking quietly. Their heads snap up at me, Katy smiles sadly where as Sasha glares at me and muffled a growl.

I smile sheepishly but focus my attention on Katy. "Uh.. Where are the guys? Tyson and Ky-" I hear a growl come from Sasha. I glare at her then look back at Katy and smile. "Where are Tyson and Kyron?" I ask politely.

"They're in the lounge room" she smiles back at me.

"Thank you" I nod.

"You're such a bitch" Sasha growls. I spin around and storm up to her, I bend slightly so I am right in her face. I Roughly pointing at her chest with my index finger

"I'd watch your tongue if I was you!" I hissed. "I just might have saved your ass by convincing MY mate, to not kick your sorry ass out of here. I would gladly have you thrown out onto the streets but I am busy looking out for YOUR mate! So don't you dare call me a bitch when you are just a pathetic slut who doesn't give to flying shits for your mate!" I yell at her causing her to flinch and cower down. She bows her head in submission.

"That's right" I stand back up straight with a proud smirk. I spin around and walk out of the room and find my way to the lounge room. When I walk in I see three men sitting on the double couch. Kyron, in the middle, with his head hung low.. And is he- crying? To his left, Tyson sat with his hand on Kyron's back. And to the right Dylan sat rather uncomfortable. He looked sad for Kyron but didn't quite know how to show it seeing how they only met yesterday.

"It's ok man, she's just a little no one who's gonna get her ass kicked out of here by tonight" Tyson muttered.

"Are you sure you want her to go though? I mean she is your mate after all, I wouldn't be surprised if you wanted her to stay-"

"No Dylan I don't want her to stay. I want her gone. I can't believe for two whole years I've trusted her- LOVED her.. When all she has done is lie to me and really, all she cares about is Jayden" Kyron snapped. Dylan sniffed the air and all three heads snapped up at me. I looked down but walked in, stopping right in front of Kyron.

"Are you ok?" I ask sympathetically, while placing a hand on his shoulder. He sniffed.

"Why do you care?" He snapped. I retrieved my hand quickly.

"I-I don't know, because I feel sad for you. I can't even imagine what you must be going through right now and I think you just need your friends to support you" I say quietly, feeling stupid for even coming. I turn around about to leave when Dylan grabs my wrist gently.

"Avery you don't need to leave, Kyron's just going through a hard time and I guess he's going to snap out like that" I smile at him

"Thanks Dylan but I think he needs to be left alone a while with you two and Jayden. I'll go get him to come down" he nods and moves his hand down to my hand and holds it for a minute.

Kyron jumps up from his seat. I immediately let go of Dylan's hand and watch Kyron storm out of the room, Tyson following him. Dylan looks at me then walks out of the room following the two guys. I follow along to. Walking into the kitchen I see Kyron standing right in front of Sasha, his arms folded firmly over his chest.

"Baby, please don't do this! Not to me!" Sasha pleads

"And why the hell not? Sasha you ripped out my heart dammit!" He yelled causing her to flinch and look down at the ground.

"I'm sorry" she whispered

"You think I care?" He snapped.

"Please don't reject me. Don't send me away-"

"Give me ONE good reason why I shouldn't Sasha" he growled.

"B-because I'm your mate" she whispered slightly raising her head to meet his fiery glare.

"Not good enough" he whispers his voice mixed with emotions; anger, sadness, love, hurt, guilt and regret. Mainly hurt and anger though.

"I Kyron Dauton-" he starts off in a clear tone, standing up straight.

"Please don't do this" Sasha whimpers, but Kyron continues.

"Reject you Sasha Paters, as my mate" his voice cracks at the end. It hurt him to do this but he needed this. Sasha dropped to her knees and cried. Pathetic. Shes the one caught 'trying' to cheat, and she begs for forgiveness. And now she cries. Kyron clears his throat.

"I want you gone by sundown. So I surest you start packing up your things and get going" he demands emotionless, and he walks out the room. Sasha's head snaps up.

"N-no! You can't! Please don't kick me out! I can't be a rogue!" She cries. But Kyron ignores her and with in seconds he is out the back door and off into the woods. Everyone starts to depart the room but Katy and I stand there. Only then did I realise Jayden too was in here, because he wrapped his arm around my waist.

"Well ok then.." I trail off now uncomfortable. Sasha snaps her head up at me. She growls.

"This is all your fault!" She screeched and charged at me, knocking me to the ground. She straddles me, I start kicking my legs up and scream at her to get off but she starts throwing punches at me. The first one I dodged by moving my head to the side, but the second punch she got my left cheek, and boy did it hurt.

The third swing I grabbed her clenched fist. She screamed at how tight I was holding it. Jayden stepped Im and dragged Sasha off me, and he threw her to the side making her skid along the floor until her back hit the wall. He held out his hands which I grabbed and he pulled me to my feet.

"Are you ok?" He asked concerned looking me over. He gently rubbed his thumb over my bruised cheek bone, causing me to wince slightly.

"Yeah I'm fine, it's just a bruise. It'll heal" I push his hand away. I turn to Sasha who sits on the floor. She looks up at me, glaring at me. I glare back. "And Sasha? You can forget about leaving at sundown" I see her relax slightly. Jayden looks at me shocked and confused, but I smile cruelly "because I want you gone and out of the boarder with in the hour" I order calmly and walk out the room with Jayden on my tail. I hear a loud scream come from Sasha which causes me to laugh.

"I hate you Avery Jedson!" She screeches.

"Good because now you can leave in thirty minutes instead!" I call back at her. Jayden chuckles.

"Since when were you so cold hearted?"

"From the moment she called me a bitch" I reply simply causing him to nod.

"Fair enough" he smiles. When we reach the lounge room, I spot Kyron, Tyson and Dylan seated on the couches, Kyron and Tyson both on single couches and Dylan alone on the double. I smile and take a seat beside him. Jayden stays standing. I look at him confused.

"Im sorry Avery but Kyron, Tyson and I have some pack things to attend to. Dylan because you are knew here, you won't be able to attend to pack meetings until we know you enough and until you have settled in" Jayden appologised. He bent down and pecked my lips. "Have a good day out with Katy" he whispered. I smile against his lips.

"See you later Jay" I say with a pout.

"Bye love" he waves and exits the room with Kyron and Tyson on his tail. I turn to Dylan. He pats the top of his legs out of boredom, making it a drum tune. After a minute of awkward silence he turns to me.

"So what are you two ladies planning on doing today?" He asks with a smile. I grin

"Watching this new movie out in the cinemas. You should join us!" I invite him. He thinks for a moment.

"Hmm It depends on what kind of movie" he smirks. I bite my lip.

"It's called The Other Woman" I state quietly. He groans

"But that's a chick flick" he falls back on the couch onto his back.

"I know but Dylan I really want to spend time with you! I want to- I need to do this. I need to get to know you better! Two years we've wasted and it's time we start getting to know each other!" I grin standing up. Dylan groans but holds up his hands which I grab and hoist him to his feet.

"Eh I'm probably going to regret this but you're right Avery" he mutters witha smile and follows me out into the kitchen. The kitchens empty and

I am left wondering where Katy and Sasha are. Using my wolf listening, I hear for where they are. I hear draws being pulled open and cupboards being slammed shut from up stairs.

"Ugh! I still can't believe it! I'm like a rogue now!" Sasha growled.

"Look, Sasha it'll be ok. Maybe go to the White Dawn pack or the White crescent Moon or some pack we have taken outs, territory and live their a while?" I hear Katy suggest quietly. I hear Sasha scream. I drop to my knees and instantly cover my ears and tune my listening back down to normal.

"Avery! Are you ok?" Dylan asks bending down to my level.

"Ugh, I wasn't expecting that" I mutter as Dylan helps me up. "Guess that's what I get for having my hearing turned up all the way" I grimace. Dylan chuckled. Minutes later I hear feet coming down the steps. I spin around to see Sasha carrying two large suit cases. She grumbles and walks straight past me.

Katy smiles sadly at me. "I know she's not a nice person Avery, but she is my friend, I've known her since diapers" she says with a frown I nod and look down at the ground, starting to feel guilty for having her sent away so soon.

"I'm sorry" I whisper and look up at Katy. She smiled sadly

"It's alright Avery. She called it on herself by acting out so wrong. I'm not surprised she's finally being kicked out" she admitted. "And honestly, I'm glad she's finally going to be out of my life" she laughs "because she's always given me shit and I'm so done with her" Katy smiled. I nod and return her smile, not really sure what to say.

Katy left the room and followed Sasha to the door. I turned to Dylan and smiled, "So.. Any thoughts?" I ask raising an eye brow. He laughs

"Just that I should be careful not to get on your bad side" he says with a chuckle. I hit his arm playfully and sit down at the bench, Dylan sits down next to me and we start talking about random things like what my life has been like the past two years.

About ten minutes later, Katy walks back in with a smile. "Well I'm glad she's gone" she says with a grin. She faces Dylan and I "Now let's go see that new movie shall we?" She raises an eye brow at me. I nod

"Yes lets! But do you think Dylan can come with please?" I ask looking over my shoulder at him. Katy beams

"Of course!" She squealed and raced up stairs.

"Where are you going?" I call out to her.

"Going to get changed!" She yelled back. With in minutes she returned now dressed in a white and blue cotton summer dress, that cut off at the knee.

"Well? Let's go!" She said grabbing her purse off the bench then walked outside to the garage. Dylan and I followed. Walking into the garage I see several cars lined up. Katy walked to the end where a black Ford was parked. She pulled out a set of shiny silver keys and unlocked the car. She turned to us with a questioning look.

"Are you coming?" She asked in a duh tone. I exchanged glances with Dylan. He looked at me knowingly and before he could take one step I grin and make a bolt to the car.

"SHOT GUN!" I yell and reach the passengers door.

"Aw no fair!" Dylan whined as he got in the back seat. I stuck my tongue out at him like the five year old I am and spun back around to face the front ignoring all of Dylan's protests. Throughout the whole car ride (about an hour because the pack house is so far away from civilisation) Dylan and I sat in silence and listened to Katy ramble on and on about little things like Tyson, and pack stuff.

We pulled up outside the shopping centre. I glanced at Katy raising my eyebrow. She just laughed. "The cinemas are in the shopping centre silly" she spoke to me in a child tone. I roll my eyes and hop out of the car. I follow Katy and Dylan in and we walk around a bit. After a short while we reached the escalators and we took the 'up' one.

At the top we found a large area, covered in dark red carpet. Lounges were everywhere and at the back was a large, very long bench, on one side is where you bought the tickets, on the other side you bought food. We went and stood in line for the tickets, which wasn't that long, maybe only about ten people?

After a minute or so of waiting Katy turned to Dylan and handed him a $twenty note. "Can you please go get some popcorn?" She asked with a smile. Dylan nodded and walked over to the other line which compared to this one was extremely long. Wow, Dylan is doing great for his first day out in public, in a whole new world to him. I expected him to be on high alert or freaking out at the slightest new noise to him, but he isn't at all. In fact he looks like the calmest person you will ever meet!

We finally reached the counter. "Next" the woman at the counter said in a monotone. Katy dragged me over and grinned at the woman and held up her three middle fingers.

"Three tickets please" she says in an overly chirpy tone.

Fourteen

Sorry for any spelling or grammar errors

Jayden

Walking out of the kitchen I looked over my shoulder at Kryron and Tyson. "Guys, Remind me if I ever see that bitch Sasha ever again, to rip her throat out" I growl. I can not believe that little bitch hurt my mate!

As we walk into the meeting room I am snapped out of my thoughts when everyone stops talking and looks at me. I clear my throat and walk to the front of the room where the white board with the map of our territory drawn on it. Still noticing all eyes are on me, I Clear my throat again and watch Kyron and Tyson take their seats.

"Ok.. As you all know, the past few weeks, rogues have been sneaking their way into our territory! They have been spying on us, trying to figure out our battle strategies! So as of now, I am setting out patrol wolves on different areas of our boarder line making sure no other rogues 'stumble' onto our boarder line" I almost yell. The anger was boiling away inside me.

"Yes but what do we do with any rogues that decide to try and cross the boarder?" One of my warrior wolves, David asked.

"Well question them, make sure they aren't spies, if they prove to be who they say they are, run aways or wolves who have been kicked out of or separated from their pack, may live and be apart of our pack. But if they are spies or our enemies, kill them" I say the last part in a venom laced tone.

There were a few Yes Alpha's and others whispered other things to each other. After a few minutes of small chit chat I spoke up again. "Now! I want you all to go out now and patrol the areas you are assigned to. If you don't know your areas and what times you are patrolling or not come look up here on the map. Now get going!" I ordered in a completely serious tone

"Yes Alpha!" They all yelled and walked over to the board behind me. I stepped aside allowing them to pass. When I saw Tyson and Kyron I grabbed their arms and dragged them outside the room. They looked at me confused.

"You two are on patrol with me in the afternoon, around four" I told them. They nod slowly.

"But where?" Tyson asked.

"By the old cabin out to the right side of the boarder line" I answer. They nod again. "Ok meeting over" I say walking back into the room. Everyone nods and walks out, some off too their rooms because they have night shifts, others went out straight to their patrol area.

I leave the room with Tyson and Kyron following. We walk into the lounge room and plop ourselves down on the couch. I pick up the remote and turn the TV on and football covers the screen. Well this should keep us occupied for the next few hours...

.

.

.

.

.

Avery

"That movie was so good!" Dylan yells all cheerful. I grin.

"It was wasn't it?" I respond with a nod. Katy laughs.

"I told you guys, you'd love it" she smiled. Walking out of the cinema we make out way to the car. I decided to be nice a let Dylan take shotgun. The ride home was full of chit chat, mainly about the movie we watched. At about 5:30 we arrived home. I walk into the kitchen in search of food. Pulling open the door to the pantry I look in and find a few packets of easy mac, chicken flavour.

Pouring the two packets into a bowl I add water and chuck it in the microwave. And dinner is on the way. I walk out the room while I wait for it to cook, and I find Dylan and Katy on the double couch but on one of the other couches is a wolf Ive never seen before. He looks up at me and bows his head.

"Evening Luna" he greets. I smile

"Please call me Avery. And you are?" I ask

"David Samuels" he smiles. he holds out his hand for me to shake. I shook it with a firm grasp.

"Nice to meet you" I say with a smile then walk over to the other free couch and sit down. "Do we really have to watch cricket?" I groan. Dylan and David laughs and Katy frowns.

"I know right? This is so stupid!" She grumbles.

"Hey.. Wheres Jayden and Tyson?" I ask finally realising they weren't inside.

"Out on patrol" David said simply. I nod and go back to watching the boring TV show. After a couple minutes I hear the microwave beep so I jump up and race out of the room to the kitchen and pull out my chicken flavoured paster out from the microwave. I find a fork in a draw somewhere and sit myself down at the bench. I took a bite and moaned at the taste. I then continue to eat the rest.

.

.

.

.

.

A few hours later and Jayden still hadn't returned. It was starting to get late so I excuse myself from the lounge room and go upstairs to Jayden's bathroom. After grabbing myself out a towel I twist the taps on in the shower and strip. I let the hot water hit my back, making all of my muscles relax.

After washing my hair I twist the tap off and get out. I wrap a towel around my body and one around my hair. I then unlock the bathroom door and walk back into the bedroom. I jump from fright and look down at Jayden who lies comfortably on the bed.

"You scared me" I placed a hand over my racing heart. He chuckled and placed both hands behind his head.

"Sorry" he smiled.I rolled my eyes and walked to the wardrobe and pulled out my pjs. I grab them then walk back to the bathroom to change. I hang the towels back up and walk back into the bedroom.

I crawled onto the bed and layed down next to Jayden. He wrapped his arm around my waist and I rest my head on his chest. I feel him breath out heavily and I look up at him. "Is something wrong?" I ask noticing how tense he was. He looks down at me and smiles

"Don't worry about it sweet heart. Get some rest" he rubs up and down my shoulder gently. Realising he doesn't want to talk about it right now I decide to let it go. I nod and close my eyes. Darkness hit me quicker than I expected it to, but I welcomed it anyway.

.

.

.

.

.

.

The next morning I woke spread out across the bed on my stomach, my head buried in the fluffy pillows. I look up noticing Jayden wasn't here. I push my self up and roll over onto my back. I sit up and look around the room. There was no one in here. I sigh and force myself to get out of bed and drag myself over to the wardrobe. I pull out some black track pants and a loose green shirt. After I changed I chucked on some sneakers and left the room.

As I enter the kitchen, I notice it is deserted. I sigh again. Lonely, lonely me. I crack a small smile as I find my favourite cereal in a cupboard. I then go for the sugar but realise it onCE again, is at the back in the top cupboard. Well poop. I shrug and sit down at the bench and pour the cereal into a bowl. I then get back up and grab the milk. Dylan walks in minutes later. I look at him with a smile.

"Hey, morning" I greet chirpy.

"Good morning Avery" he yawns.

"Tired?" I chuckle. He nods and sits down.

"Oh before you sit down- could you please get the sugar for me?" I smile. He nods and walks over to the cupboard and grabs the sugar out and hands it to me. "Thanks" he nods with out a word and sits back down.

I grab a spoon out of the draw and start eating my cereal beside Dylan. "Do you know where everyone is?" He asks. I shake my head.

"I don't even think Katy is here" I mumble. He nods and looks down at the bench. After I finish eating I stand up and grab Dylan's hand. He looks at me confused.

"Well seeing how we have the whole place to ourselves, we might as well have some fun!" I chirp. He nods, but doesn't look so excited. I see the purple bags under his eyes. I tilt my head to the side slightly.

"Hey you never told me, why are you so tired?" I ask. He shrugs.

"Bad dreams" he replies quietly.

"About...?"

"About being locked up in your dungeons.. Just memories of the past. Don't worry about it" he smiles reassuringly. I nod and decide to drop it. Dylan stands up and walks over to the sink and turns the taps on. He splashes his face with cold water then turns back to me.

"Well? Let's go" he grins. I grab his hand and lead him outside the back door. However, when is swing open the back door I collide with a large hard back. The man turns around and stares down at me with a frown.

"Luna" he bows his head slightly. His voice sent bad vibes through me. Something about this guy was off.

"Yeah um.. Excuse me if we could just get past-" I tried to push past him but he blocked the door.

"No one leaves the house. Alpha's orders" he growls loudly. I flinch and step back. Dylan grabs my arm gently.

"You ok?" He whispers. I nod. He then pulls me behind him and he steps forward right in front of the buff werewolf that growled in my face. He stares down at Dylan questionably.

"How dare you talk to her that way" Dylan growls at him. "She is your Luna and she deserves some respect!" The man looked taken about but quickly replaced his shock with anger.

"How dare YOU speak to ME that way!" He growled. "Do you know who I am!?" He roared.

"Yeah some rat that died in a whole a few years ago-" Dylan replied simply but was cut off

"I wouldn't get on my bad side if I were you little punk" he snapped at Dylan. I then stepped forward and looked the guy in the eye.

"What is your name?" I ask as politely as I could.

"Joe Barks" he replied through gritted teeth. I stood as straight as I could and glared at him.

"Well, 'Joe Barks' " I sneer "as you should have well known by now, I am your Luna you are just a mere pack warrior wolf. You have no power over me, but I however, with the snap of my fingers I could have you killed!" I threaten causing him to flinch and take a step back. Of course I wouldn't have him killed, I mean no one really deserves to die here..

"Sorry Luna" he bows his head and stands to the side allowing us to pass. We walk straight pass him but I spin around to face him.

"Now, before this all got messy, I was just going to say we were going for a walk through the woods, and if anyone would like to know where we are or how long we will be tell them where we are and we'll be back in a few hours" I order. He nods but keeps his gaze on the ground, avoiding eye contact with me. I then turn to Dylan. "Let's go" I say. He nods and follows me out into the woods.

We walk around for a while talking about random things until we decide to go back to the pack house. "So you mother and Finn are coming down here in a couple days?" Dylan asks looking at me. I smile

"Yes they are. I can't wait to see Finn but I also feel a bit like.." I trialled off frowning

"Like what?" Dylan asks concerned. Walking up to the pack house I stop walking when we reach the back door and turn to Dylan.

"I fell like something bad is going to happen" I answer then swing the door open and walk back inside. Walking into the kitchen I notice Dylan is following closely behind me. I spot Jayden sitting at the bench with Kyron beside him. They both have worried expressions across their faces. I walk over to them, both their heads snap up at me.

"What's up guys?" I ask nervously.

"Don't worry about it Avery" Kyron says quietly. I raise an eyebrow up at Jayden. He sighs and rubs his forehead. I fold my arms over my chest. What is with all the secrets?

"We uh.. We seem to have a bit of a rogue problem" he answers looking up at me.

Please vote and comment! :)

Fifteen

Sorry for any spelling/grammar errors :)

Enjoy!

Jayden

This morning I woke at four o'clock to the sound of a ear piercing scream through my head. I jolt up and my hands go to my ears, trying to block out the intensifying screeching, only then realising it is only in my head so there is no way to remove it. One of the pack members are in trouble. I quickly get out of bed careful not to wake Avery. Aw she looks so sweet when she sleeps. My beautiful angel.

Walking over to the chest of draws I quickly pull out jeans and a black shirt. I slip them on and run out the room. I stop outside Kyron's door and knock. "What?" He groans.

"Get out here now!" I whisper yell. In seconds he is out the door his hair all ruffled up and he looked tired as hell. He glared at me

"This better be good Jay" he growled quietly. "It's four in the morning!" He whispered hitting my arm.

"Someone's hurt!" I whispered back, watching his angry expression turn to concern and worry.

"Who?" He asked quietly.

"I don't know, I just heard them screaming through the mind link between him and me" I answer. He nods

"I'll go wake Tyson and Katy and we'll meet you out there" he replied. I nod

"Alright, see you shortly. And in your wolf forms" I say and run off down stairs. I sprint through the house to the front door. I swing it open and run out. I jump in the air, shifting into my pure black wolf in the process.

'Hey where are we off to?' I hear Shadow, my wolf, ask. I start running into the forest to the right of the house.

'To the border line, off to the right' I reply, my paws pounding against the hard ground. I hear another scream ring through my head, the noise so loud it stung my ears. I shake my head and feel myself stumble, however I quickly regain myself and continue to sprint through the woods.

I see a clearing so I run out of the woods and into the large grassy area. Looking around I don't see anyone. I sniff the air, David's scent rushes though my nostrils. Looking down at the ground before me, I see skid marks, and claw marks everywhere. Some of the thick grass was flattened in some places. I walk around a bit and then new scents rush through my snout.

I growl and spin back around to face the woods. I lower my head and let another growl out. 'Show yourself' I growl out again. Shady figure emerge from the forest. Seven very large werewolves appear before me. 'Where is David?' I ask through mind links to them. They snicker and look at each other.

'Shift' one commands. I shake my head. They must be really stupid if they thought I'd ever do that.

'Why would I do that? I'd be defenceless' I reply in a duh tone but still crouched down in defence form.

'You will if you want your friend to live' the same brown wolf growled. I hear a whimper and two more wolves come out from the woods, one of them, the colour sandy brown, the other dark brown. The sandy one happened to be David. I growl again.

'What do you want?' I ask

'For you to shift' one simply replied. Not what I meant.

'What do you want?' I repeat slower with another growl.

'For you to come with us' another answered.

'Why?' I ask still suspicious.

'Enough of the questions!' The brown wolf beside David, growled out. He bit into David's front paw causing him to yelp in pain. I lift my head quickly and step forward.

'Kyron! Tyson! Where are you!?' I yell through the pack link.

'Right behind David and that rogue' Kyron answered. I look back at David, and fair enough, right behind him, just in the forest, I see three shadowy figures. The third wolf must be Katy. One of them crouches down ready to pounce.

'Wait guys! I want to see what these rogues are doing here in the first place' I quickly tell them.

'Ok' Katy answers back. I look back at the rogues who stare back at me questioningly.

'Look, you guys aren't going to take me with out a fight and let me tell you, this fight you won't win. Because my beta, his mate, and my third in command are just mere seconds away from here, and with them by my side we make an unstoppable team. So I suggest to you kindly, that you leave now' I finish with a growl. Most of them cower down and take several steps back. I look over my shoulder. 'The border lines that way' I nod behind me.

Five out of eight rogues run off behind me. I let them pass. I turn to the three wolves that stayed. One had David beside him, the others stood a few feet away. The taller one stepped forward glaring at me.

'Incase we couldn't take you with us, which clearly, now we won't be.. Our Alpha told us to give you a message. He told us to tell you that we declare war. Expect us soon but not too soon' was his final words before the three last rogues ran off behind me and back over the border line from where they came. Wait.. Did they just say Their Alpha? Rogues don't have alphas.. They aren't a pack. What is going on here?

I here a whimper and I look at David. He lies on his side, trying to push himself up but failing each time. He had bites and large deep claw marks all over him. I run over to him and bend down by his side. Seconds later, Katy Kyron and Tyson are beside me. Tyson and Kyron shift back into their human forms.

"Shift back David, it's alright bud" Tyson places a hand on David's back.

"Come on David, it won't hurt that much" Kyron adds. David nods once then minutes later he shifts back into human form. Bruises, deep cuts and bites cover his body. There is blood everywhere, and there are probably several broken bones. I know that if we don't get him to the pack doctor quickly, we might loose him.

'Put him on my back' I order Kyron and Tyson. They nod and carefully place David on my back. 'David, I need you to hold on tight alright?' I say through pack link. I feel him nod and I turn to the others. 'I'll meet you at the pack house' I say. They nod and I run off.

I'm a lot faster than anyone else in my pack, partly because I am alpha and naturally, alphas are ten times faster and stronger than your average werewolf. But the other reason that makes me extra fast is because I am a black wolf. And any wolf from The Warrior Pack are way stronger than any other wolf.

With in minutes of full speed running, I reach the pack doctors house. He lives just a few minutes away from the pack house. I run up to the door and bark loudly. A minute later Doctor Mewton came walking outside. His smile vanishes when he sees the sight of David.

"Let's get him inside" he says quietly. I nod and crouch down. Doctor Mewton takes David off my back, and I shift back into human form. I help him carry David inside. David's eyes were closed, but every now and then her would groan quietly, signalling he was still conscious, but barely.

Walking quickly into doc's surgery room I remove David's arm off my shoulder and we lay him on the table and Doctor Mewton gets straight to work. Minutes later, Janice, doc's wife enters the room carrying a pair of denim knee length shorts.

I give her a grateful smile and take the shorts from her pale hands. She nods avoiding eye contact and she leaves the room with out a word. I slip the shorts on and turn my attention to David. He lies completely still. No noise could be heard except the faint breathing and his weak heart pumping in his chest.

I pace back and forth nervously while Doctor Mewton starts bandaging and sticking needles into David. "Is he going to be ok? Can you fix him?" I ask worried.

"All I can do is slow the bleeding down. David will heal on his own, slower than usual because of how much blood he has lost but still much faster than human pace" he answered as he wrapped the last bandage around David's arm. I nod.

After an hour or so of sitting in a very uncomfortable wooden chair, I stand up and wipe my palms on my shorts. I look over at the doctor. "I'm sorry but I have to go, my pack needs me. Please call when David wakes and starts healing" I say. He nods

"Will do" he replies. I give him a small smile and walk out the room and out the front. I jog back to the pack house. I walk in through the back door and into the kitchen. Kyron, Tyson and Katy sat at the bench, their heads in their hands. They looked up at me when I walked in.

"He'll be ok" I say quietly. Katy smiles and the guys sigh in relief.

"But what did the rogues want in the first place?" Tyson asks confused. I sigh.

"I'm not sure exactly, but from what they told me, is that they and several other rogues have come together to form a massive pack. They have a leader, well they called him an Alpha so that got me wondering if their 'Alpha' is actually an Alpha, like from one of the packs we destroyed. But anyway.. They are declaring war on us, so Tyson, Katy? Could you guys please go round the pack up and get them all in the meeting room?"

"Sure" Tyson said getting up. He walked out the room with Katy following. Kyron looked at me questioningly?

"Is there a reason you wanted me to stay behind with you?" Kyron asked tilting his head slightly,

"Not really, I just wanted to let you know that.. What ever we are going up against.. It won't be anything like our last battles" I say running a hand through my

"Ok.. Anything else?" He sighs.

"Just that.. Whoever this Alpha is... He wants revenge. And he's coming after us" as soon as that word left my mouth, the back door opened and the fresh scent of strawberries flowed through my nose. I inhale deeply.

"What's up guys?" Her quiet voice rang through my ears. I look up at her, trying to not to let the worry become evident. Kyron looked up at her and opened his mouth.

"Don't worry about it Avery" Kyron answered and looked down again. I smile at how Kyron was acting, not wanting his Luna to get all worried. But she needed to know. Maybe her pack- what's left of her pack.. Could help us?

Avery looks over at me and raises an eyebrow. I let out a sigh and rub my forehead stressfully. "We uh.. We seem to have a bit of a rogue problem" I admit looking her in the eye. She freezes and looks at me with shock.

"W-what? How big of a problem? Is it just a few or..?"

"There appears to be a whole army of them with their own Alpha" Kyron answers her.

"And they're planning an attack" she whispers. I nod.

"Yes and I was wondering.. How many pack members from your pack survived?" I ask. She glares at me

"You mean the ones who you didn't end up killing?" She asked angrily.

"Look love, I know it's a touchy subject but we need people to help us win this battle.. I have this feeling that-" she cuts me off

"That something bad is going to happen. That this will be the strongest battle you have ever fought" she finishes for me. I blink at her a few times.

"How did you know?" I whisper.

"I just.. Have this feeling. I don't know" she answers quietly. I stand up and walk over to her. I wrap my arms around her waist and pull her close. She closed her eyes and inhaled deeply. "I'll call my family" she whispered. I smiled down at her and kissed the top of her head.

"Thank you" you could not imagine how grateful I was. It was at that moment that I felt the urge to say those three words. I wanted to at that very moment I wanted to say, I Love You Avery, but I knew she wasn't ready for it.

So I just left it at that. I pulled away and dug my hand into my pocket and pulled out my iPhone. I handed it over to my sweet little mate. She smiled and took it. I know it's cheesy and all but that one little smile made a thousand butterflies erupt in my stomach.

I watch her dial away with my phone, and I took a seat at the island next to Kyron. I patted the empty stool beside me and Avery sat down next to me. I tuned my wolf hearing up so I could here what was going on, on the other side of the phone. It rang a few times before someone answered. Avery cleared her throat.

"Hello?" She spoke clearly.

"Avery?" Her mothers voice rang through, worry evident in it.

"Mother, look I know it's a bit crazy to ask this right now, but how many pack members survived? How many do we still have?" She asked her voice starting to go shaky. I held her soft hand In mine and rubbed small circles on the back of it. It seemed to calm her because her muscles relaxed.

"Not many, about fifty, all of our warriors too" she said sadly. "why?" He voice held curiosity

"Um.. I know it's a big ask an all but could you please bring everyone here? As in the whole pack, everyone that survived that is" Avery asked hopefully.

"I don't think so. Why?" Her mothers voice was a little more harsh.

"Because Jayden's pack might be under attack and there is going to be a big war soon and he- WE" she smiled over me "we need as much help as we can get" she said more confidently. I heard whispering on the other side, too hard to make out.

"Fine. But we are coming over ourselves, tell us where you are"

"Wait when are you going to come?" Avery asked quickly.

"Tomorrow morning" her mother replied. Avery looked over at me for confirmation. I nodded and Avery started to tell them how to get here.

Katy and Tyson walked in. "Everyone's ready for that meeting now" Katy announced with a small smile. I nod

"Thank you. I'll meet you there in a few minutes" they nod and walk back out the room. Avery hangs up the phone and passes it to me. I smile down at her. "Come on babe, we got a meeting to attend to" I chirp. She looks at me confused but takes my hand. I lead her out of the kitchen and too the meeting room.

Avery

Walking into the meeting room, Jayden leads me to the front of the room to the white board that stood in front of two very large, stain glass windows. Looking properly at the board, I could see a map of the territory and small dot points all over it.

Turning around to face everyone who was currently seated at the long rectangular table, I see they all have their eyes on us.

I also notice that these werewolves are not from The Warrior Pack. These ones were just your ordinary werewolves. Jayden cleared his throat and stepped forward.

"Good afternoon everyone.. Now I know we only just had a meeting earlier yesterday, but earlier today David was attacked by a bunch of rogues. He was severely injured but in time, he will heal. Now these rogues.. They were different to your every day rogue. They were traveling in their own kind of pack, and from what they told me... in this pack of rogues, there are many more rogues and they even have their own Alpha.

This Alpha... I think he was from a pack we destroyed, like The White Dawn Pack or the Red Curse Pack, or any other pack we have destroyed... In that case he could have come from one out of thirty packs. All I know is that he is an actual Alpha, not some rogue they picked to be leader. He has alpha blood in him" Jayden explained, his tone was loud and clear.

There were whispers coming from the pack but they shushed after a few minutes. Then Jayden continued.

"Not only are they trying to invade our territory and spy on us... They have declared war on us. And from what I know so far, this battle will not be easy. They will be stronger then any other pack we have faced, stronger than The White Dawn Pack even. These rogues that came today, they had a different scent to other rogues. It's like they had their own mark" he paused and looked around the room.

"And we need to train, we need to start to prepare for this 'epic battle' and we should be ready with in a week. Train as hard as you can, we will have other wolves from other packs help us out, they will be arriving here tomorrow to start training with us.

In this battle, all children under the age of fifteen and certain woman, ones with out children and ones who aren't too old or weak, will be required to fight in this battle. Mothers, the Elderly and the sick will sit out, they will flee the territory with all the children ages fourteen and under and they won't come back until the battle has completely ended." he finished.

Everyone nodded and replied "Yes Alpha"

"Meeting over. Thank you for attending" Jayden muttered. Everyone stood up in a hurry and left the room, well except Kyron, Tyson and Katy. They walked over to us. Kyron dug his hands into his pockets and looked at the ground. Tyson wrapped his arm around Katy's waist and she buried herself into his side and rested her head on his shoulder. Kyron was first to speak.

"So what do we do now?" He asked glumly.

"Hell if I knew" Tyson muttered.

"We follow through our daily routines. Act normal, but train more often. If there are rogues that sneak into our territory tomorrow they will be spying on us, knowing our every move and battle plan. We can not have that. So we'll just see how it all goes down tomorrow" Jayden said with a shrug. He squeezed my hand lightly in his which caused me to smile.

Katy and Tyson nod and leave the room. "We'll see you at dinner" Katy called over her shoulder. I smile at her perkiness. Jayden then walks out the room, tugging on my hand so I follow closely behind. Kyron then follows us. We walk straight into the lounge room to find it abandoned. I sit down on the double couch and Jayden walks over to the TV and turns it on. Kyron walks in the room.

"I'm going to go make dinner, I'll call you when it's done" Jayden says walking out of the room. Kyron sits down next to me, keeping his hands buried away in his pockets. He looks kind of sad and I know what it is about. I slowly lift my hand and place it on his arm. He looks at me slightly confused.

"I know it hurts now Kyron, but it will get better. Just give it time, you'll find someone better" I say reassuringly with a small smile. He smiles sadly.

"Thanks Avery, but I don't think I'll find anyone as amazing as I thought Sasha was" he replied looking down. He takes his hands out of his pockets and fidgets his fingers. I grab both his hands and held them nn mine. I look him in the eye, his eyes held nothing but sadness and sorrow.

"Kyron, believe me on this one ok? One day, you WILL find someone incredible. She will love you for who you are and you will love her no matter what. She might not be your mate but you two will be so in love it won't matter. And when you find that girl, don't let her go.

I know she won't let you go either. Kyron, you are an amazing person and you need to know that. You just have to open your heart and keep it open, don't shut out the world ok? When that girl comes along, you'll feel it, and you will know she is the one. Sasha was just some piece of shit that didn't deserve the love you gave her in the first place." I finished my long speech with a small smile.

Kyron smiled down at me. But then sighed, "but what if Sasha was 'The One'? What if I never find anyone as good as she could have been?"

"In my theory, there could be many 'the ones' it just takes a while to find them. You don't know what you have until you loose it but trust me on this, Sasha would never have been a good mate. She only cared about herself, not bout anyone else, not even you. And it's her loss." I answer honestly. He smiles again and wraps his arms around me.

"Thank you Avery" he sighs "you're such a great person, a kind soul. You truely are an amazing friend and I never thought I would have said this but I'm glad you're here, and I'm glad you are our Luna. I don't think anyone else could play that role better than you. You have also changed Jayden's life so much, I bet you haven't even realised" he says pulling back. I tilt my head to the side.

"How so?" I ask confused.

"Well before you came along into our lives, Jayden was cold hearted, he didn't care much about us. All he wanted was power and he didn't even have one concern for who ever got hurt. Now look at him. He's always smiling, he hasn't frowned once since you walked in and I've seen the way he looks at you Avery. He truely does love you. He might not say it but I know he does" Kyron answers truthfully, not once breaking eye contact with me.

"But he's been a little.. Distant lately. It's like he's scared of me" I answer, the thought finally coming out of my head. Ever since the day when we were all in the pool and I snapped, I've felt that things haven't been the same with him, he's more cautious, it's like he's waiting for me to snap again.

"Of course he's not scared of you Avery. He's just waiting, until your ready to take the next step. Until you are ready to be with him" he explains. I nod and look up at him.

"Thanks Kyron. You're such a good friend" I say, I kiss his cheek and stand up. "I'm going to go see how dinners going" I say walking out of the room.

"Avery?" Kyron calls. I stop and spin around to face him. "Thanks." I smile at him.

"Anytime" I answer him and walk out of the room. Who knew Kyron and I would be so close? I feel so connected to him right now, it's so weird. I always thought he wasn't a nice guy from the moment he called me a bitch, but now... Wow.

I walk into the kitchen as silent as I could. Jayden was standing at the stove in front of a fry pan, with a spatula in his left hand. I crept up behind him and hugged him from behind. I here him chuckle.

"Hey beautiful what's up?" He asks turning around to face me. I cup his cheek, stand up on my tiptoes and kiss his lips softly. "What was that for?" He murmurs his, eyes were closed though. I smile.

"I just... Felt like it" I suggested. Jayden smiled and opened his eyes. He looked down at me and slithered his arms around my waist. He brought his head down and kissed me back, but this time more passionately. My arms made their way up to his neck and I tangled them in his hair. He ran his tongue over my bottom lip and we deepened the kiss. Our tongues battled for dominance but of course he one.

We were interrupted when a horrid smell of burnt chicken filled my nostrils. I pulled away breathless. Jayden pouted and I grinned. "Your steak is burning" I murmured. That caught his attention. His eyes opened wide and he spun around and quickly took it out of the fry pan and placed onto a large plate.

"You distracted me" he grunted. I laughed and peck his cheek.

"See you at the table" I tease and walk out the room and into the dining room. I sit down in my chair. Katy looks over at me and grins

"I saw you and Jayden in the kitchen getting it on" she winked "it looked rather heated in there" I blushed and looked down at the table.

"Aw look Avery's blushing!" Tyson laughed. I glared at him playfully which caused him to laugh harder. Kyron and Katy joined in too and soon enough so did I. Minutes later Jayden walked in carrying a tray full of steak in one hand and a large plate of steamed vegetables in the other hand. He placed them down on the table and sat down next to me, and pecked my cheek. I smile and start grabbing food off the plates.

Dinner passed quickly and before I knew it Jayden and I were walking upstairs, when we reached the top Jayden scooped me up in his arms and carried me bridal stile to his room. I squealed in surprise. He kicked open the bedroom door and shut it once we got inside. After carrying me over to the bed, he gently lays me down then climbs on top of me, placing either arm on either side of my head. He bends down and kisses me. I return the kiss and wrap my right arm around his neck, pulling him close. This kiss deepens and I let out soft moans.

I arch my back as Jayden trails kisses down my neck and back up again. He kisses the tender spot over and over which causes me to moan again. I tangle my hands in his hair. He then trails kisses back down and stops just above the crook of my neck and shoulder.

"Jayden, Mark me" I murmur. He raises his head slightly so he can look into my eyes.

"Are you sure?" He asks unsure. I nod and close my eyes, trying to calm myself down.

"Yes I'm sure" I breath. He nods gently moves my hair to the side with his thumb and goes back to kissing my neck. I moan and tilt my head to give him better access. I feel his teeth graze along my skin in the spot where he is going to bite. He sinks his teeth into my neck, the bite stings a little at first but then it brings nothing but pleasure. He pulls back after he is finished and he pecks my lips. I smile and pull away and rest my forehead on his. Wrapping my arms around his neck and pull him impossibly closer, I sigh in content and close my eyes.

"I love you Avery Jedson" he whispers. My breath hitches in my throat. He actually does love me. Did I love him? Of course I did, there was no question about that. Nothing in me could doubt my feelings for this boy.

"I love you too, Jayden Byson" I finally admit opening my eyes and looking into his dark eyes. They held nothing but happiness and love in them. He lies back down on the bed beside me and pulls me close to him. I suddenly grew very tired and I found myself closing my eyes. "Good night Jay" I mumble and I feel the darkness swallow me.

Vote, comment? :)

Sixteen

Avery

With the excitement of seeing my family today, I couldn't seem to sit still on the kitchen stool. Dylan chuckled at me noticing how unfocused I was in the conversation the six of us were having.

"Avery, you with us?" Tyson asked looking slightly irritated. I looked over at him confused. He rubbed his forehead tiredly. "We were saying that all of the werewolves from The Warrior Pack except Jayden will be fleeing with the elders, children and mothers" he answered my unasked question. I silently ohhed but then the thought popped in my head,

"You never told me what will happen to me. I'm from The Warrior Wolf pack, but i want to fight" I say looking into Jayden's green eyes. Is it just me or do his eyes change colour a lot? Like yesterday they were brown, the day before I'm pretty sure they were blue, and now they are green! That's pretty cool-

"Avery, I will not have you fighting out on that battle field. You could get hurt-" I cut Jayden off with the wave of my hand.

"No, Jayden I am fighting whether you like it or not. I want to fight. I want to be with you" I answer the last part quietly. Jayden sighed in frustration. Katy and Kyron looked at me confused. I tilted my head at them curiously.

"When did you get that?" Katy pointed at my neck. I blushed and slapped my right hand over my new mark.

"Last night" I murmur looking down at the table. My cheeks flush deep red as all the scenes from last night rush through my mind. Oh how I wouldn't mind replaying them over and over again.

"Don't be cover it up love, I think my name looks good on you" Jayden said proudly with his famous smirk. I laugh at him and remove my hand.

"Ok don't change the subject, Jayden let me fight please? Let me fight with you. What Luna would I be if I wasn't there to defend my pack? What Luna would I be if I fled from battle?" I point out.

"An alive one to keep the generations going" Tyson muttered. I snapped my head at him and locked eyes with him. What did he mean by that? I hear Kyron sigh loudly so I looked over at him. He rubbed the back of his neck nervously.

"Avery what Ty means by that is, that there is a possible chance that we could all go down on that battle field. We have no idea what we are up against here, and if Jayden dies out there- which I'm sure he won't" he adds quickly, and then continues "you need to be there for the rest of the pack. They will need a leader, someone that can protect all the others. So you need to sit out of this one alright?" Kyron says frustrated.

I frown. "Nice try. I'm still fighting" I say still confident. they all let out a series of groans.

"I'm making Katy sit out" Tyson points out suggestively. Katy raises an eyebrow at him.

"You said last night that I could fight" she crosses her arms over her chest.

"Oh yeah of course baby" he nods then looks at Jayden and shakes his head. I almost laugh at that.

"Good luck with that Ty, the only way Katy will sit out is if she suddenly becomes pregnant or hurt or what ever your rules are" I mutter. Katy grins over at me. I smile back. Dylan chuckles but doesn't say anything. "Dylan, are you going to fight?" I ask him quietly. He looks from me to Jayden. Jayden shrugs.

"It's up to you man, I mean I suggest you don't because you haven't had good fighting experience and because you are from The Warrior Wolves pack and we need all wolves from that pack to stay alive and out of this mess, no one can know about them. But like I said, it's up to you" Jayden answers.

"I'll get back to you on that one" Dylan winks at me. I frown at him. If I have to sit out- which I won't be! - so does he! I hear a car door slam shut. My head snaps up as three familiar scents rush through my nose. I jump up and run to the front door and swing it open.

I look down at the bottom of the steps to see my dad's old ute, with my mother still seated inside it, and Finn and my father are grabbing bags out of the back. Finn sniffs the air and he looks up at me. He gives me a small smile but looks away after a second. I walk down the steps and run into my fathers outstretched arms.

"I missed you" I admit in a whisper.

"I missed you too pumpkin" he mutters. I pull back after a minute and walk over to Finn. He grabbed a bag out of the back but I took it from his hands and placed it on the ground. He looked at me with a blank face.

Right now I was on the verge of tears. I pulled him in for a hug but he kept I is arms pinned down by his side and made no attempt to return the hug. I didn't care though, I just continued to hug him.

"Finn you have no idea how much I have missed you!" I cried. He was silent, and very still I might add. After a minute of no movement I looked at him with a frown, "you do realise I won't let go of you until you hug me back mister" I scold him playfully. He sighs and rips himself out of my grip. I stand there shocked and watch him grab the large bag off the ground and carry it up to the house.

"It was nice to see you again too sister" he says almost emotionless, although I could swear I heard the slightest tone of guilt and sadness in it. He walks inside past my very confused looking mate.

I stand still, frozen in place. I wanted to have a melt down, right then and there. What happened to him? Why does he hate me? I hear my mother clear her throat and I spin around to face her. She is just inches in front of me. Her face is straight, no smile, no frown, no worry or concern like I had heard over the phone. She outstretched her arms slightly for a hug.

I glare at her. "Who do you think you are!?" I screech and walk straight past her, brushing my shoulder roughly against hers. As I walk past my dad I see his confused expression. Don't look at me like that, I know you have done something to my younger brother. You have filled his head with lies! I so badly wanted to yell but decided not to.

"You all will be sleeping in the attic" I say as calmly as I can then run off to the house. Jayden who stands in the doorway, catches my wrist as I try to run past him. "Let me go. please just let me go" I sob. Jayden pulls me in for a hug. And I cry into his chest.

"Shh, it's alright love. Everything will be ok" he says soothingly and gently sways us from side to side.

"Just take me upstairs" I whisper looking up into his eyes. He looked pained to see me like this. He nods and takes my small hand in his and entwined our fingers. As we make our way to the stairs we pass Kyron.

"Make sure Avery's parents and her brother find their way to their room, and please with any of the arriving werewolves from other packs, lead them to the guest house?" Jayden orders calmly. Kyron nods,

"Yes Alpha" he answers with a straight face and walks outside. Jayden leads me upstairs and into his room. I sit down at the end of the bed and Jayden sits beside me.

"Now would you like to tell me what's going on here?" He asks quietly. I rest my head on his shoulder as his delicious scent rushes through my nose.

"My parents.. They've changed Finn. I don't know how but they've said something to him to make him hate me. He can't even look at me!" A few tears roll down my cheek. Jayden gently brushes them away with his thumb.

"It's ok baby, I'm sure he doesn't hate you." He whispers in my ear.

"What do I do Jay?" I ask looking up at him.

"Why don't you talk to Finn? Find out what really is going on, then you two can come join us and the other packs for training" he suggests. I nod and stand up. Jayden stands up too and wraps his arms around my waist.

He bent down slowly and I felt his lips brush against mine. He pulled away all to soon though. I open my eyes and look into his, which now were light blue. I tilt my head at him and he looks at me questioningly.

"What?"

"Your eyes" I murmur "do they always change colour?" I ask cupping his cheek. He nods

"Yeah they do. I don't know why and I have no idea what triggers each colour but they just do" he answers. I nod. I take my hand back off his check but wrap it around his neck.

"Well thank you Jayden. You make things so much better for me" I smile up at him. He nods and kisses my forehead.

"Your welcome love, but I have to go. I'll see you soon though alright?" He cups my cheek and looks into my eyes. I nod and he leaves.

"I love you" I whisper.

"Love you too!" I hear him call from the hall. I smile. I raise my fingers to my lips still feeling the tingles from the kiss. After a minute or so I regain my self and leave the room. I find the stairs that lead up to the attic and I slowly walk up them.

When I reach the top I see a queen size bed set up in the middle of the room. A wooden bedside table set up on either side of the bed, to the right was a large oak wood wardrobe but to the left was a regular sized, circular shaped window that had the perfect view of the back yard.

In front of the wardrobe was a large blue mat, that had a white duvet over it and two small cream pillows. I'm guessing Finn will sleep here. "How uncomfortable" I mutter aloud.

"What are you doing in here?" A small familiar voice rang through my ears. I spun around to face my eleven year old brother. He frowned at me. I clasped my hands together.

"How very nice it is to see you too Finn" I answer sarcastically, which only causes him to frown more. I roll my eyes. "Finn take a seat" I say trying my best to remain chirpy. He sat down on the edge of the bed.

"Are they making you sleep on the floor?" I ask sympathy lacing my tone. He rolled his eyes.

"Nooo I get the bed to my self and the two douch bags we call parents get the floor" he answers sarcastically.

"I can get you an actual bed if you'd like" I offer with a small smile. Finn just rolls his eyes and ignore me. I sigh and sit down next to him. "Finn, the reason why I came up here, is I wanted to talk to you" I say placing my hands in my lap. Finn nods and looks down at the floor.

"About what?" He asks quietly.

"About why you are acting this way, what have I don't to make you despise me so much you can't even look my the eye?" I ask pleading for an answer. He sighs

"I don't have to explain myself" he says standing up. I grab his wrist. He glares down at me.

"Yes you do" I spit. He tries to yank his wrist out of my hand.

"Let go of me!" He yells and tries struggling with all his might.

"No Finn answer me" I try to remain calm.

"You're hurting me!" He cries. As the words leave his mouth, Memories flash through my mind.

Flash Back

I walk in to see Finn sitting on my mother's lap, his arms clinging to her as he cries hysterically. I look from Daniel to father. They both look at me, rage through their eyes. Daniel stands up and walks over to me roughly grabbing my wrist. "Why did you tell him all that?" He growls.

"Ouch Daniel" I wince "your hurting me!" I try to pry his hand off my wrist but he only grips tighter. "I don't know why I told him. A couple words slipped out of my mouth, he harassed me to tell him what they meant so I obliged. He's my brother, he deserves to know"

"No! He doesn't need to know! Look at him, look how scared he is" Daniel growled gripping my wrist tighter. If he grips any tighter I Swear it will break!

"Daniel! He's not a baby anymore! He's eleven years old for christ's sake!" I yell. Daniels face goes redder with anger. I hear a crack, fear rushes through me as pain surges through my arm.

A look of realisation crosses Daniels face and he immediately lets go of my wrist. I snatch it to my side and cradle it. The pain, it hurt. Tears streamed down my face.

End of Flash back

I look down at Finn, I quickly release his wrist as guilt washes through me. He rubs his wrist and looks at me a little petrified but anger I think over road that. "Finn I'm sorry" I apologise quickly. He just stares at me.

"I don't know what happened" I say with a sigh. I wait for Finn to walk out the room and leave me here on my own but he doesn't. Instead he sits down beside me.

"Avery, I should be the sorry one" he mumbles. I look at him slightly shocked. "I guess I should tell you my story huh?" He chuckles quietly. I nod

"Yes, from the beginning please" I say with a smile. He sighs and runs a hand through his hair. He looks so much like Daniel when he does that...

"Well it was right after you had called us for the first time since you were kidnapped...

Flash Back

Finn's POV

It had been only a day since Avery had been kidnapped, and all chaos had gone loose. Running around inside our pack house I carries bowls of warm soup and fresh water bottles. There had been few survivors from the battle we had just fought and right now it was my job to help them get better. I heard John groan down on the ground next to my foot. I bent down and gave him a bowl of soup.

"Thanks lad" he smiles at me weakly. I nod and continue to walk around. I hear the phone ring in the kitchen so I race over to it and pick it up.

"Hello?" I ask a little shaky.

"F-Finn?" I hear a familiar voice stutter. I gasp in surprise. It's her! She's alright! She's alive!

"Sissy!" I yell her nick name for me.

"Yes Finn! It's me" she cried through the phone. Why is she crying? Is she ok? Where even is she?

"Finn! Let me talk to her!" My father whisper yells at me. His eyes are red and puffy and he still has tears running down his face. I nod at him, as much as I would like to talk to Avery longer, I have many things to tell her! But I think papa needs to talk to her first.

"Avery Papa wants to talk to you" I say.

"No Finn, I want to talk to you, don't go" she begs. I shake my head as a tear runs down my cheek. How I missed the sound of my sisters voice, it had only been one day and I was going crazy with out her! I need her here to cradle me and tell me everything was ok. I missed her smile and her calm soothing voice. But right now, I knew what I had to do.

"Love you Avery" I said and passed the phone over to my father. Immediately he started to yell. He yelled so loudly I had to cover my ears.

"Avery Michelle Jedson! Where are you!?" He used her full name. He looked so angry but sad too. I used my special hearing to see what Avery was saying. I might not have shifted yet but I still have all the perks, speed, strength, smell and listening.

"Father, calm down, I'm ok-" Avery tried but dad cut her off.

"You're ok!? When I returned home this morning your mother tells me you were stolen by the Dark Shadow pack!" He yelled. I covered my ears again.

"Father please, I'm alright" I hear Avery's faint voice.

"Well where are you? Why did they take you?"

"Well, I uh... Im Jayden Byson's Mate" She answers quietly. Who is he again? Oh right! The Dark Shadow Packs Alpha! I smiled. My sister found her mate! Yay! I couldn't keep the grin off my face. At least I know she is alright now. I mean that Jayden guy would do anything to protect my sister wouldn't he? They are mates after all.

"YOU'RE WHAT!?" My father screamed. Why is he angry about this?

"Yeah.. Um.. Hey have you heard from Daniel?" Avery asked randomly.

"Don't change the subject missy!" Father continued to yell.

"No, dad, really. Is Daniel ok?" She was more concerned this time when she asked. Dad sighed and rubbed the back of his neck.

"No. I haven't seen him" he finally answered. I looked down at my hands. I miss Daniel. I can't help but wonder myself where he is. Mother tells me he is still alive but I just don't know. She doesn't look like she is telling the truth.

"W-what do you mean? Is he ok? Is he even alive!?" Her voice started to tremble.

"I mean exactly what I said. I haven't seen him. Or Brandon, or Mark. The three of them have gone missing and so has a whole lot of warrior wolves. They might be dead, they might be alive in hiding I don't know" he said running a hand through his hair.

"I-I have to go in a minute. Put me back on to Finn please" my ears perked up and I looked at my father pleadingly. I needed to speak to her. He nods and passed me the phone.

"A-Avery?" A tear ran down my cheek.

"Finn, I just want you to know that I love you ok? I have to go now. If you see Daniel tell him I love him too and I'll be home soon" no wait don't go! The thought ran through my head.

"Avery wait, there's something you should know" I quickly say.

"What? What's wrong?" She asks worriedly.

"It's ah that guy that you were talking to earlier today..." I trailed off.

"Finn, be REALLY careful about what you say right now.. We have ears on us"

"Ok I just wanted to tell you he's missing" I answer simply.

"W-what?" She stuttered.

"Th-they took him" I say quietly.

"Ok, thanks Finn. I love you ok? Don't forget that" she rushed but I know she meant it. I nod.

"Ok sissy, love you too" I say and she hangs up the phone. My father tilts his head at me. I sigh,

"She's alright" I say. He nods.

"Look Finn, your sister has made friends with the enemy. She is not alright!" He yelled. I flinched at his tone. "I don't want you to talk to her anymore. She is a stranger to us, she is no longer family. Do you hear me?" His voice boomed. I was frozen in fear. I finally shook my head, anger boiled inside me.

"No! She is family! She's my sister and no matter what she does, no matter who she loves, I will ALWAYS love her. And there is nothing you can do to change that!" I yell. Dad was about to retort when mother walked in, tears streaming down her face.

"He's right James" she said quietly looking at my father. "She is still our Avery. No matter how much she disgraces us she is still our daughter. And it is up to us to show her who her real family is. We will find a way to get her back home. We will make her choose between him and us" she sticks her nose in the air.

"Why can't she love Jayden? He is her mate" I defend my sister.

"Because Finn. Avery's 'mate' destroyed OUR pack. He almost wiped us all out, and as far as I'm concerned... He is not family. We are her family and she belongs to us. Not him" she answers venom lacing her tone.

"Finn, if you go around pretended nothing is wrong especially in front of your sister, things will not go down well. I forbid you to act all loving to her. You are to guide her to come home and to stay away from this Jayden guy! Do you hear me!?" My father yells.

"Wait, so you are telling me.. I can not be nice to my own sister? You're telling me I have to tell her to reject her own mate, otherwise I won't be her brother?" I ask confused. They nod.

"It's him, or us" mum spat and walked out the kitchen in a hurry. Well that's my family for you. They are so strange aren't they? I mean I get where they are coming from, Jayden did kind of kill our pack but I'm sure he had his reasons... Anyway, he loves Avery and she loves him. They're mates, they belong together. So I am not going to get in the middle of this family feud.

End Of Flash Back

Avery POV

I sat there in shock. "So my parents are only here to take me home? They don't care about my mate? Are they even going to help us in this battle with the rogues?" I ask still shocked.

Finn grimaced. "Yes, yes and no. They plan to leave tonight, you coming with us" he answered. "But please Avery! I didn't tell you ok? Dad will kill me if he knew that you knew" he said all worried. I nod.

"Don't worry Finn, you're safe with me ok? Hey, when they leave home, why don't you stay here?" I suggest with a smile. I couldn't care less my parents didn't care about my wants or needs and they were going to abandon me if I didn't go with them. But Finn doesn't deserve to live with their restrictions and orders.

"So I take it you aren't going back home?" Finn chuckled. I nod and wait for him to answer my question. He sighs, "I'll think about it ok?" He says with a smile. I grin and hug him. I stand up and take his hand in mine.

"Come on, let's go train" I say with a grin. Finn laughs and follows me out the room and out the house.

We walk straight outside and turn left, we walk about a kilometre through the woods and we reach a large clearing. It's all grass but there are obstacles set out everywhere, tires, punching bags, those walls with ropes that you climb up and climbing obstacles, there were rings set up and people fighting in them.

Everyone was training so hard. I find Katy and Tyson over at the rock climbing wall.

I drag Finn over. Katy is half way up and Tyson is holding the ropes. Tyson smiles over at me and down at Finn. "Hey Luna" he says in a teasing voice. I frown at him.

"Hey Blondie" I say poking my tongue out at him. He glares at me playfully. "Uh.. Finn, meet Tyson, Jayden's beta" I say with a smile. "Tyson, meet my brother, Finn"

Tyson lets one of his hands let go of the rope and he shakes Finns hand. "Nice to meet you bro" he smiled. Finn grinned

"You too." He looked up at the wall, "can I go next?" He asked. Tyson nods with a smile

"Sure!" I hear a scream and Katy comes flying off the wall. Tyson's expression changes to worry but he quickly pulls on the rope, making Katy stop in the air. She looks down at us, glaring at Tyson.

"You could have dropped me!" She screeches. Tyson chuckles

"I would have caught you though babe" he answers with a laugh. She rolls her eyes and swings back over to the wall and continues to climb. After a few minutes of watching, Katy reaches the top and makes her way down.

I feel two arms wrap around my waist and by the electrifying feeling I got, I could easily tell it was Jayden. "I'd like to see you climb up that wall" he whispered in my ear. I turn my head to look up at him and raise an eyebrow.

"Why? So you can get a better view of my ass?" I smirk. He laughs.

"You know me too well" he grins.

"What even is the point of this?" I ask confused. I mean, it's not like we're gonna have to climb this wall in the middle of a battle.

"It helps with your sense of surroundings, and it helps you to learn to focus more. It also helps with your strength and speed too I guess" he explains with a shrug. I nod. Katy's feet touch the ground and she unbuckled herself and slips the harness off.

Finn walks over to her and she happily slips it on over his head. He immediately starts climbing the wall. "So did you's sort everything out?" Jayden asked resting his chin on my shoulder and looked up at Finn.

Wow it's been like ten seconds and he's already climbed over ten meters. The wall is huge, it's about 30metres high and it's covered with red, green, blue, white and black rocks.

"Yeah we did actually" I say with a smile. I turn my head to look at Jayden.

"And...?" He asks me to continue

"My parents aren't going to fight in your battle, neither is my old pack, they hate you, they want to take me home with them tonight, they want Finn to have kept that a secret and they will hate me forever and I won't be considered their daughter if I choose to stand by you" I tell him everything Finn told me. "Oh and shh we don't know this" I add. He nods but frowns.

"So your parents only came up here to make you go back home with them?" He asks confused. I nod

"Yeah and if I don't, they don't want me in their lives anymore. I wish Daniel were here to tell me what he thinks of this situation" I sigh.

"Would he approve of us?" Jayden asks. I nod

"Yes of course he would. He's always had this thing about him where he understands all about mates all though he's never had one of his own... I just now him" I smile at all the memories I've shared with him. I hear someone clear their throat. I spin around to face both of my parents.

"Um... Hey guys..." They frown at me with disapproving looks. "How much did you hear?" I ask biting my lip. Jayden's arms tighten around my waist slightly. I smile at his protectiveness.

"All of it" my father growls.

"Don't you growl at me, you're the ones wanting me to reject my own mate!" I yell causing my mother to flinch. She quickly regains her posture and glares at me.

"Excuse me young lady but You're the sleeping with the enemy!" She screeches. I blink a few times.

"Mum, I'm still a virgin" I state calmly. "And you are the one wanting me to come home with you so I can help you and the pack with god knows what!" I yell.

"Darling, your mate is a selfish bastard who destroyed our pack for no reason! You are to reject him now and we will be off with out another word" my father growls. My mother nods. I step forward, out of Jayden's arms and fold my arms over my chest.

"You have no idea how hard it would be for me to reject my mate, my other half, my soul mate! I love him and I always will! And if it comes down to choosing my mate over my own selfish ignorant parents then It will be him!

It's always been him" I smile over my shoulder at him. I notice everyone is crowded around us watching our fight, including my old pack. I smile evilly.

"And you have no idea what it's like for me because you yourselves haven't even found your own mate!" I yell with a grin. My mother gasps and my fathers growl almost shakes the ground.

"What?" A wolf from my old pack gasps

"What is she talking about?" Another whispers.

"Yes that's right! These two people, James and Samantha Jedson, who sadly I am ashamed to call my parents, are not mates!" I yell. My parents glare at me but Jayden on the other hand is laughing his ass off. There are a lot of gasps. "Oh and they wanted me to reject my mate" I add pointing up my idex finger. I smile and skip off to the wall that Finn has just finished climbing.

"I told you not to tell them" he whined taking off his harness and passed it to me. I smiled at his cuteness.

"I didn't tell them, They over heard" I say simply and put the harness over my head. I did up all the buckles and turned to Finn. "Does this look right?" I ask him. He nods.

"Yep, oh and that off you gave me on staying here, is it still open?" He asked hopefully. I nod with a grin.

"Of course it is lil bro" I say and ruffle his hair. He smiles

"Thanks sis" I nod at him

"Your welcome" I say and look over at Tyson who is still holding the ropes in his hands.

"You ready Avery?" He asks raising an eyebrow. I nod and start climbing the wall. I look around carefully, debating which rock to place my hand and foot on next. I see a medium sized red rock with a dip at the top on it to I grab hold of it. Looking down I find a good rock to place my right foot on.

"You alright love!?" I hear Jay call. I smile down at him, wow he is so far away!

"Yep!" I call and look back up, realising I only have ten more metres to climb. As I reach the top I look back down. "Alright! I'm ready to come down now!" I yell. I hear a muffled voice, probably Tyson telling me ok so I start to climb back. I don't think I trust the rope to lean my self back.

After ten minutes it was getting tricky to climb down the way I came up so I leant back and kicked off the wall. Instead of the rope pulling me down slowly I felt myself sailing down to the earth quickly.

I screamed as it felt like I was falling off a twenty story building. I felt to strong arms catch me and he held me bridal stile. He was so tense.

I shook in his arms and buried my head into his neck breathing in his scent. "W-what was that?" I whispered still shaken.

"I don't know" Jayden whispered. He looked over at Tyson as did I. He looked shocked.

"I don't know what happened, honestly!" He held his hands up. "That didn't happen for Finn or Katy, someone must have cut the rope or som ething..." He trialled off. He pulled the rope down and just as he had said, it had been cut off. But who would have tried to do such a thing? Kyron, Katy and Finn run over to me.

"Oh my god! Avery are you ok!?" Katy screeches. Jayden holds me tighter.

"Avery what happened? Are you hurt?" Kyron's concerned voice rang through my ears.

"Sissy are you ok?" Finn's scared voice echoed through my mind. I look over at Tyson to see Dylan yelling at him. A high ringing sound goes through my ears and I find it very difficult to hear what anyone around me is saying.

Out of the corner of my eye I see a man in black track pants and a black hoodie run out around the crowd of werewolves and make his way to the forest.

I point at him. "Rogue" I manage to cough out. Jayden's head snaps up just in time to see the man slip into the woods.

"Go! Get him! Bring him to me!" He yells, werewolves from different packs nod and run off after him. "Avery, shh it's alright" he cradles me close to his chest.

After a minute or so, I start to feel a whole lot better. The shock had left my system and I could think straight. Currently Jayden was seated on the ground with me on his lap, his arms firmly wrapped around me, afraid to let me go.

"Ok, I'm all good now" I say, my voice muffled due to the fact Jay had squashed the side of my face up against his chest. If anything, Jayden only held me tighter. "Seriously Jayden, I'm fine now" I say trying to push myself away. He didn't budge. "Can't. Breath" I wheeze.

"Dude your suffocating her!" Dylan explains. Thanks, point out the obvious. Kyron laughs as he tugs Jayden's arms off me.

"He's in shock just as much as you were" Kyron whispers in my ear. I nod with a smile as Dylan struggles to hold Jayden back.

"No, let go of me" Jayden growls. Dylan chuckled

"Sorry man, but not until you calm down" he answered. Jayden took several deep breaths, his eyes were pitch black. I walk over to him, Kyron grabs my wrist and looks at me warningly.

"I wouldn't if I were you" he warns me, I smile at him.

"Thanks but I'll be fine" I say confidently. He nods and lets go of my wrist. I walk over to Jayden who still has both his arms pinned behind his back, being held there by Dylan. I gently run my fingers up his right forearm.

"Sh Jay, I'm alright see?" I say and peck his cheek. That causes him to calm a little. His deep breaths become more slower and lighter. I brush my lips against his and he kisses me back. Dylan lets go of Jayden and Jay instantly wraps his arms around my waist and tangles his hand in my hair as we deepen the kiss.

"Get. A. Room" Tyson says monotoned. Kyron and Dylan burst out laughing and Katy grins at us,

"Aww they're just so cute together!" She squeals. I smile against Jayden's lips and pull back causing him to pout. I turn around so my back is against his chest and I look at everyone.

"Why would someone do that? I mean if it's a rogue yeah I get why they want to kill you but with you only falling twenty metres or so wouldn't have killed you and I'll bet you they were expecting that Jay would catch you..." Kyron says looking deep in thought. Everyone thinks for a few minutes. I close my eyes and think hard. After a few seconds my eyes pop open.

"It's a distraction" I whisper. Everyone snaps their heads at me. I look to my right, the way to the pack house. I see thick smoke clouding up the sky. I gasp as does everyone else and we make a run to it.

After ten minutes of solid sprinting, we find ourselves in front of a massive building, aka the pack house, at it was covered in flames. Tears are streaming down Katy's face as Tyson holds her tight. Jayden is completely shocked and Kyron and Dylan are well... Shocked too I guess.

I spot a piece of paper on the grass a few feet away from us. I hop over to it and grasp it in my hand. I unfold it and start to read the messy writing. I looked at everyone and they looked at me questioningly. So I read the note out loud to them all.

"This is just the beginning. Game on mutts"

Seventeen

- -

Here chapter seventeen! Please don't forget to vote and comment :)Sorry for any spelling/grammar errors

Avery

After the massive fire had been put out, we had all slept in one of the guest houses. Would you believe how many guest houses there are here!? There's like six of them!

Anyways, the next morning, my parents left but my old pack refused to go with them. They called my parents liars and traitors and refused to trust them anymore. So my parents fled and made a run to god knows where and I'm so thrilled that they have left.

That rogue that cut the rope on me, was never caught, however some of the wolves from from my old pack could have sworn they had smelt several scents that belonged to some type of rogue, but multiple rogues, there wasn't just two or three, more like ten of them at least.

The week had passed slowly, we had done lots of training. I flop down on the bed beside Katy, completely exhausted. I let out a groan and roll over onto my left side to face her.

She had this gigantic grin all over her face and a knowing look. Her eyes danced with excitement. I looked at her questionably. She just shrugged but continued to smile happily. I sat up now frustrated and I looked her in the eyes, demanding to know what she was so cheerful about.

"Alright missy. Spill" I say pointing my index finger at her. She laughed and nodded.

"Alright alright!" She says throwing her hands up and sitting up in the process. Her smile vanished when she continued and it was replaced with a look of complete seriousness. "But Avery, you must know I only found out this morning and I have not told ANYONE. Not even Ty and I'd really appreciate it if you too kept this a secret ok?" She asks with pleading eyes. I nod with a friendly smile.

"Of course Katy. You can trust me" I say reassuringly and I place my hand on her shoulder. Katy takes a shaky breath and looks down at her hands.

"Ok... I don't want to fight in the battle anymore. I just can't." she admits quietly and looks up at me waiting for my reaction. My eyes almost pop out of my head. I thought she wanted to do this! Why has she changed her mind? What's happened?

"What? Why not!?" I almost yell, still shocked and extremely confused.

"BecauseImPregnant" she rushes out.

"Ok. I. Did. Not. Here. A. Word. You. Just. Said" I say slowly and calmly. "Please repeat?" She takes a shaky breath.

"I can't fight in the battle because- because I am pregnant" she squeals. I scream with joy and immediately pull her in for a hug.

"Oh my god!!! Katy congratulations!!" I could not contain my excitement for her. This is amazing! Wow, Katy is going to be a mother! This is just incredible. "Katy, you'll make an amazing mum" I say with aw. She smiles.

"Thanks Avery" she says. I smile but pause. "So I did hear the bed squeaking the other night!" I point out with a grin. She gasps and smacks my arm.

"Avery!" She giggles. I laugh with her but rub my arm."Ouch" I pout. She sticks her tongue out at me so I stick mine out at her.

The rest of the night, Katy and I stayed up in Jay's and my room, having a movie marathon and pigging out of popcorn and chocolate. With great difficulty I had finally managed to convince Jayden to sleep else where while Katy and I had our girls night. And let me to you, he wasn't very happy about not getting to sleep in the same bed as me, but he'll get over it... Eventually.

"Th-this movie- is so- sad!" Katy cried, sniffing between each word. She grabs her fifth tissue and wipes her tears away again. We were currently in the middle of watching titanic, up to the part where the boat is sinking.

A few hours later, at three in the morning, we had decided to call it a night. We got into bed and I snuggled deep under the warm blankets. I rolled over onto my side to face Katy. Her eyes open and she stares at me.

"You need to tell him" I say with a sigh. She nods"I know, I will tomorrow" she yawns and shuts her eyes again. I smile and feel myself drifting off into a blissful slumber.

dream

I wonder around our spot. The grass is so green and the flowers are all blossomed and it is really, really pretty. I look over at Jayden who is swimming in the lake, Tyson, Kyron and Dylan are with him. Katy and I are climbing the large oak tree in the centre of our spot. "I've reached the top!" I yell with a grin. Katy grumbles

"I can't climb any higher" she says frowning. I laugh at her. "That's alright haha"

"Mama! Mama come quick! Jasmine's hurt!" I hear a small boy yell from the bottom of the tree. Is this Katy's son? From where I am I can see He has short chocolate brown hair. I look at Katy and she looks at me confused.

"Avery? Aren't you going to go see what the matter is?" She asks."W-what?" I stutter. That couldn't be my son. I'm not a mum.

"Your son Scott, he's calling you. He said Jasmine's hurt" she says a little worried."Ugh who's Jasmine again?" I ask trying to think.

"Avery! This is no time to be joking around! Your daughter could be hurt!" Katy screeches at me. I flinch at her tone. I quickly climb down the tree to meet my 'son'. Tears are streaming down his face.

"S-Scott? It's ok" I say soothingly and I pull him in for a hug. Just tell me what happened ok?" I ask calmly and pull back to look at him. Getting a better look at him, he looks no older than ten, his chocolate brown hair shines brightly with hints of gold in it, and his eyes... Wow they were just mesmerising.

His left eye was a light forest green but his right eye, was the colour ocean blue. And just around the brim of each colour, was a thin line of gold that glittered in the sunlight.

"Mum we were climbing in the old oak tree at home a-and Derek and Jasmine were mucking around. They were pushing each other and Jasmine's foot slipped and she fell out of the tree. She says she can't walk or stand up and her leg is really sore!" He sniffs.

"It's alright Scott, everything will be ok" I say calmly. "Who's Derek?" I ask confused. Scott looks at me like I had grown two heads.

"My twin..?" He says just as confused. I nod"Ok take me to Jasmine" I say standing back up. He nods and grabs my hand and leads me away, looking back over my shoulder I see no one there. Katy, Jayden, Tyson, Kyron and Dylan had completely vanished. Weird.

As my feet leave the soft green grass and we enter the bright light that should take us into the forest.. My eyes are blinded by how strong the light it. I cover them with my right arm but I feel my left hand slip out of Scott's hand. I stop running and start to walk slowly.

A minute later the brightness tones down back to normal. I'm in a kitchen. This room isn't familiar to the eyes but I get this feeling in my gut that I know this place. "Mummy! Mummy! Mummy!" I hear a little girl cry. I walk around trying to find her.

"Where are you?" I call. Her crying gets louder and I walk into the living room to see her curled up on the floor, her black hair covering her face. I crouch down beside her. She sobs and looks up at me, he chocolate brown eyes bore into mine. "You almost lost me mummy" she whispers a few tears slide down her face. What is she talking about?

Doing exactly what came to the mind, I pull her in for a hug and gently rock her back and forth "Sh baby, it's ok" I whisper in her ear. I pull back after a minute and stare into her brown eyes. This small girl looks no older than five but oh my, she is beautiful. "What's your name?" I ask. She looks at me confused.

"What do you mean mummy? Don't you know who I am?" She asks tilting her head to the side. I shake my head and close my eyes."Of course I do sweet heart, you are my daughter" I say with a smile. But really, who is this child? "Why were you crying?" I change the subject.

"Derek stole my dolly and he lit her hair on fire and it all fell off!" She sobbed. I have a strange feeling that this is 'Jasmine'."Aw it's ok darling, we'll just get you a new dolly" I say with a small smile. The girl looks up at me and smiles. It's funny how that one small smile could make her whole face light up."Really?" She beams. I nod and laugh

"Sure!" I grin. I stand up and take her small soft hand in mine. I help her to her feet and we head for the door. Again, I am blinded by a bright light. I feel 'Jasmine's' hand slip free of mine. I squeeze my eyes shut, the brightness too much for me to handle.

End Of Dream

"Avery! Wake up! I'm hungry!" I hear Katy's voice whine. I blink my eyes, the sun rays shine brightly through the windows. No wonder why it so so bright in my dream. That was a dream right? It just felt so real! But seriously... Three children? This is to much for me to think about right now!

"Avery? What's up?" Katy asks shaking my shoulders lightly. I groan and cover my eyes, blocking the sun out."I just had the strangest dream" I sigh. She beams "Ohh details please!" She squealed. I laugh and tell her my dream.

....

She blinks a few times then her lips break into a large grin. "Oh my gosh! You're going to have babies!" She squealed. I laughed and shook my head."I seriously doubt it would be any time soon if I was" I chuckle.

"So you want to have children?" She smiled. I thought for a minute. Did I really want children? I must admit the concept of children did always seem to make my mind ponder. After a few minutes I finally nod.

"Yeah I guess but not until all of this rogue business has died down and the battle is over" I say with a nod. Katy nods her head furiously."Yep good idea" she says. "Oh and guess what?" "What?" I tilt my head to the side.

"I will be ready to give birth in only six months because of being beta and you'll only go through four months, isn't that cool?" She grins to herself.

"Yep" I say with a nod then stand up. I walk over to my draws and grab out a pair of black trackies and some sneakers. I tied my hair up in a loose bun then walked to the door. I looked over my shoulder at Katy who had just slipped on her favourite grey shirt that had white long sleeves.

"Well come on" I say. She looks at me confused, I roll my eyes then grin. "you have to tell Tyson about Blondie junior!" I squeal. She laughs and runs over to me and we walk out of the room. After walking down the stairs, we walk into the kitchen to find Jayden and Tyson seated at the bench.

I sit down on the stool in the middle of them. I couldn't stop myself from smiling, so I sat there grinning like an idiot while I waited for Katy to blurt out her surprise. Jayden raised an eyebrow at me.

"Why are you so cheerful this morning?" He asks. I shrug and look over at Katy. Jay pecks my cheek and whispers in my ear "how was your girls night?" I grin again.

"It was really good. It felt nice to finally get a good night sleep with out your snoring" I say playfully elbowing him in the ribs. He gasped and placed a hand over his heart.

"I do not snore!" He breaths dramatically. Katy and Ty chuckle."Uh.. Yeah you do man" Tyson says with a smirk. Jayden frowns and slumps his shoulders.

"..Shut up" he grumbles. I laugh and kiss his cheek."Love you babe" I whisper. He smiles and cups my cheek. He places his lips on mine. I wrap my arm around his neck as we deepen the kiss. In the background I hear Katy clear her throat impatiently. I smile and pull away and turn to Katy and Tyson.

"Hehe sorry" I smile sheepishly. Katy smiles"As I was saying before you two decided to have your little.. Make out session- I Will NOT be participating in your battle with the rogues" she states looking from Jayden to Tyson. Tyson smiles in triumph.

"I'm glad you have decided that" he says and pecks her lips. He pulls back and looks at her confused. "Why did you decide that?" He asks slightly tilting his head to the side. Katy grins.

"Ok don't be mad, I only found out yesterday and haven't really had a chance to tell you..." She trailed off. Tyson looks at her weirdly.

"Katy?" He growls "haven't had the chance to tell me what?" He frowns. Katy looks down with a sheepish grin.

"I'm pregnant" she whispers loudly. Tyson's facial expression is replaced with shock and surprise, Jayden's is no different than Ty's. After a minute of Tyson being frozen, he snaps out of his trance. He stands up, picks Katy up by the waist and spins around in circles, grinning from ear to ear. She squeals in surprise.

"I'm going to be a daddy!" He yells excitedly. I laugh and look over my shoulder at Jay. He smiles warmly at Tyson and Katy. "Congrats bro" he says standing up and walking over to Tyson. Tyson places Katy down and turns to Jayden. They shook hands but then Jayden quit the tough act and pulled Tyson in for a bro hug. Naw.

Kyron walks in the next minute. On the way to the fridge he stops and looks at us. He looks like he's trying to figure something out. "Wait.. Don't you all usually sit around the bench all bored as hell? Why are you all dancing around like chimpanzees?" He asks confused. I laugh at him.

"Kyron, I'm pregnant" Katy grins at him. He looks at her surprised." For real?" He blinks. She laughed"No cos we're all dancing around like "chimpanzees" for no reason" she laughs. He grins and runs over to her, embracing her in for a hug. She pats his back.

"Congrats Katy" he whispers."Thanks Kyron" she smiles. He pulls back and walks over to Tyson and gives him a bro hug. "Congrats man" Kyron says patting Ty's back,"Thanks bro"

...

I take another bite out of my ham and cheese sandwich and look at Kyron who sat beside me at the bench. "Kyron, it's like lunch time and I still haven't seen Dylan!" I whine. "Do you know where he is?" I ask hopefully. Kyron frowns and shakes his head.

"Sorry princess, but no. I haven't seen him and I have no clue where he could be" he shrugs and takes a large bite out of his sandwich."What if something's wrong? What if he's in trouble?" I worry. Kyron chuckles.

"Avery, he's a big badass warrior wolf. I'm sure he can take care of himself by now" he says placing a hand on my shoulder. I nod

"Yeah I guess so. I just worry about him you know? I mean I just have this feeling that I need to protect him no matter what. I was devastated when I thought my father killed him two years ago and I had only known him less than five hours! So devastated in fact, I kept myself locked away for two whole years" I chuckle lightly although to me this is no laughing matter. Kyron looked at me startled.

"What!? First of all you thought Dylan was dead? And you locked yourself up for two years because of it?" He asked surprised. I nod and look down.

"I spent two whole years being mad and hating Daniel because he didn't defend Dylan, and now Daniel might be dead! I wasted two whole years with him!" I cried. God I am such a mess right now. I wipe my tears away and look at Kyron. He pulls me in for a hug."It's alright Avery" he cooed. "I'm sure your brother is still alive, out there hiding somewhere" he reassures me. I nod and sniff. He pulls back and looks at me with confusion. "So this pull you have towards Dylan, it's like a guard thing... You must be... No it's not possible." He talks to himself. I look at him questionably.

"Kyron. What's not possible?" I ask sitting up straighter. He sighs and looks down at me.

"It just might be possible... Avery do you know what a wolf-guardian is?" He asks hopefully. I think for a moment, the name did sound familiar...

Flash Back

Several years ago...

"Daniel please read me a bed time story?" I begged my older brother. He chuckles,"Alright. Let me go grab a book. I will meet you in your room" he grins at me. I nod with a smile and run off to my room. I jump into bed and make myself comfy. Minutes later, Daniel walks in with a small book I had never seen before.

"Daniel, what's that book called?" I ask looking at the front cover. Daniel passes me the book and I examine the cover properly. On it is a girl with jet black hair, she's dressed in black pants and a blank long sleeved shirt, she also has black boots on.

Behind her in the shadows is a small boy crouched down. His hair too is jet black but his clothes are all ripped. The girl has a fierce and scary look on her face, but the boy looks scared and defenceless.

Daniel smiles down at me "It's called 'Wolf-Guardian' "

End Of Flash Back

I look up at Kyron who looks down at me expectant. I sigh and rub my forehead and look down at my hands that rest in my lap. "Yes. I've heard of it before but I can't quite remember what they are" I answer furrowing my eyebrows as I try hard to remember how the story went. But my mind comes out blank.

"They are these female werewolves, that are destined to protect this one werewolf. He could be anyone, someone from another pack, someone from your own. But the Wolf-Guardian is to protect him no matter what. If he dies, well I don't remember what happens but something bad does. By the sounds of it it can't be good. But anyway... Avery I think you are a Guardian-Wolf sent to protect Dylan from what is to come" Kyron announces.

"Oh. Wow ok..." I look up at him still slightly confused. "So something bad is going to happen to Dylan and I have to be there to protect him because if he dies something bad will happen to me?" I ask. He nods. "Ok then I have to go find Dylan-"

I was cut off when somebody walked in through the door. "Speak of the devil" Kyron chirps. Dylan smiled over at us warily. "Uh hey guys..." He trails off sheepishly. A strong scent wiffs through my nostrils. I look at Dylan raising my eyebrows.

"Really Dylan? Have you learnt nothing the past week about rogues?" I raise my voice standing up. Dylan holds his hands up in surrender."Avery before you say anything, let me explain-" I cut him off

"Dylan! How can you just let a rogue come in here!? Why is one standing right outside the door right now!? They have been attacking us for days on end and you decide to let one come live with us!?" I yell at him.

What if that rogue had tried to attack him? Or worse, killed him? I walk past Dylan and to the door. I swing it open to come face to face with a teenage girl, who looked no older than sixteen. She looked so scared and.. Innocent. She takes a few steps backwards and looks at the ground, I sigh and turn to Dylan.

"You have two minutes to tell me your story" I snap at him, still rather angry he would be so reckless. I turn to the girl. "What is your name?" I ask her softly."B-Belle" she stutters quietly. I smile at her.

"Well Belle, why don't you come in here, take a seat. Tell us your story" I say and wave my hand at the island where Kyron and Dylan sit. She nods and takes a shaky breath. She walks over to Dylan and sits down beside him. He holds her hand in his reassuringly, and he entwined their fingers. I smile at how sweet he is being to her. But why is he looking at her like that? He has that puppy love struck look written all over his face...

"It's alright Belle, just tell them what you told me" he smiles at her. She nods, Kyron and I lean forward and place our elbows on the bench top, and rest our chins on our palms.

"O-ok. I'm not really sure where to start but my names Isobelle Colliah" she introduced herself quietly. She tucked a few of her blonde hair strands behind her ear and continued. "A-and I'm from th-the White D-Dawn pack" she stuttered. I gasped and stood up. I walked over to her and hugged her. She rested her chin on my shoulder and cried.

"Shh it's ok sweet heart, I know what your going through" I murmur. Poor girl! Her pack got wiped out too! By Jayden..."M-my father was the Alpha a-and he, my mother and younger sister Delilah were murdered right in front of my eyes" she sobbed. I smiled sadly.

"Belle?" I say pulling back to look into her bright blue eyes. She sniffs and wipes her tears away."Y-yes?"

"My name is Avery Jedson. My father was the Alpha of The White Crescent Pack. My old pack was demolished by the Dark Shadow pack only weeks ago, my parents and younger brother survived but my older brother... I haven't heard from him. I'm not sure if he's alive or not. A-Anyway, I found my mate and now I am here. I know what you are going through, and believe me it must be tough, worse for you because everyone around you has died but trust me-" I place a hand on her shoulder and give her a small smile "it will get better" I say with a nod.

She smiles sadly "It won't though. My life was perfect! I had the perfect parents. The perfect sister. The perfect best friend. The perfect boyfriend" I look over at Dylan to see his fists clench up. Well that's not at all weird... I was snapped out of my accusing thoughts when Belle continued,

"A-and now they are all dead! That horrible son of a bitch Alpha Jayden of The Dark Shadow Pack had to ruin everything!" I clenched my hands into balls of fists trying to contain my anger. She called my mate a son of a bitch! Well I guess he deserves it but still! I take a deep breath and calm myself.

"How old are you?" I ask calmly."Fourteen, turning fifteen in a few weeks" she answers. So she hasn't shifted yet..."Has your wolf started to talk to you yet?" I ask tilting my head. She nods

"She started talking to me today, right before I ran into Dylan. I had stumbled onto this land and Dylan had sniffed me out. He thought I was an intruder but when he saw me in my human form he wondered why I was so young and why I was a rogue so I told him my story." She explained. She looked over at him and gave him a small smile.

"Well Belle Colliah, as of today you are now apart of my pack. - I'm the Luna so if I say you can be in it, you can" I wink. She smiles"Thank you Avery" she cries and hugs me again. I pat her back."Yeah... I wouldn't thank me yet..." I trail off squinting my eyes shut. She pulls back. I open my eyes slowly to see her staring at me confused.

"Why?" She asks confused. I turn to Kyron and Dylan. They smirk at me."Go on Avery, tell her" Dylan nudges me. I turn to Kyron, he holds his hands up in surrender. "Don't look at me!" He yells. I laugh for a bit but sigh when I see how serious Belle's face is.

"Ok I'm going to need you to not to freak out ok?" I say pointing my finger at her with a small smile. She nods "that Alpha, Jayden Byson... The one who destroyed both our packs... He's my mate and right now you are in his territory.- but don't worry! He won't hurt you, and he's a completely different person now than what he was before" I add quickly.

She didn't look as scared as I though she would but she was frowning at his name. "You don't look as scared as I thought you would be" I state with a chuckle. She shrugs.

"I don't really have anything left to lose, so I wouldn't care if he killed me. That's why I'm not scared" she mutters and stands up. She walks out the room "I need some fresh air" she mumbles and disappears out the back door. Dylan stands up.

"I'll go make sure she's alright" he tells us and follows after her. I turn to Kyron.

"Well that wasn't at all weird" I mumble. He laughs and pats my back gently.

"You make a great Luna" he tells me, I can see the honesty in his eyes. I smile"Thanks Kyron." He nods. The next minute Jayden and Tyson walk in talking about 'the baby' and Katy's plans for the battle. Jayden smiles over at me and sits down beside me. He grabs hold of my hand and entwined our fingers.

"Um Jay?" I ask quietly. He stops talking to Tyson and faces me."Yes love?""You know the pack you destroyed a couple months ago... The White Dawn Pack?""Yes, vaguely, why?" He asks confused as to why I would bring it up.

"Well, the Alpha of that pack, has a daughter, Belle her name is. And she just so happened to stumble onto our territory this morning. And because she has no family- or anyone, for that matter... I have invited her to stay with us" I finish with a smile. Jayden thinks for a moment.

"Alright she can stay" he sighs. I squeal with excitement and hug him."T hanks Jay" I breath.

"Well it is the least I can do for her. I mean I did kind of murder her entire family..." He trails off with a look of disgust. "How was I so cruel for all those years? I used to jump at the idea of killing someone from another pack but now, my stomach flips ten times at the mention of it" he says sadly. Tyson and Kyron chuckle.

"Feeling guilty man?" Tyson laughs "Yeah, thought I'd never see the day!" Kyron adds with a grin. Jayden rolls his eyes at them then looks back at me.

"Just remember to make her feel welcome ok?" I say and pat his cheek. I peck his lips then stand up. I then jog upstairs to find Katy. I can't wait to tell her about Belle. Was it just me or did I see some kind of a pull between her and Dylan? They couldn't be mates.. First of all she hadn't come of age yet, and second, she would have to be a pure white wolf...

I knock of Katy's bedroom door. She swings it open and I grin at her. "I have so much to tell you!" I yell.

So.. What did you guys think of chapter seventeen?

Eighteen

Sorry for any spelling/grammar errors

Enjoy :)

Avery

The next few days was filled with training. Dylan had dedicated himself to be Belle's personal trainer. I have to admit though... They do look really sweet together. I watch the two do one on one, combat fighting.

Belle throws a full forced punch at Dylan's face. He catches her fist right before it hits him. She grunts and throws her other fist but he catches that one too. Belle smirks and goes to knee him in the groin but Dylan simply steps the the side. He sticks his foot out behind Belle's leg which causes her to fall down onto her back, only she drags Dylan down with her.

Dylan straddles her and he gives her his famous smirk. Using Belle's super speed and strength, she flips themselves around so Dylan lays on the ground and she straddles him. Dylan brings his hand slowly up to her face and tucks a few strands of her hair behind her ear. He then trails his thumb over her cheek softly. She bends down so her lips are just centimetres above Dylan's then-

My vision was cut off when Jayden stands in front of me, his arms crossed firmly over his chest. I move my head to the side to try and look around him but he too steps to the side. "Aww but it was just getting good!" I whine.

The past week, Dylan and Belle have been getting closer and closer to each other. They've even started kissing each other! They're just so cute together! I really have this strong feeling that they are mates. I guess we'll find out in a couple weeks when Belle turns fifteen.

"Avery? Avery are you even listening to me?" Jayden snaps his fingers in front of my face. I blink a few times and stare up at him. My eyes trail up his well toned body. My eyes roam over his v-line and up his eight pack, my mouth starts to water. Why does he always have to be shirtless? It really has been distracting me lately... "Avery" he sighs frustrated.

I blink again and snap my eyes up and lock with his eyes. Right how they are the colour forest green, so beautiful they are, I could just stare into them forever and never get bored.

"I- uh. What were you saying?" I ask trying to snap out of my trance. I was really finding it hard to ignore all both my wolf and my own horny thoughts that were rushing through my mind right now. I stand up and look into Jay's eyes.

"I was saying that I want you to get back up and keep on training" he mutters. He stares at my lips and I stare at his. I feel myself leaning in and his lips brush against mine. Jayden wraps his arms around my waist to keep me in place.

I wrap my arms around his neck and tangle my hands in his hair. He licks along my bottom lip, asking for entrance which I gladly granted. We stayed like this a very long time, Jayden's hands constantly trailed up my back and all the way down again.

"Jayden.. I th-think I'm ready. To complete the mating process" I stutter. He pulls back and looks at me raising an eyebrow.

"Are you sure?" He asks concerned. I nod and peck his lips. He smiles

"Good because I wasn't sure how much longer I could last" he chuckles. He picks me up bridal stile and carries me back to the guest house we've been living in the past few weeks.

Our lips stayed locked the whole way there. After a few minutes Jayden pulled back and with his right hand he dug it into his pocket and pulled out a set of keys. I open my eyes and look around me to see the sun had almost set but everyone else was still out training.

Jayden finally unlocks the door and kicks it open. He kicks it shut after we enter and he carries me upstairs. I couldn't stop smiling. I really was ready for this.

.

.

.

(I'm going to go ahead and skip this scene sorry! :p)

.

.

.

.

I wake up with my hands tangled in my hair. I tug them out carefully and look over at Jayden, who slept peacefully. I smile and blush as the memories come flooding back from last night. I bite my lip as I replayed the memories over and over.

Nothing could explain how happy I was right now. I think I will go take a shower... I hop out of bed only to realise I was my skin was still bare. I tug a sheet off the bed and wrap it around my small body. Jayden groans and rolls onto his side to face me.

His eyes open, I stare into his now dark brown eyes that were filled with lust. He smiles "morning beautiful" he greets, his voice is husky. I smile,

"Morning" I mumble tiredly. "I'm going to go take a shower" I mutter and walk into the shower.

"And I shall join you" Jayden says now interested. I laugh and walk into the bathroom with him behind me. Jayden walks over and turns the taps on and he hops in. He looks at me with a smirk. "You coming in?" He asks. I bite my lip nervously but nod. I dump the bed sheets on the floor and hop in the shower. Honestly, that's all we did. Just showered.

.

.

.

I walked over to the wardrobe and pulled out some black shorts and a tank top. I took my towel off and slipped into my clothes. I turned around to see Jayden already dressed. He looked at me, still smiling. I gasp.

"Jay we didn't use protection last night" I look at him shocked. He shrugged,

"Oh well" he smirked. I rolled my eyes,

"Well I don't actually mind having children at all. I just wanted to wait until after the battle that's all" I say. He looks at me surprised.

"You actually want to have children?" He asked blinking a few times. I nod and smile.

"Yeah, I mean why not? I've always loved the idea and I'm not getting any younger here so..." I trail off smiling. I actually really hope I get pregnant...

"Let's go get breakfast" Jayden says with a grin. "I'm starving" I nod agreeing with him and we walk downstairs hand in hand. Reaching the bottom of the stairs, the fresh smell of eggs and bacon flows through my nose. I inhale deeply and follow the delicious scent.

We walk into the kitchen to see Kyron cooking at the stove, Dylan, Tyson, Katy and Belle all sat around the island digging into their breakfast. I see three spare plates covered in bacon and scrambled eggs. I take one and sit down beside Dylan.

Jay grabs a plate too and sits down beside me. Kyron turns off the stove and grabs his own plate and piles extra bacon onto it. He then sits down on the other side of Jayden.

The room became silent and everyone tuned their attention onto Jayden and I. I awkwardly finish chewing my mouthful and swallow. "What?" I ask looking at everyone. They stared back at me, looking completely serious. Katy was first to burst into a fit of giggles, Belle then cracked and started to grin and the others started to laugh.

"You guys finished the mating process last night!" Katy squealed so loudly I had to cover my ears. I nod and Jay winces at how loud Katy was. "OMG tell me everything!" She yells.

I laugh, defiantly not here in front of all the guys, I mouth at her 'Not Now' she got it and nodded. Breakfast passed by quickly and because it was a Sunday, we don't have to train! Yay!

Katy, Belle and I run off outside. "Where should we go?" I ask. Belle shrugs but Katy grins.

"How about 'the spot'? You know the one Jayden took you too not long ago? As children we all used to hang out there growing up but I haven't been there in a long time" she laughs. "Oh but weren't you there the other night?" She raises an eyebrow at me. My dream comes flying back to me, the spot where Katy and I were climbing the oak tree and Scott came running up.

Belle looks between us confused. "What are you guys even talking about?" She laughs. I smile and tell her the dream I had the other night.

"Oh! Wow, that's cool. Do you think you'll actually have three children later on? Three sounds like quite a handful to have" she laughs. I smile

"I was one in three" I state. She looks at me surprised.

"Really?" She asks. I nod.

"Yep, Finn, you met him yesterday at training, he's my little brother. He doesn't have to train so much because he's not going to fight in the battle, and Daniel my older brother... Well I haven't seen him in a while lets just say." I explain. She looks at me confused.

"Whys that? Jayden and the guys told me everyone was fighting in the battle, even the children" she says confused. What? Why would they tell her that? I look over at Katy. She looks at me her eyes wide and she shakes her head. I suddenly hear her voice in my head.

'Dont tell her anything about the evacuation plans. She might be apart of our pack now but the less people that know about these plans, the better. And because she would have shifted by the time the battle comes, she is required to participate in it' Katy explains through our little mind link.

'But what if she's Dylan's mate? Won't he want her to sit out? Dylan isn't participating in the battle because of this whole guardian thing and he won't want his mate to go out on the battle field with out him' I reply.

'What makes you so sure that they are mates?' She raises an eyebrow.

'I don't know, just the way they act around each other' I answer. And that aura of love they give off when ever they are around each other. I add mentally to myself.

"Hello?" Belles confused voice rang through my ears. I look at her confused expression.

"Oh right um, well everyone is participating in the battle but I'm going to hide Finn because I won't be able to handle it if he dies so I'm forcing him to sit out on this" I cover. She nods believing me. Well that is half true...

"Oh ok" belle mumbles. All of a sudden I don't hear leaves crunching under my feet anymore. I look up and see we had arrived. The spot still look as beautiful as it did the other week. I run over to the oak tree and start to climb it. Katy follows me up and so does Belle. I started to tell the girls all about last night on the way up the tree.

I finally reached the top. I sat down on a stable, thick branch and Katy sat just below me, with Belle next to her. "So he didn't use a condom?" She squealed. I laughed and nodded.

"So your dream could come true very soon!" She yelled with a grin. I laughed again and Belle laughed too. We started talking about the most random things.

"Katy, have you thought of any names for your child?" Belle asks. Katy beams.

"Yes I have actually"

"Well spill then!" I order grinning.

"Ok so if it was a boy, I was thinking Max or Tyler..." She says biting her lip.

"Tyler sounds a bit like Tyson, don't you think?" I ask sticking my tongue out at her. She rolls her eyes but smiles.

"That's the name I've had picked out since I was ten!" She laughs.

"Hmm I like the sound of Max. Ok now for the girls" Belle says with a grin. Katy and I laugh.

"Ok for the girl names I was thinking April or Kirsten" Katy smiles. I smile

"I like those names" I say.

"Mmm me too" Belle agrees. Katy grins

"Thanks guys" she says.

A few hours later we were all siting by the lake, our feet dangled in the crystal clear, shallow water. Little gold shiny fish swum by, their Finns sparkling in the sunlight. "So Belle..." I trail off. Belle sat in the middle of Katy and I. Katy looked at her and grinned.

"You and Dylan huh?" She nudged Belle's shoulder. Belle blushed and looked down at her feet.

"Are you guys like a thing now or something? I saw you's kissing the other day" I say smirking at her which caused her cheeks to fume.

"Y-yes I guess so..." She answered shyly.

"Do you love him?" Katy asked grinning from ear to ear.

"Yes do you?" I ask excitedly. Belle is silent for a moment.

"Yes" she finally answers, it comes out as a mere whisper, I had to strain my ears to hear. Katy and I start to squeal.

"Aww so cute!" I grin

"You guys are adorable!" Katy yells. Belle just laughs.

"Hehe thanks guys" she blushes. I stand up.

"It's getting late" I say waving my hand at the sun that was starting to set behind the trees.

"Yeah let's head back" Katy says standing up. We both extend a hand to Belle which she takes and we hoist her too her feet. We start walking back bumping each other's shoulders every now and then.

.

.

.

"So Avery I was wondering..." Jay trails off. I roll onto my side to stare at him. I pull the fresh new bed sheets up to my neck and snuggled deeper to get warm.

"Yes Jayden?" I ask him to continue.

"Well while you and the girls were out today, Tyson, Kyron, Dylan and I were catching up on things. Tyson wouldn't shut up about having a baby, and he was telling us the names they might call the baby... And it got me thinking..." Jayden trailed off again. I smiled and looked into Jay's now light blue eyes.

"Thinking about what?" I whisper.

"Well if we were to have a child, what would you want to name him?" He asks staring back into my eyes. Or her! It could be a girl you know.

"Well I've always like the name Derek if I ever had a boy" I say, I guess that's why one of my 'children' in my dream was named Derek. "AND for the girl I've always liked the name Jazzlin" I admit. Jazzlin is Quite similar to Jasmine... "What about you?" I ask.

"Well if it were a boy I was thinking.. Scott, and for the girl I got no idea. But I don't like Jazzlin" he admits with a shrug. "Jasmine though, that's similar and it sounds sweet" he says smiling warmly at me.

I smile and let a yawn escape my mouth. Well no wonder the other child was called Scott. But how? Will I actually have three children later on in life, children identical to the ones I saw in my dream?

"Good night Jay" I mumble deciding I should actually get some sleep.

"Good night love" he whispers.

Comment? Vote? Let me know what is on your minds! :)

Nineteen

Prepare to be amazed haha bit of a surprise comes in this chapter but I'm sure most you you will be able to guess what is going to happen :) but there will be a big twist later on in the next few chapters that you probably won't be expecting.

Anyways here is chapter nineteen, enjoy :) Don't forget to vote and comment

Sorry for any gramma/spelling errors

Avery

The burning sensation in my throat didn't seem to want to leave. The feeling in the pit of my stomach felt like I was on fire and the pain hurt like crazy. I had never experience this before.

I gripped the toilet seat harder and I leant forward. My knees hurt from kneeling on the cold hard tiles the past half an hour, puking my guts out. I felt Jayden's warm hand return to my back and he rubbed it soothingly. I felt another lot of bile rise In my throat.

I coughed and spluttered as it rushed out my mouth and into the toilet bowl. I felt the back of my throat burning again, and the after taste was just feral. Jayden continued to hold my hair back and rub my back gently.

"What's wrong with me?" I cough. "This has been going on for a week now" I say, reaching my hand up. I press the flush button on the toilet and I fall back onto my bum. Jayden squats down beside me.

"I don't know sweet heart-" he was cut off when Katy walked in carrying a glass of fresh water. She passed it to me and I took it gratefully. I took a large mouthful and gargled it at the back of my throat, then spat it back out into the toilet.

The burning feeling eased a little and my stomach started to settle. Out of the corner of my eyes I could see Katy whispering to Jayden. He looked over at me unsure but nodded and left the room. Wait, where is he going?

Katy sighed in relief and walked over to me. She squatted down beside me. "You alright?" She asked sympathetically. I nodded then shook my head. I cleared my throat and swallowed.

"Yes. No. Maybe. I don't know Katy what's going on with me? Why am I vomiting? I have never vomited before" I coughed. Katy smiled "When was the last time you had your period?" She asked.

"A little over a month ago why?" I thought for a minute then it clicked. "I'm late!" I whisper yell.

"And we all no that werewolves cannot get sick unless of certain reasons... Can you think of what could be going on right now?" She grins. My eyes widen.

"No! Really!? Oh my gosh!" I screamed. Katy laughed. "Looks like I won't be the only fat one" she says sticking her tongue out at me. Oh my god, I'm pregnant! But we only did it once and it's been about a little over a week or so since then...

"Katy! This is... Amazing! But bad. Very bad" I say sadly."Whys it bad? I thought you wanted children?" She asks. I sigh

"I do, but the battle is coming up soon. I'm not sure when, but with me being pregnant Jayden definitely won't want me to fight and I want to be out there with him and-" Katy cuts me off my rant

"Avery. Calm down, we don't have to tell him until after the battle" Katy said reassuring. "The battle won't be too far from now, a week tops maybe? I don't know but we can keep a secret for a while" Katy winked.

"Really? You'd keep this a secret for me?" I ask surprised. She nods with a grin.

"But we have to tell Belle" she says in complete seriousness. I nod. We stand up and walk down stairs. I see everyone seated at the island in the kitchen. Everyone except-

"Where's Dylan and Belle?" I ask confused. Kyron chuckles "Well as you guys already know... It's Belles birthday tomorrow and we've decided to throw her a surprise birthday party!" Tyson whisper yells. I nod with a grin.

"What a good idea! I love parties!" Katy squeals."Yes anyway, Dylan took Belle out for the day so we could set it all up. We are setting this up in the party house, which is on the right side of the guest house that is furthest away from here." Kyron states with a nod. I blink at them.

"No way! You guys have your own Party House!?" I yell shocked. They nod and grin.

"Come on" Jayden says standing up. "We've got a party to organise" we cheer and follow the guys outside and we make our way to the Party House.

My smile falls as we are walking. How am I going to keep this a secret from Jayden?

How can I not tell him? Well I need to tell someone other than the girls. I need a guy's advice. And looking at the guys it was obvious who I was closest to.

I skip over to Kyron and tug on his arm. He raises an eyebrow at me but continues to walk."Kyron I have to tell you something... It's very important and I need your advice" I say quietly. He looks around at the others then at me.

"Who are we keeping a secret from?" He whispers with a smirk."Jayden" I whisper back catching him off guard.

"Woah I though you were gonna say Katy or Dylan but your own mate!?" He whisper yells. I slap my hand over his mate. Tyson was the only one that heard him because he turned to us and raised an eyebrow. He mustn't have heard word for word because he turned back around and continued to talk to Jayden.

"Yes now come with me" I whisper. "Jayden are there any party streamers or balloons at the party house?" I ask loudly. Jayden's head snapped up and he clicked his fingers.

"So that's what I forgot" he mutters loudly."Kyron and I will go get some, we'll meet you at the party house soon ok?" I say. He nods

"Alright see you soon, love you!" He calls after us."Love you too" I reply and I spin around, grabbing Kyron's hand and we start walking back to the house. "Fine forget about me then" Kyron pouts playfully."All good Kyron, I was already planning on it" Jay answers teasingly.

As we walked back to the house, Kyron dug his hands into his pockets and kept them buried. "So what was the big secret you wanted to tell me?" He asked quietly. I sighed and stopped walking. The house was only about twenty metres away. I looked from the house and back to Kyron.

"Kyron.. I'm pregnant" I say quietly

------------------Short chapter I know, sorry. Vote? Comment? :)

Twenty

A very

Kyron walks into the kitchen and over to a cupboard. He grabs out blue, red and pink streamers and three bags of multi coloured balloons. "Kyron, say something" I beg. He looks at me.

"It's great, fantastic, really Avery. I'm thrilled for you" he says calmly. When I told him twenty minutes ago he was all jumping around, yelling and cheering but as soon as I told him I didn't want to tell Jayden until after the battle, Kyron has been all quiet.

"Why are you acting this way?" I ask quietly.

"Because Avery. How am I supposed to keep a secret like this from my best friend? My Alpha!" He raises his voice and runs a hand through his hair.

"Woah calm down. It's not like we are keeping this secret for a long time, it's just until after the battle, which I have a feeling will be quite soon" I explain. Kyron sighs in frustration.

"Avery I can't keep this from him. Neither can you, he's your mate and yes he will make you sit out of the battle but it's for your own good and your baby's sake" he waved a hand at my stomach. I sigh in defeat.

"Fine you win. I'll tell him" I mumble. Kyron raises an eyebrow.

"Win? This wasn't an argument Avery" he states and walks back outside with the streamers in one hand and the balloons in the other. I sigh again and follow him out. We walk to the party house in silence. We stop about ten metres away. I turn to Kyron confused. Why did he stop?

"Avery, I'm sorry. I really am happy for you ok? I just want you to know that. I think this is amazing and you will make an incredible mother" he laughed. I laughed too and hugged him.

"Thanks Kyron" I mumble into his chest.

"Anytime Avery" he replied with a smile. We then walked to the large double storied building. It was made of bricks, and on the outside it looks old and dusty, kind of like an abandoned building. We walk inside however, and it looks like it was built yesterday!

The floors are made of wood, they are dark and polished and the lights shine off it. The walls are a creamy colour with posters hanging everywhere. Katy was hanging a banner up with Tyson that reads 'Happy Birthday Belle!' And it is written in a different colour for each letter.

Jayden is handing up sparkly, colourful paper letters on the wall in a long line next to each other and it reads 'Happy Birthday!' He has done this on all four walls.

"Looking good guys" I nod my head in approval. Katy laughs. Kyron and I walk over to the back wall were several long, rectangle, wooden tables are set up beside each other along the wall. Kyron opens up the bags of balloons and dumps them all over a table.

"Dibs not blowing them up!" I shout and laugh.

"Dibs not!" Katy says raising her hand.

"Kyron and Tyson, you two can blow them all up" Jayden passes a balloon pump to Tyson. Kyron frowns

"If Tyson gets to use the only balloon pump to fill up the balloons, what do I use?" He asks confused.

"Your mouth silly!" I laugh at him. He frowns and huffs in annoyance. I tear open one of the streamer packets and I take out a pink roll. I pass a purple one to Katy and a blue to Jayden. We start throwing them around and hanging them up.

"Oh! The food! What are we going to do about that?" I ask suddenly. Jayden chuckles

"I got some of the werewolves from our pack to cook party food, enough food for everyone. Because Everyone that is here is invited" he smiled. I nod.

"Good"

After a few hours Jayden pulled out his phone. "It's Dylan. They're on their way back and they've got bad news to share with us" he mutters. We nod and pack up all the extra things we didn't use and all of the equipment, and chucked them in the storage room. We then headed back to the guest house we are living in.

Just as we got back, Dylan and Belle run in to the kitchen to meet us, they were panting and huffing, trying to catch their breaths. "R-rogues" Belle puffs worriedly. We all become alert.

"What? where?" I ask on high alert.

"W-when we were walking through the woods-" Dylan swallowed then continued "we saw five rogues. They told us they were coming in four days including today" Dylan rushed out. Belle nodded, her eyes were all teary. I pulled her in for a hug.

"It's alright, you're safe now" I coo.

"Th-they were so scary" she whimpered. Dylan nodded and I pulled back and gave Belle a reassuring nod,

"It's ok now, we'll protect you. Especially Dylan" I wink at him. He steps forward and wraps his arm around Belle's waist protectively.

"Changing the subject" Kyron cleared his throat "at midnight tonight, Belle you will shift into your wolf form for the first time!" He tries to get her mind off the rogues. I give him a grateful smile. He nods and looks back at Belle. "You excited?" He asks grinning. She nodded and smiled.

"Y-yes but does it hurt?" She asked quietly. Kyron grimaced

"A little I guess, but it will only hurt for a minute or so" he answers.

"And I'll be right there with you the whole time" Dylan smiled reassuringly. She nodded again and pecked his lips. Dylan smiled and kissed her back, more passionately.

"Aw" I smiled. Kyron laughed

"Get a room you two!" He waved them off. They pulled apart, Dylan chuckling. Belle was blushing like crazy. She rested her forehead against Dylan's. Katy smacked Kyron's arm.

"You meanie" she frowned at him, which caused him to laugh harder. Tyson chuckled and pulled Katy towards him, spinning her to face him. He smashed his lips to hers and she instantly wrapped her arms around his neck and flicked her leg up.

I feel two strong arms wrap around my waist and I am pulled back into a hard chest. I smile up at Jayden and lay my head back on his chest. I hear Kyron clear his throat.

"I'll uh.. Be up in my room" he mutters and walks out the room and up the stairs with out another word. I look over at Dylan and Belle, and Tyson and Katy. Both couples are making out. I instantly feel guilty. Poor Kyron. I step forward out of Jayden's grip. He looks at me confused.

"I'll be back ok?" I hold my hands up in front of me signalling Jayden to stay down here. He nods and I run for the stairs. I jog up them quickly and make my way to Kyron.

Poor guy, he's the only one here with our a mate, because his ex-mate was a bitch and I'll bet he's still struggling with the fact that she never loved him. And see all of us down there being all lovey and dovey, probably made him feel a whole lot worse.

I knock on his door. He doesn't answer so I open it anyway. He's lying on his back on his bed. His hands are under his head and he stares up at the ceiling. I walk over to him and sit on the bed beside him. "Kyron?" I speak softly. His eyes lock with mine, although his eyes are pure black signalling his wolf is out.

"Avery" he greets in a growl. He smiles softly.

"What's your name?" I ask him.

"Zander" he replied staring back up at the ceiling.

"Zander- I'm sorry, we should have been more considerate-"

"No, no it's alright" he cuts me off. His arms fall to his side and I stare at his hand.

"No. It's not" I reply picking up his hand and hold it in both of mine. He looks up at me again and sighs.

"I'm fine, really Avery. I'm not upset about that bitch anymore I swear"

"You just lied to my face" I frown at him. He was silent. I took a deep breath and sighed sadly. "Zander- And Kyron... you both need to know, it's ok to be upset. It's ok to be angry, you lost your soul mate and for a werewolf, that is the hardest thing in the world to go through. It's ok to be frustrated. It's ok to be mad." Zander sits up beside me and looks at me tilting his head to the side slightly. And I continue

"It's alright to take your frustration out on something. Kyron, it's ok to be upset, you lost someone dear to you, you lost your other half. It is ok to let yourself fall, you don't need to stand strong 24/7 you are allowed to show your emotions. You weren't made of steel" I say the last sentence in a whisper. I rub my thumbs softly over his hand. I sigh "Kyron It's ok to be sad" I smile sadly at him.

I look back into his eyes to see they have gone back to their normal forest green colour. They hold sadness, and I see a tear slide down his cheek. I instantly pull him in for a hug. He hugs me back and I here him sniff a few times. I pat his back softly. After several minutes he finally pulls back and looks at me. His eyes are slightly red and slight puffy, and a little watery. With is thumb, he wipes his eyes and blinks hard a few times. He smiled at me sincerely

"Thank you Avery" he whispers. I nod

"Sometimes you just need a shoulder to cry on" I shrug and I give a small smile.

.

.

.

.

.

"Are you ready Belle?" I ask. She nods and walks forward in front of us all. We all stand out the back on the lawn. Dylan steps forward and holds her hand,

"I'm right here ok?" Dylan smiles reassuringly. I look up to see the moon has reached it's highest point.

"Alright man, take a step back" Tyson says to Dylan. Dylan nods and stands back beside Katy. Belle arches her back and throws her head back. She screams and drops to her knees. I wince, I remember the first time I had shifted it hurt like hell. But Daniel and Finn were right there by my side. Belle lets out another agonising scream. Dylan steps forward but Kyron places a hand on his shoulder and shook his head.

Dylan bowed his head and stepped back. After a couple minutes I hear the last bone in Belle's fragile body, crack. Her head snaps up to up, her eyes are the colour gold. She opens her jaw, Her fangs extend. She growls and shifts into her wolf. It's fur is pure white, exactly like mine, however On her front left paw there is a tiny black spot but that's it.

"A Warrior Wolf" I gasp. I look around and everyone looks just as surprised. Dylan's jaw drops. After a few minutes she shifts back into her human form. She curls up in a ball and looks up at Dylan. Dylan lets out a viscous growl.

"Mate!" He growls and steps in front of her protectively. He glares at Kyron, Tyson and Jayden.

"Guys he wants you to look away" I say in a duh tone. They blink, snapping out of their trance, and they quickly spin around.

"Oh right" Kyron says quickly.

"Oops" Jayden mutters.

"Sorry!" Ty apologised

Dylan takes his shirt off in one swift movement and looks down at Belle. She hides her body from him. He growls

"You don't need to hide yourself from me" he growls out. She whimpers and looks up at him. She stands up and Dylan quickly slips his shirt over her. His shirt is quite large on her small body, it goes down to her mid thigh.

"Aw! I just knew they'd be mates!" I squeal excitedly. Dylan snaps his head at me. His eyes are pitch black, so his wolf is out.

"So what's your name may I ask?" I asked him. Jayden, Tyson and Kyron spun back around. Katy couldn't keep the grin off her face.

"Asher" he growls.

"Alright Asher" I clasp my hands together. "Wow, facing two angry were-wolves in one day! Record!" I mutter enthusiastically causing Jayden and Kyron to chuckle. "Anyways, Asher your scaring the poor girl" I look over at Belle who hides behind Asher. He raises both his eyebrows and spins around.

"Am I scaring you?" He asks. She nods quickly. "Oh. Sorry" was all he said before his eyes turned back to normal. "I'm sorry Belle! I ugh.. I couldn't control him" he admits sheepishly. He rubs the backs of his neck nervously. Belle laughs and pecks his lips.

"It's alright Dylan" she whispers. He smiles and holds her hand and they walk back inside. The rest of us follow. Aww aren't they sweet!?

.

.

.

.

.

.

The next morning I woke bright an early. I grabbed out the dress I had planned to wear for the party and I slipped it on. It was a white summer dress that reached mid thigh. Along the edges of the skirt part it had patterns of flowers, laced into it. The shoulder straps were about an inch thick and the fabric was just nice and light. I also slipped on my white sandals that matched the dress. I walked into the bathroom to do my make up. I applied very little and I then brushed my hair and French braided it neatly.

"Wake up Jay! We have set all the food up!" I whisper yell. He groans and rolls over onto his side.

"Five more minutes" he grumbles and shuts his eyes again. I frown and grab the glass of water that was on the bedside table and I poured it all over Jayden's face. He jolted up. "I'm awake! I'm awake!" He says alert. I laugh at him so hard I was doubling over in pain from my stomach that really hurt so much now from all the laughter. I clutched it and stopped laughing, however I couldn't keep the grin off my face. Jayden frowned at me.

"Grr" he grumbled and got out of bed. He walked into the bathroom and when he came back out minutes later, his face was completely dried. He smirked and got dressed into more formal clothes than what he usually would wear. He put on a red and black checkered shirt and denim jeans. He chucked on some black boots of his then he went into the bathroom. He came back out minutes later, his hair combed back. I smile.

"Hawt-e" I say nodding my head in approval.

"Not so bad yourself" he teases. I stick my tongue out. He walks over to me and places a soft kiss on the to of my head. "You look beautiful, love" he whispered. I blushed and stare into his green eyes. Ok, I defiantly can not keep this secret from him any longer.

I take a deep breath.

"Jay, there's something important I need to tell you" I whisper. He looks at me concerned and worried.

"What's wrong? Are you hurt?" He asks all worried. I shake my head and smile.

"No, but what I'm about to tell you.. It may come as a bit of a shock... Anyway even after I tell you this I want to fight in the battle with the rogues. Do you pinky swear that you will still let me fight?" I ask holding out my tiny finger. He sighs and shakes it.

"I promise now spill" he says frustrated. My serious look brakes into a grin.

"I'm pregnant!" I squeal excitedly. Jayden stares at me in shock.

"W-what?" I let him let it sink in for a minute. He finally registered it, and his lips too, broke into a grin. He picked me up by the waist, the same way Tyson had with Katy not so long ago, and he spun me round and round. "This is amazing!" He laughs. How I loved to see him this cheerful and happy. It made me happy to see him like this. "Oh, we must tell everyone at the party but at night after Belle has had her fun time" he smiles. He then frowns.

"But you aren't fighting against the rogues" he says with complete seriousness. I shook my head.

"You pinky swore" I stick my tongue out at him. He sighs

"Why do you want to fight so badly?"

'Yes why do you want to fight so badly? You could kill both of us and your child' Jackie my wolf scolded me. I frown and look back up at Jayden

"Because I want to be there with you" I sigh. Jay smiles at me.

"I want you to be the too but Avery, I need you to stay safe. I couldn't live with myself if you died. I'd be a mental reck, I wouldn't able to keep myself together and both our pack and children would be doomed." He says with a long sigh. I smile sadly and cup his cheek.

"I can take care of myself you know" I smile and peck his lips.

"Prove it" he smirks. Using his speed he pins me to the wall. I go to knee him in the groin but he dodges me easily.

I bend my head forward and kiss his soft lips. He kisses me back which is exactly what I thought he'd do. Using my speed and strength. I catch him off guard by tripping him. He land on his back with a grunt and I quick sit on top of him, straddling him.

"There" I peck his lips. I see the lust cloud his eyes as he stares at my lips. I stand back up. In a flash I am out the room. I knock on Tyson and Katy's door. Katy answers it with a yawn. She stares at my her eyes barley open. I laugh at her appearance.

She was in one of Tyson's large grey shirts and her hair was like a birds nest. "Had trouble sleeping last night?" I ask her with a wink. She rolls her eyes and smiles. I nudge her "fun sex?" She nods.

"The best" she mumbles. "Ty and I will meet you down stairs" she yawns and shuts the door. I laugh at her. I look over my shoulder to see a well dress Kyron and a hottie Jayden walk down the stairs, I quickly go and follow them. The three of us eat breakfast and discuss how the party is going to go.

"Dude why do you look so happy?" Kyron yawns. Jayden smiles but doesn't say anything. I roll my eyes.

"Jay he knows" I mutter. Jayden looked at me confused,

"You told him before me!?" He points at his chest, I nod like it's no big deal, cos really, it isn't. "Ugh" he grumbles. I laugh

"Don't worry bout it Jayden" I pat his shoulder, "I guess I didn't really have time to tell you yesterday..."

"You had heaps of time to tell me" he mutters.

"I'm sorry, I just... Well at least I told you today instead of waiting until after the battle like I had intended to in the first place" I smirk. Jayden snaps his head up at me.

"You were going to wait three more days to tell me!?" He yells surprised. Well today, tomorrow and then the battle is the next day... So yeah three days.

"Eh..." I waved my hand. What? I knew he wasn't going to let me fight if I had told him yesterday... Well he probably still won't let me fight but I'll find a way... Why do I even want to fight so much? You may all be asking.

The answer is simple, I want to be there for Jayden, I want to have his back, and I don't want him to go through this alone.

"Anyways..." Kyron clears his throat. "Let's get everyone and all the food into the party house" he says standing up. I give home a grateful smile for changing the topic. He nods in response and the three of us go to the guest house next door where the other werewolves had cooked the food.

"Alright everyone!" Jayden calls out as we enter it through he front door. "It's time to start taking the party food over to the party house and set it all up!" Jayden yells. People come running down the stairs and run into the kitchen. We follow them, as we enter the kitchen I gawk at the sight before me.

Plates full of all sorts of delicious, luxurious party foods are set up everywhere. My mouth waters at the sight and I feel the strong urge just to take a piece of chocolate off one of the plates and- I slowly reach my hands out to one of the plates that held chocolate rum balls.

My finger inches away from one, I look around to make sure no one sees. I pick the small chocolate ball up but out of the blue someone smacks my hand from behind me. The rum ball drops back onto the plate, I flinch out of surprise.

I look over my shoulder to see Kyron folding his arms smirking at me. "Caught ya red handed" he tsked. I poke my tongue out of him. "Why don't you take one of the fruit plates to the party house, because I know how much you LOVE fruit" he laughs at me. I pout and pick up the plate beside the rum balls, it contains nothing but neatly sliced oranges.

"I just wanted to test them and make sure they weren't poisoned!" I lie. Kyron smirks again.

"That's what I'm for" he says picking up the chocolate ball I had picked up before and he plops it into his mouth. My jaw drops to the floor and I gape at him.

"You. Did. Not!" I scream. I place the fruit platter down and dive my hand in to the plate filled with chocolate balls however Kyron smirks and in one swift movement, he picks up the plate and holds it out to his right. I frown and try to reach for it again. He holds the plate high above his head. I pout. That's too tall for me. "I just wanted one" I look down at the ground.

I see Jayden waking up behind Kyron, he takes two rum balls of the plate, popping one into his mouth and he walks over to me. He wraps an arm around my waist and holds out the second chocolate ball. I grin and hold out my hands.

Jay smiles and drops it into my hand. I flash him a grateful smile and plop the little ball of chocolate into my mouth. I moan as I devour it, the sensational taste explodes in my mouth.

Jayden kisses the top of my head. "Now take some plates to the party house" he smirks. I laugh and pick up the plate full of oranges and carry it outside with Kyron following me. I walk over to the second guest house where more werewolves were staying.

I knocked on the front door, walked in and yelled "ITS PARTY TIME!" And then went to the third guest house and the fourth. The last guest house had no one living in it so we walked to the party house to set up.

Once we had finished setting up all of the food I smile over at Katy. "We ready?" I ask her. Tyson walks up to her and wraps his arm around he waist, and she lays her head on his shoulder. She smiles. "Yep! We did it!" She grins I laugh.

"Ok onto the last step of the plan" I announce. I walk over to Jayden. I hold out my hand. He raises an eyebrow at me.

"You wanna use 'my' phone?" He laughs. I frown at him.

"Don't ruin the mood" I point my index finger at his chest. He laughs and digs his hand into his pocket and takes out his phone. He unlocks it and passes it to me. I smile in thanks and dial Dylan's number.

It rings five times before he answers.

"Hey, we all good to go?" He whispers. I grin

"Yep! See yous in five?" I suggest.

"Avery! This party is going to be awesome!" Finn says tugging on my shirt. I smile down at him and ruffle his hair.

"You bet it will lil bro" I smile at him.

"Alright, see ya" Dylan says hanging up. I smile down at my little brother and give him a hug.

"Hey Finn, tomorrow, you and the other kids and some of the adults are leaving ok?" I tell him. I crouch down to be level with him. He looks at me worried.

"Are you coming with me?" He asks his voice shaking. I smile sadly

"No.. But.. Katy and Dylan will be there with you, and possibly Belle" I say looking up in thought.

"But I want you to be there with me" he whimpers. I pull him in for a hug, his sad face makes me melt.

"Aw Finn it's ok. I need you to be a big boy for me ok?" I ask pulling back and looking into his eyes. He nods and holds his tears back.

"I love you Avery"

"And I love you Finn" I smile at him.

"They're here!" Someone whisper yells.

"Get the lights!" Jay replies. We all crowd together in the centre of the room. Tyson runs over to the light switch and turns it off and he then sprints over to us.

"A-are you sure we're allowed back here?" I here Belle ask unsure. Dylan laughs

"Yeah of course we are! Last I heard, it hasn't been used in over ten years" he chuckled. The door handle squeaks and the rusty door creaks open. I hear Dylan run his hand along the wall for the light switch. He flicks it on, and Belle gasps.

"SURPRISE! HAPPY BIRTHDAY!" We cheer. She clasps her hands over her mouth and she stares at us in shock.

"You guys! This is amazing!" She gushes. Dylan pecks her lips.

"Happy birthday babe" he murmurs. Aw! Jayden, Tyson, Kyron, Katy and I walk over to the adorably cute couple and we circle around them

"Happy Birthday Belle!" I squeal and pull her in for a hug. She grins and pulls back

"Thank you Avery!" She laughs. Katy grins and squeals in excitement and puls Belle in for a hug.

"Happy Birthday beautiful!" She screams with a grin.

"Thanks Katy!" She beams. She pulls back and looks at all of us. "You guys really did this, for me?" She asked surprised and her eyes fill with aw. We all nod with a grin.

"It was practically Jayden's idea!" I wink at him. He chuckles and Belle smiles at him.

"Happy birthday Belle" the guys say stuffing their hands into their pockets. She smiles at us all gratefully and she looked extremely happy. I see another emotion flash through her eyes, guilt is it? Why? What does she have to be guilty of? I was snapped out of my thoughts when I hear a loud howl come from outside deep in the woods.

'Alpha! There are three rogues here! We have them cornered, come quick!' I hear David through the pack mind link. Ever since he's recovered, he has been determined to guard this place with his life. He is such a good patrol wolf. I suddenly become alert and I look at Jayden. It seems as though everyone in the room had received that message because they were all staring at us.

Jayden held up his hands "everyone please remain calm, my mate and I will go see what the matter is with these rogues.. Mean while, whilst we are gone, enjoy the party!" He smiles. Everyone nods and goes back to talking.

'Ok David, I'm on my way. Keep those rogues there' Jayden says through mind link.

'Yes Alpha. Oh one more thing!' David quickly adds

'Yes David what's that?' Jayden asks walking out the door with me on his tail.

'One of the rogues, the one that seems to be leading the other two... His fur is pure black, just like yours' David says confused. Jayden turns to me.

'Looks like we found another pack member' Jay announces. I nod, excitement coursing through my veins. We run through the woods in our human forms. After a few minutes, a strong, yet familiar scent could be smelt.

As we run towards the scents I see ten of our wolves, all in a circle. They were crouched down, with their heads below their knees, as if ready to pounce. Jayden holds his hands up.

"I want you all to take one step back" he commands his pack. "And relex a little would you? You all look so intimidating" he shivers with a grin. Jayden walks past our wolves and into the circle. I follow but the wolves stand closer and do not let me enter.

I frown and try to peak over. Just as David had said, there was indeed a pure black wolf. He stood in between and slightly in front of the other two protectively. I gasped and pushed my way forcefully through into the circle and I ran up to Jayden's side. I stared the black wolf into his eyes. I can not believe my eyes.

"Daniel?"

Vote? Comment? :) let me know what you guys think! :)

Twenty One

A very

The black wolf stares at me with wide eyes. They hold nothing but pure relief, love and regret in them. I run forward, but Jay grabs my wrist. I snap my eyes up to him and glare at him.

"Let. Me. Go" I growl at him. I hear I low growl escape the black wolf's snout. Jayden looks taken aback and I feel his grip slacken. I snatch my wrist away and I run over to my brother. Tears of joy stream down my face and I run in for a hug. I wrap my arms around his fluffy neck and bury my head away in his black fur.

"D-Daniel" I sob. He nuzzled his head into the crook of my shoulder and neck. "I-I though you were d-dead" I cry. I hear him sigh sadly. I turn to face Jayden. He was shocked, yet relieved and happy. "C-can you please fetch them some c-clothes?" I stammer.

He nods he looks at David. David nods at all the other wolves and they run off. Minutes later they return, in their human forms dressed in nothing but shorts. They chuck three pairs at me and I catch them and smile in thanks at David. He just nods and smiles back at me.

I spin back around to look at my brother. I hold out the clothes. "You guys can shift back now. They won't hurt you" I say looking over my shoulder at Jayden. I smile at him and he smiles back reassuringly. I look back at Daniel. He nods at the other two wolves and the three of them shift back into their human forms. I blink several times looking over at each one.

"B-Brandon?" I stutter. He smirks and bows.

"Luna" he greets teasingly. Daniel raised an eyebrow and me. I shrugged and chucked him the clothes.

"I'll tell you later" I say, I then look back at Jayden. He too smirks at me. I roll my eyes and grin. I then look at the third wolf.

"M-Mark? But you were at home- you answered the phone when I rang once and-" he cut me off by holding his hands up.

"Yes I know I was at your old home when you rang" he nods. "You aren't going crazy" he chuckles. I tilt my head curiously at him.

"B-but how? You said you didn't know where Daniel was and now you are running around with him? Why did you lie to me?" I whisper. Mark sighed and ran a hand through his hair.

"Daniel was in hiding Avery. I hadn't even let your parents know he was alive. I'm sorry I lied to you but I had to" he explains. I nod and look back at Daniel, my eyes trap under his sorrow filled gaze. With out thinking, I smack his arm. He winced.

"You put me through hell!" I screech at him. After a few heavy pants, my anger dies down. I take a deep breath and recompose myself. "I'm good now" I say calmly with a smile. Daniel stares at me surprised for a minute but shrugs with a sly grin. I spin around and walk over to Jayden. I look over my shoulder at Daniel,

"Well come on! We have a party to attend!" I say with a grin and we all make our way back to the part house.

"So when are you going to tell Daniel about us?" Jayden smirks down at me. "Looks like that Brandon guy already figured it out" he laughed. I smile.

"I'll tell him during the party- before we announce the baby thing" I add. He nods.

.

.

.

.

.

I grip Daniel's hand in mine and drag him away from the party food. "Daniel you've been pigging out the past hour!" I explain. He laughs.

"I did meet your friends Tyson and Katy, and the party girl and her mate" he adds matter-of-factly. "And I caught up with little Finny" he laughs. I smack his arm lightly.

"He doesn't like it when you call him that! It's just Finn!" I hiss. "And besides, you know the 'party girl's' mate?" I ask raising an eyebrow. Daniel looks down at me confused.

"Yeah what about him?" He asks looking around to find him. His eyes roam the dance floor before they lock onto Dylan, who dances happily with Belle.

"That's Dylan, do you remember a Dylan I once introduced to the family?" I smirk. Daniels eyes widen.

"Oh god, is that him?" Daniel asks, his eyes almost popping out of his head. I laugh and nod. "Oh wow" he sighs running a hand through his hair. I nod.

"Mmm" I mumble knowingly.

"Boy do I feel guilty right now" he mutters under his breath.

"As you should" I scold.

"I'm going to go apologise although I don't deserve his forgiveness. Excuse me a minute won't you?" Daniel asked looking at me sincerely. I nod with a small smile.

"I'm sure he'd appreciate the gesture" I call after Daniel who has already started to walk over to Dylan. "Alright, I'll just.. Wait here then.. By mys elf..." I mumble to myself.

"Hey babe" I feel Jay's arm slither around my waist as he plants lots of small kisses on the top of my head. I giggle and turn around to face him. I place a soft peck on his lips. He then steps back, bows and holds a hand out to me, still bowed.

"May I have this dance?" He asks looking up at me, just as one of the songs ends and a slow song starts. I nod with a grin.

"You may" I giggle. I curtsy and place my hand in his and he leads me away to the dance floor. The song 'All I Need', started to play softly and we started to dance to it. Jay's hands made their way to my hips, and they held onto them softly.

I wrapped my hands around his neck and rested my forehead on his. We stayed like this for not long enough, as the song ended all to soon. We walked off the dance floor and over to the tables of food where Dylan and Daniel were happily chatting to each other.

Belle was wrapped in Dylan's arms, her back was in his chest and his arms were wrapped around her waist. They looked so sweet together! Perfect match, right here guys! We walked up to them and they looked at his. Daniel raised his eyebrow at me. I grinned and couldn't keep it in any longer.

"Daniel, I'd like to formally introduce you to my mate, Alpha Jayden of the Dark Shadow Pack" I smile between the two. Daniel looks at Jayden a little distastefully but covers it up well with a warm smile. He held out his hand and Jayden did not notice the hatred that radiated from my brother for he shook his hand. I will admit Daniel covered his emotions well. I glanced at Jayden warily.

"Nice to meet you" Daniel fake smiles. Jayden nodded

"You too, welcome and please enjoy your stay. Any family of Avery is family of mine" Jayden smiles down at me. That statement sent a million butterflies to erupt in my stomach. When No one is looking at Daniel, I see a spark of anger in them.

"Daniel" I say through gritted teeth, he looks at me his eyebrows slightly raised.

"Mm?"

"May I have I word" I say in more demand than request. He nods and I walk to the door, with him following, we walk outside and towards the woods where the party noise could not be heard as much. I turn around to face my brother and fold my arms over my chest.

"Ok spill. What crawled up your ass and died?" I asked dead panned. Daniel raises both his eyebrows in shock.

"Excuse me?"

"You know what I'm talking about Daniel. I saw the tension in the room as soon as I said the word 'mate' " I growl out. I see Daniel's eyes darken and he turns his head away from me and suddenly the ground became very interesting to him. "Why do you not accept him Daniel?" I ask ever so quietly.

"He destroyed our home Avery. They all did" he waves his hand at the building.

"Actually not all of them-" I add but then know it's not worth it because it won't change Daniel's opinion on Jayden. I sigh sadly "Daniel, he's my mate. I love him. And he loves me" I point out. "Yes he has done terrible things in the past but a wise man once said:

'A mate is your equal. You will cherish them for who they are, for the rest of your life. You will forgive them no matter how many terrible things they have done. And if you love your mate and your mate loves you, your true family will except them no matter what, and your true family will always fight by your side' "

I recite what Daniel had told me few years ago. I had been afraid that when I find my mate, my parents would not except him and I asked Daniel about it and he told me the meaning of love and family. That if my parents truly loved me, they would except my decisions and except my mate no matter how much they despised him.

Daniel raises his head and locks eyes with me. He sighs in defeat, knowing I had caught him out. "You're right, I'm sorry Avery. I know I will get over it in time but for now... I just need some time to clear my head. Ok?" He asked placing a hand on my shoulder. He gives me a small smile which meant he would be true to his word. I nod and smile at him. I pull him in for a hug,

"I love you big bro" I whisper.

"I love you too sis"

"Hey Daniel...?" I trail off pulling back. He looks at me curious.

"Yes Avery?"

"Have you ever heard about the Midnight Warrior Pack?" I ask raising an eyebrow and grin.

.

.

.

.

.

After telling Daniel the whole story of the Warrior Pack, how it is true, and how Jayden has been finding more of the warrior wolves, I told Daniel that he too, is from The Midnight Warrior Wolf Pack. He was rather surprised and very suspicious but he excepted the fact that I was telling the truth.

"I can show some of the werewolves from our original 'secret' pack, if you'd like?" I offer. He nods.

"Alright, my mind seems to be telling me that is a good idea. So lead the way" I smile and lead Daniel back into the building.

"Oh but first- I want to introduce you to one of my closest friends here. Actually I think he is my closest friend, out ranking Katy. But don't tell Katy I said that" I quickly add. Daniel chuckles.

"Alright then" he replies holding his head high when we walk inside.

'Could all of the Warrior Wolves from the Midnight Warrior wolf pack please meet me right outside the party house in a few minutes?' I ask them directly through mind link.

'Yes Luna' they reply

'Please! Avery!' I chuckle.

I spot who I was looking for and my grip tightens on Daniel as I lead him over. "Kyron!" I call excitedly. Kyron, who was talking to Jane- I think her name is, spun around to face me. He smiled and waved me over.

Daniel and I stood in front of him. I of course was grinning from ear to ear. I looked at Jane, I'm pretty sure she was just a year or so older than me. She was constantly smiling flirtatiously at Kyron. I rolled my eyes at her. She looked at me and smiled.

"Luna" she greeted and smiled friendly, although I could see right through her act. She flipped her platinum blonde hair over her shoulder and battled her eye lashes at Kyron. He's either really blind or he totally uninterested, either way I'm good with that.

"Janet" I fake smile back at her. She frowns at me.

"It's Jane" she says matter-of-factly, I roll my eyes.

"Sure, what ever you say 'Janet'. Listen, if you could please go find someone who's actually interested in you to stalk, that would be real nice. I have to speak with Kyron, with out you here" I snap. She gasps and glares at me. Kyron and Daniel chuckle.

"How dare you talk to me like that!? I was just talking to Kyron nicely and you accuse me of stalking him!?" She shrieks at me. I wave my finger from side to side and shut my eyes disapprovingly.

"Tsk tsk tsk, Janet you wouldn't want me to kick you out how I kicked Sasha out would you?" I glare at her, her eyes fill with fear. She cowers down and bows her head in submission.

"N-no Luna. I-I'll talk to you later Kyron" she winked at him. Ugh the nerve of her! No way was I letting some whore, walk all over Kyron.

"No you won't" I snap. She looks at me startled.

"I can talk to him if I please" she says stepping forward. I just love it how the guys are clearly amused by our cat fight.

"Like hell you can" I snap taking my own step forward.

"He wants to talk to me too you know! He wants to get to know me! I'll bet he even likes me!" She screeches in my face. I laugh.

"Hahaha- no." I say dead panned. "I'm sure he'd rather talk to a tree than with you" I bitch at her, I raise an eyebrow at Kyron to make sure I'm right.

He nods, "yep" he laughs. Jane glares at me.

"Ugh! I hate you!" She screams. I smile sweetly.

"Sweet heart, why don't you go join all the other haters, sit at their table and wait for me to actually care" I point at the door signalling that she should leave. She screams and breaks into tears and runs for the door. Everyone around me cheers. Wow I didn't know they were all listening...

"Good job Luna!" Some would say

"You sure showed her!" Others would remark. I smile in thanks and then turn to Kyron and Daniel.

"Sorry you guys had to witness that" I almost laugh.

"Most interesting fight I've seen in years" Daniel commented with a laugh.

"I reckon" Kyron agreed. I laughed at them.

"Ok anyways... Kyron, I'd like you to meet my older brother Daniel" I wave my hand at him. "Daniel, meet Kyron" I chirp. Kyron smiles and holds out his hand. Daniel shakes it.

"We've heard much about you" Kyron smiles widely. Daniel raises an eyebrow and looks at me. I smile sheepishly.

"Really?" He asks surprised. Kyron grins and nod.

"Oh yeah. Avery over here wouldn't shut up about you! It got painful to listen to sometimes" Kyron winked. I slap his arm.

"Yeah, because most of that time I thought you were dead" I point out looking at Daniel. Daniel chuckles.

"Yeah, I can imagine what was going on through your mind whilst I was gone" he laughs. I roll my eyes.

"Any who..." I trail off, "everyone's waiting for us outside, let's go. Kyron would you want to come with?" I ask him. Kyron smiles.

"Sure" he said and the three of us walk outside to be met by over twenty faces. I spot Dylan, Belle and Jayden talking to each other and I wave at them. They wave back and start to walk over. Daniel sniffs the air and inhales deeply. I see his eyes go from brown to black.

I follow his gaze to one of the warrior wolves. Her name was Clarise I think. Her hair really stood out, a few weeks ago she had died it hot pink and it looked really pretty.

She was currently talking to one of the guys, Matt. Uh oh. "Mate" Daniel growled. I see Clarise sniff the air and she looks around, she locks eyes with Daniel and her lips break into a smile.

She runs over to us, abandoning mate. And she runs straight into Daniel's arms. He buries his face into the crook of her shoulder and neck and he inhales deeply.

I feel Jayden's arm slither around my waist and he holds me tightly. Belle and Dylan smile at Daniel and Clarise. "Um guys" I cough. They pull back and look at me.

I glance at the crowd of people before us and back to the couple. I then glance back at the crowd and back to my brother. "Everyone's watching" I whisper. Clarise blushes and pulls away, only to have Daniel pull her back into his chest.

I look around at everyone. They smile at me. "Hello Luna!" They greet. I groan.

"Avery please!" I laugh. They laugh too.

"Sorry Avery" they answer. I smile, that's more like it.

"Ok guys. This man here, is my brother Daniel Jedson. He is one of us, and as you can see he has finally found his mate- Clarise!" I yell with a grin. They all cheer. My eyes roam the crowd of people and they stop at Matt.

He glares at the new couple. His hands are clenched and he looks as if he would rip Daniel's head off. His eyes were pure black which meant his wolf was on the urge of shifting.

"U-uh everyone can go enjoy the party now! I just wanted to introduce you too my brother. Enjoy the rest of your afternoon/night!" I say looking up seeing the sun was about to set. Everyone smiles and starts chatting with each other as they abandon us to rejoin the party.

Everyone walked back inside except Kyron, Dylan, Belle, Jayden, Daniel, Clarise and Matt. Matt stood there, his face fuming red and I could have sworn I saw smoke puffing out of his nose and ears!

He storms over to Daniel and Clarise and wrenches her out of Daniel's grip. Hey! Daniel growls deeply and Clarise looks petrified. I take a step forward but Jay pulls me back. "Let them sort this out themselves" he whispers in my ear.

I nod and watch. Daniel goes to take a step forward but Matt steps back dragging Clarise with him. Daniels eyes too, change to the colour of black. Just as he was about to shift, Clarise holds her hands up to stop him.

"Daniel please wait" she pleads, he takes a deep breath and takes a small step back. Clarise turns to Matt. "Matt, I-" Matt cuts her off.

"No Clarise! We are together! You are mine! Not him" he growls.

"Hell to the no!" Daniel growls. Clarise holds her hand out to Daniel telling him to stop. He huffs in annoyance.

"Matt- what we had.. I'm not going to lie, it was special. And I loved every moment of our time together- but Daniel is my mate. He is my true lover- you will find yours I'm sure-"

"Save it Clarise! You are my mate!" He growls.

"No Matt. I'm not" she tries to pull away, his grip tightens on her though. Daniel takes a step forward, his face was as red as a tomato!

"Yes you are!" Matt growls

"No Matt. I'm Daniel's-"

"If I can't have you, no one will!" Matt growls. Daniel shifts into his wolf form and growls loud enough to make the ground shake. Matt looks taken aback. He pulls Clarise roughly behind him, "don't worry love, I will protect you from this beast!" Matt growls and shifts into his wolf form.

I swear Matt has lost his mind. It is Matt whome she needs to be protected from. He is the one being cruel. Clarise whimpers as Daniel charges forward and tackles Matt to the ground.

I wave Clarise over and she runs quickly over to me. I pull her in for a hug. "It's ok, you're ok" I say soothingly and I pat her back gently.

"I know I'm fine-" she sobs "it's Daniel I am worried about. M-Matt is r-really strong" she sobs harder and she starts to shake. "D-Daniel might not s-stand a chance" I chuckle at her. "Why are you laughing?" She asks.

"Because- Daniel is an Alpha sweetheart. He will take Matt out with in seconds" I laugh but then my face turns serious. "He's going to kill Matt" I whisper worry starts to course through my veins. I look up at Jayden worriedly. As if reading my mind, he nods and quickly strips. I look at him weirdly,

"What? These are good clothes!" He defends. I laugh at him for a second. Jayden then shifts. He growls but Daniel and Matt continue to roll around on the ground. Jayden growls loudly and walks over to them.

Matt looks up and bows his head at Jayden, but Daniel being so blinded by rage continued to fight. He bit down hard into Matt's paw causing him to yelp and jump away.

Jayden roars, which catches Daniel's attention. Daniel stands up and glares at Jayden. Matt pushes himself up and staggers over to Jayden and hides behind him. Pfft, coward.

Daniel growls but Jayden growls louder asking Daniel to submit. Daniel shakes his head and roars. Jayden lowers his head ready to attack. No! This fight Daniel defiantly won't stand a chance to win. I see the fear in Clarise's eyes.

Just as Jayden in about to pounce, I run over to them. "No!" I yell and jump in front of Jayden. I don't face either of the wolves but I hold my hands out to both of them. I look between them, my breaths coming out in shallow pants. "If you're going to fight, you're going to have to go through me first" I stand my ground.

Neither wolf moves. They stare at me pleadingly but I shake my head. "I will not watch you fight to the death. I will not choose between my brother and my mate. This is ridiculous!" I shout. "Stop this right now! Shift back!" I order.

I hear a sigh of annoyance and Daniel shifts back into his human form. I hear Clarise sigh in relief and she runs over to Daniel, however she stops a few feet and looks at him from head to toe. Daniel raises an eyebrow.

"Like what you see?" He smirks. She blushes deep scarlet. I almost laugh. I then turn to Jayden. He stands frozen, I can still see a hint of anger in his eyes. I walk over to him slowly and I cup his furry cheek and look deep into his brown eyes.

They soften under my touch and he sighs. I watch him shift back into his human form and I can't help but gape at this glorious sight before be. Jayden chuckles.

"Gosh, you're worse than Clarise!" He exclaims. I blush and look at the ground. He laughs and walks over to his clothes and slips them on. Matt to shifts back into his human form, his body covered in scratches and blood, and his leg looks twisted, it is also missing a deep chunk of skin from it. He should heal in an hour or so providing he doesn't lose too much blood.

I walk over to him and slap him. He looks at me confused. "That was for even thinking you could beat my brother at a fight" I spat. I then slapped him again, this time much harder, his head snapped to the right and I could already see a Hugh red hand print starting to glow. "And that was for Clarise" I answer quietly but not too quiet.

I then walk off leaving him stand there. Daniel walks over to Jayden and I and Jay tosses him a pain of shorts.

"Hey were did Dylan, Belle and Kyron go?" I ask only just realising they weren't out side. Jayden chuckled.

"They went inside to rejoin the party right after Daniel shifted into his wolf form." He explained. I nodded.

"Oh" and the four of us walk back into the building, leaving Matt there by himself. Jayden entwines our fingers as we walk in. After an hour or so we noticed the children were starting to grow tired so we knew some people would be leaving shortly. I turn to Jayden and grin.

"Want to tell everyone now?" I ask. His head snaps up, he now becomes alert.

"About the-"

"Yep" I cut him off with a grin. He nods enthusiastically and we make our way to the back of the room where the DJ is situated. We stopped the music and grabbed a microphone.

"Hello? Uh we- my mate and I would like to make a very important announcement, so if we could have all your attention, that be great" Jayden clears his throat. Everyone stops talking and looks up at us smiling. I take the microphone out of Jayden's hands and swallow the lump in my throat.

"Um.. First off, I'd like to wish Isobelle Colliah, a very happy fifteenth birthday! We all wish you had a fabulous day Belle!" I say, everyone cheers. My eyes catch hers. She flashes me a grateful smiled filled with aw. "Now let's sing happy birthday!" I grin, her eyes widen and she waves her hands in front of her face mouthing the word 'no' over and over, I chuckle at that.Everyone laughs and we all chant together:

"Happy Birthday to you

Happy birthday to you

Happy birthday dear Belle

Happy birthday to you!"

The entire time we sang, Belle kept her face hidden in Dylan's chest, and when we had finished singing and Belle had looked around, her face was bright red from embarrassment. I chuckle a grin at her. I then clear my throat.

"Ok, the second thing is the today, we fully welcome everyone here that has no pack, into our pack. I am truly sorry for your losses... Of your family, your loved ones, of your pack, your home.. And the least we could do, is invite you to join our pack" I say looking around the room.

I see lots of sad faces but then they all smile at me with aw and gratitude. I smile up at Jayden and he grins down at me.

"I like your speech so far" he murmured in my ear. I blush and then continue.

"And last but not least, my third and final announcement..." I look up at Jayden and see the joy and pride in his eyes "I have a feel, that Alpha Jayden would like to tell you all just what exactly I am about to say, so here Jay" I say and pass the microphone to him.

He smiles down at me and brings the microphone to his lips. He inhales deeply.

"Ladies and gentlemen, children of all ages... I am happy to announce that, Avery, your Luna, my queen," he looks into my eyes with desire, lust, passion and mostly love. I feel my heart swell with joy.

Jayden then looks back out at everyone "Avery is pregnant" he announces with a gigantic grin covering his face. The room erupts with cheers and gasps. I feel my cheeks blush even further and I take a step back, into Jayden's back.

"Thank you everyone for joining us today to celebrate Belle's birthday! We'll see you all bright an early tomorrow!" Jayden excuses us and everyone starts to leave the hall. I look up at Jayden.

"When will we clean this out?" I ask, the thought only just crossed my mind. Jayden chuckles

"Sometime after the battle" he says with a nod.

"Ok" I smile and we walk to the centre of the room where the rest of our friend are. Kyron waves us over and we walk faster. We stand beside Tyson and Katy. I look over at Belle to see she is starting to doze off.

I can only imagine how tired she is, after all she is the youngest here. Dylan shifts his weight onto his right foot so he can keep her balanced easier. Looking over at Daniel and Clarise, I'm not surprised to see them making out.

"I'm going to take Belle to bed" Dylan says, picking her up bridal style.

"Alright, good night you two" I smile.

"Sweet dreams!" Katy squeals quietly.

"Night" the others say in union. Dylan carries her out with out another word. Jayden turns back to the group and we all loo at him waiting.

"Ok, so first thing tomorrow, I want all the mothers, children, midnight warriors, elders and any injured, to be gathered up... In here. Make sure everyone is accounted for and then at 8am, get them out of the boarders and to a safe distance" Jayden orders looking at Kyron. Kyron nods.

Jayden throws him some kind of look that I can't read. His eyes are hard, his eyebrow furrowed. Kyron seemed to get it and he nods. What ever they're talking about, well thinking about.. it doesn't matter, it's probably something not battle related. But I don't bother to ask.

"Ok, and for everyone who battles, you know the large spacious grass field to the left of our house, of the other side of the woods? Where the hills are?" He asks Tyson. He nods, however I have no clue where he is talking about because I have never explored that far. "That is where the battle will be held" Jayden explains. We all nod.

"Hey, you said all the midnight warriors will not fight, I think you could use my help in this fight" Daniel interjects. Clarise grips his arm tightly and shakes her head.

"You could get hurt" she whimpers. He smiles sadly down at her.

"Clarise, I am an Alpha. If I can survive bent attacked by his pack-" he nods at Jayden, I roll my eyes at him. Typical for my brother to bring that up. "Then I can survive being attacked by a pack of rogues" he finishes holding her closer to him. She nods and a tear slips down her cheek.

"Yes, you may fight" Jayden nods. I look up at Jay and shake my head.

"No! He is my brother, I don't want him to get hurt!" I cry. Daniel looks at me sadly.

"I will be fine Avery" he reassures. I shake my head.

"These rogues will be stronger than anything we've ever faced Daniel" I argue.

"Avery Michelle Jedson" he raises his voice slightly but not in an angered or cruel manner, in fact he has a small smile play his lips. I look into his eyes and he continues, "have I ever lost a fight?"

He asks raising an eyebrow. My brother has been in many battles, one on one, team, rogues, almost every battle he has fought, he comes off the field dripped from head to toe in blood, but EVERY single battle he has fought, he has won. And obviously, he always lives.

I finally shake my head, no. He smiles and hugs Clarise tighter. "Then you must know I will be fine" he replied. I smile and nod although I had other thoughts on my mind.

"Ok guys, let's try to get a good nights sleep for we have two big days coming a head of us" Jayden muttered. We all nod and walk off to the guest house. Daniel and Clarise score the last bedroom in our guest house.

.

.

.

I walk out of the bathroom, wrapped in a towel. Jayden lays on the bed staring at me like a hawk. I see the lust and passion in his eyes. "No. Not tonight" I hold my finger out.

He frowns and groans, then he bends his head back and chuckles. I smirk and walk over to my draws and change into my nightie. I then crawl into bed beside Jayden, he holds me tight. I feel his breathing change after a short while, so I know he's asleep.

After a while of tossing and turning, I find I can not sleep. I sigh and wriggle out of Jayden's grip. Perhaps I am hungry? I skip out the room and rush down the stairs. I walk into the kitchen to see it is not empty.

Daniel is seated at the island, munching on an apple. His head snaps up at me as he hears me enter. His muscles relax when he sees me. I give him a small smile and walk to the fridge. I grab out the chocolate cake that was already half eaten.

I place it on the island and then grab a knife out of the draw. I look at Daniel who stares at the cake longingly. I raise an eyebrow. "You want a slice?" I offer.

"Mm I shouldn't.. But yes please" I laugh at him and cut him a slice. I grab out two small plates and two cake forks. I put the cake slices on the plates then the rest of the cake back in the fridge. I pick up both plates and walk around to Dylan. He had already tossed the apple.

I place one plate down in front of him, and I sit down beside him. "Thanks" he mumbles and takes a bite. I smile

"You're welcome" I reply. We eat in silence for the first few minutes. I then must have decide to tell him exactly what was on my mind, for I found myself blurting out "You can't fight in the battle"

Daniel raises a brow and glances at me. He takes another bite out of his cake and then he places the fork down. He turns around to face me properly, I do the same.

A tear slides down my cheek and Daniel brushes it away with his thumb. "Don't cry little sister" he whispers. "I know you do not want me to fight-but I feel like I have to" he takes a sharp breath "And a wise man once said:

'A mate is your equal. You will cherish them for who they are. You will forgive them no matter how many terrible things they have done. And if you love your mate and your mate loves you, your true family will except them no matter what, and your true family will always fight by your side'

Meaning true family who cares for you, cares for your mate. If they would fight for you, they would fight for your mate. That is why I feel as though I must do this. I'm fighting for you" he cups my cheek. I stare into his eyes, they show love and sadness.

"But I don't want to lose you! I just got you back" I whisper and squeeze my eyes shut, trying to hold back the tears that threaten to escape.

"Avery.. I know. But the gods brought me here for a reason did they not? I may have stumbled onto this land by accident but maybe the gods had planned for me to for reason" he thinks aloud. "Avery, look at me" he speaks softly. I slowly open my watery eyes.

My brother smiles sadly at me, he places his finger under my chin, tilting my head up so my eyes meet his. "I love you so very much, and don't you forget that ok? If anything happens to me tomorrow- know that I will always be there with you, no matter what" he whispers and kisses the top of my head.

As soon as he pulls away I hug him. He hugs me back but I hug tighter, afraid to let go. I was afraid that this would be the last hug I ever got from him. I was afraid I would never speak to my brother like this again. I was afraid I would never see him again. I was afraid that not tonight, nor tomorrow, but the next day would be the end.

"Clarise, Dylan, Belle and Katy will be leaving with you tomorrow, please keep my mate safe-"

"Daniel, I'm not leaving. I am fighting" I say quietly. Daniels mouth drops.

"Y-you're what? But Avery! You can't! The baby-"

"Daniel, I'm not letting you and my mate go out there alone, I want to be there for the both of you-"

"We will have Tyson and Kyron" he retorts.

"I don't care!" I sob. "If any of you die out on that battle field- gods forbid- I want to be there for you. I want to be there to help you, to protect you all, to have all of your backs" I rant. Daniel smiles sadly at me.

"But what if it is you, who dies? What if you are injured and you lose the baby?" He asks propping himself up with his elbow. I shake my head and close my eyes.

"I won't-"

"But what if you do?" He cuts me off. I sigh

"I don't know alright?" I then pick up mine and Daniel's empty plates and take them to the sink. "Daniel, I'm sorry" I whisper. In a flash he is behind me. He pulls me in for a needed hug. I bury my face in his chest, breathing in his scent. Mmm chocolate. Why does he always smell of chocolate?

We stay like this for what felt like a very long time, however it was not long enough. Daniel pulls back, he kisses the top of my head. "Good night Avery. I love you" he whispers.

"Love you to big bro" I smile slightly. He smiles then makes his way for the stairs. After a minute of being frozen in place, I shrug and drag my feet to the stairs.

I crawl into bed beside Jayden and wriggle up to him. I hear the sound of a bed squeaking. I grin at the thought of anyone of my friends having the time of their lives right now.

After a while the squeaking got really irritating when I couldn't sleep. I huff and pull my pillow over my head and squish it against my ears. It worked, for I heard nothing. I then drifted off to sleep.

Dream

"You're it!" Scott yelled as he tagged Derek's shoulder. He then sprinted off onto the park's grassy area, away from the playground where Derek and Jasmine stood.

Derek looked over at Jasmine. He grinned and charged up the steps for her. She screamed and ran to the slide and slid down. I laughed as he chased her around the playground, every now and then she would call

"Haha I'm fast than you!" Or "you can't catch me!" And she ran even faster. Jasmine was the age of seven, and the boys were ten, yet she always managed to out run them. I feel a warm arm slither around my waist, and the bench creaked as Jayden sat down beside me. He pecked my cheek. I smiled and kissed his soft lips. I moaned as we deepened the kiss.

"Eww, mummy and daddy are kissing!" Jasmine yelled. I smiled and pulled away from Jayden. He chuckled and we looked at her. She stood a few meters away from us, frozen as she gawked at us. Derek jogs over to he and stopped beside her. He pushed her shoulder lightly but hard enough for her to stumble to the left slightly.

"You're it" he whispered in her ear and sprinted off to where Scott was. I laughed and watch Jasmine blink a few times before she ran off after her brothers.

"I love you Avery Byson" Jayden murmured. I smiled and looking into his green eyes.

"And I love you, Jayden Byson" I giggled as he brought me closer to him and he smashed his lips against mine.

End Of Dream

Vote? Comment? Please let me know what you think! :)

Twenty two

Prepare for a twist! :)

Don't forget to comment and vote! (:

Sorry for any spelling/grammar errors

Avery

It was a seven o'clock that morning I had woken up. It was at ten past seven, that Jayden and I walked down stairs into the kitchen to meet everyone from our small group of friends.

It was at ten past seven, that we saw Belle sitting beside Dylan, balling her eyes out. It was at ten past seven that everyone around us were shaking with both fear and anger, the anger being directed at Belle. Even Dylan could not look at her with out his eyes turning black.

I look around and notice the only two people not down here are Daniel and his mate Clarise, for they were still asleep upstairs. I have a strange feeling it was them who were getting it on last night, *wink, wink*.

Everyone snaps they're heads up at Jayden and I as we enter the room full of tension. Belle cries harder as I look at her with sympathy.

"Someone tell me what is going on? Why are you sending daggers towards this poor girl?" I ask. Even Katy, the one who I thought would not stoop so low, sent menacing glares towards Belle.

I wrapped an arm around Belle's shoulder, trying to comfort her but she only cried harder. I looked at Dylan, to see his eyes were pure black and he looked only at the bench top before him.

"Some one tell me what on earth all the drama is about!" Jayden demanded. Tyson pointed at Belle. Kyron cleared his throat.

"She has lied to us Jayden. She is not who she claims to be" he growled.

"What do you mean?" I snap.

"H-he m-means th-that" she sobs between words. She takes a deep shaky breath. "He means that I have betrayed you" she whispers. I take a step back and look at her confused.

"How? What do you mean?" I ask. At that very moment, Dylan stands up and storms out the room.

"I will go talk to him" Kyron says and follows Dylan. I nod in thanks and turn back to the crying girl. I feel Jayden's presence beside me but I spare him no glance.

"From the very beginning, from when my home had been burnt to the ground- I had no one. I fled my territory and out of the boarders and ran until I could run no more- that was when he found me" she whispered.

"When who found you Belle?" Jayden asked, his voice husky. I looked up at him to see the purple bags under his eyes.

"The Alpha Rogue" she answered. The one we all fear. Belle inhaled and continued "H-he told me his pack was destroyed by yours and he was s-seeking revenge by making his own pack to t-take down yours" she stuttered looking down at the ground. "And he offered me to join his pack, so I did" she whispered.

I gasp. So she has been with the enemy pack the whole time? "Why are you telling us this now?" I ask confused.

"Because... W-when I was with that pack, the Alpha told me how much he despised you all, he told me how evil you all were and that you needed to be stopped. I thought all he said was true so I went along with his plans. He wanted me to be a spy, and know your every move then report back to him" she explained quietly, still staring at the ground below her.

"And so I did, but when I met you all... You were nothing how he claimed you to be. I didn't know if it was an act or if it were he who was lying. And I didn't know what to do!

I had instantly fallen in love with Dylan and you were all so nice to me. I knew I couldn't betray you so when I didn't report back to the Alpha how I said that I would- he sent rogues out to look for me, to make sure I had not been killed. That was the day before the party" she explained. "When Dylan and I were out in the woods"

I felt the anger inside me. It burned, and it pained me to think that this lovely girl planned to betray us from the start. But now knowing that she had been misguided, and the Alpha Rogue had lied to her about us, he had tricked her into believing we were the evil one...

She knows the truth now and has decided to come forward and tell us everything... I think we can trust her, and over time, forgive her.

Jayden looked at me curious as to why I was so quiet and I told him exactly what was on my mind. He let it all sink in as did Katy and Tyson, the only other two in the room. Belle looked at me surprised. She probably expected me to hate her and have her killed at once.

"Belle, I need you to tell me everything. You know that we don't know" I said calmly and I sat down beside her.

"J-just that... Oh you're going to hate me when I tell you this!" She shook her head, guilt flashed through her eyes. I placed a hand on her shoulder.

"Belle, listen. I do not and will not hate you. I understand why you sided with the Alpha at first, and I am happy you decided to go against him as soon as you found out he had his facts wrong. I will only hate you if you know something, and don't tell us, and that once fact gets everyone around us killed" I say looking her in the eyes.

She nods and looks around the room. Her eyes stop on one thing behind Jay. I turn around to see Dylan and Kyron standing there amused. I guess they heard the whole story then.

"They said they were planning the attack tomorrow. They lied. They wanted to throw you off their trail, and have the advantage of surprise..." She trailed off, breaking eye contact with Dylan.

"Belle?" I grab both her shoulders and force her to face me. I looked into her watery eyes. "When are they attacking?" I ask determination in my tone. She swallowed and stared back at me. She answered in a whisper with no hesitation.

"Today"

Twenty Three

Sadly, this book is coming to an end :(but I'm happy to announce there will be a sequel! The sequel will be called: My Rogue.

Anyways, enjoy! Sorry for any spelling/grammar errors

Jayden

"Today" the word rang through my ears. It felt as if I had, had a blow to the gut. We weren't ready!

"What time?" I ask quickly.

"Mid day. Twelve sharp" she answered finally looking up at me. She bows her head. I run a hand through my hair and turn to everyone.

"Round everyone up. Kyron, get all the children, mothers, elders, midnight warrior pack, all rounded up. Tyson, get all the fighters prepared. Have them fed and watered. Avery, could you please go wake Daniel and Clarise up and tell them everything?" I ask her sweetly.

She nods silently, still in shock I guess. She stands up and makes her way to the stairs. Tyson walks straight out the back door, with Katy right behind him. I guess she wants to say her good bye.

I turn to Kyron. "You know what to do I presume?" He nods.

"Yes Alpha" he says his tone completely serious.

"Good, and make sure she has no clue" I add, and he nods and walks out the door to round up all those who won't be fighting. Incase you are wondering about who I mean "she"... I mean Avery.

Kyron and I had thought up a plan to get Avery away from the fight. When we are all set up on the battle field, Kyron is forcefully going to take Avery away to safely. I won't allow her to get hurt out there today. Things could get really messy.

I know Avery will put up a fight but it's for the baby's and her own sake that she doesn't participate in this fight. I bet you a million bucks that she has never been in a battle before, she doesn't know the feeling.

Seeing thousands of people die before you, having people charge at you trying to actually murder you, I just know she will freeze. Because when the time comes for her to fight for her own life, to fight to the death, I know she doesn't have it in her to take another's life away. She's just not that kind of person. She is just too kind hearted.

Anyways, I'm doing this to protect her. I look at Dylan and Belle to see them talking quietly to each other. Belle is apologising every five seconds and Dylan is trying his hardest to comfort her. I don't think he would be able to ever hold a grudge against her.

"Why don't you too go to the party house and wait there for everyone else who is fleeing too?" I ask them. They nod, grab a basket full of sandwiches and water bottles they had prepared for them, Katy, Clarise and Avery to share. They then leave, walking out the front door.

I hear foot steps pound against the stairs as three someone's run down them. Daniel, Clarise and Avery appear at the bottom at the stair case and they walk in grinning from ear to ear. I raise an eyebrow. I don't know how they could be so happy at a time like this.

"Why so happy?" I ask confused.

"Look at Clarise's neck!" Avery squeals in delight. I look and there on her neck is Daniel's name written in silver with a swirl to the side of it. I raised both my eyebrows.

"He marked you?" I question surprised as to how quick they have moved. She giggled and nodded

"More than that" she replied.

"You completed the mate process?" I say even more surprised. They nod and hold hands. I smile

"I'm very happy for you Clarise" I say looking into her ocean blue eyes. She nods in thanks. I turn to Daniel and hold out my hand for him to shake

"Congrats bro" I tried to keep a straight face but the corners of my lips curved upwards. Daniel smiled and shook my hand.

"Thanks" he says with a nod. I nod and then turn to Clarise. "Dylan and Belle just left for the party house, with the food. If you hurry you can catch up to them" I nod at the front door. Her smile falls. She looks up at Daniel.

"Walk me?" She asks sweetly. He nods.

"Of course" and they leave hand in hand. They are leaving soon. I have one of the elders prepared to lead them out for I need Kyron to come back and take Avery away when it's time.

I check my watch. 7:45. Everyone who is leaving (besides Avery and Kyron who will leave later) will have left in fifteen minutes.

I look over at Avery who watches me curiously. I smile nervously. "You ready for today?" I ask her. She smiles

"Yeah of course-not! I'm not ready to fight against these rogues!" She starts to stress. Her breathing becomes shallow. I rush to her side and hug her, trying to calm her down.

"Sh deep breaths" I whisper in her ear. She nods and tries to breath slower and deeper. "You know.. You don't have to fight if you don't want to" I offer raising an eyebrow. She sighs

"It's too late to back out now and I don't want to leave you" she cries. I hold her tighter, afraid to let go. I know love, and I don't want you to leave either but if you don't you could really hurt yourself out there today. I think to myself but do not say.

"It's not too late. They haven't left yet, there's still time-" I try to convince her. She shakes her head.

"No, I want to stay" she says, determined. I nod, ok then, time for plan B.

.

.

.

.

Avery

After than mini panic attack I had this morning, Jayden hasn't stopped eyeing me. He looks more tense, nervous and worried. Probably just because he thinks I'll have another panic attack or something. Anyway, just a little after that panic attack I was sitting in the toilet, puking my guts out. Morning sickness. How pleasant.

We were now standing on the battle field, waiting for battle. It was eleven o'clock which meant we had one more hour before they attacked us. I see Kyron out of the corner of my eye.

He walks over to me, his eyes are filled with sorrow. I look at him confused. He only walks faster. I get the urge to run from him but something in me told me not to. Something told me to trust him. I don't know what he's up to but-

I feel my feet lift off the ground, as Kyron picks me up bridal style and starts to carry me off. I scream. "Put me down! Kyron i swear to god if you don't put me down ill-"

"You'll what?" He mocks. No you can't do this, please no. He walks his way off the grassy field and to the forest. I spot Jayden talking with Daniel. I know I'm not going to win this with Kyron so this might be the last time I see any of them ever again.

"At least let me say good bye" I whisper. Kyron must of heard me, for he placed me down on my feet,

"No more than five minutes. We are on a very tight schedule here!" He calls after me. I nod and run faster. Jayden sees me running towards him and he opens his arms wide. I jump into them and bury my head into the crook of his neck.

"Please" I sob. "Don't send me away" i whisper. I pull back to look into Jayden's beautiful light brown eyes. He smiles sadly.

"I'm sorry Avery, but it's for your own good" he places his hand softly on my belly. "And for the sake of our baby" he whispers. He bends down and kisses my belly "bye little guy, I'll see you soon" he whispers to it. I laugh a little but it doesn't replace all the tears that stream down my face.

Jayden brings his head back up and looks me in the eyes. I see fear, worry, love yet I also see hope, all in his eyes. He leans forward and he places a soft kiss on my lips. I wrap my arm around his neck and kiss him back with everything I've got.

For that one moment, it felt as if we were the only two people in the world. It was just him, and me. The kiss was so passionate yet it was filled with nothing but love. There was no lust or desire, just pure love.

We pull apart after hearing Kyron clear his throat, signalling we had to leave. I look back into Jayden's now forest green eyes. And then it clicked. "It's your emotions that change them" I whisper. He looks at me confused.

"Change what?" He whispers resting his forehead on mine.

"Your eye colour" I still whisper, not once breaking eye contact. Jayden smiles sadly.

"Good bye Avery" he whispers and kisses the top of my head.

"I refuse to say good bye, for it might mean we won't ever see each other again, so instead I will say, I will see you tomorrow" a crack just a small smile. Jayden chuckles softly, the sweet sound rings through my ears.

"Alright then, I will see you tomorrow Avery" he smiles "I love you" he says completely serious.

"I love you too, Jayden" the smile disappears off my face as I say it.

"Come on Avery! We need to go!" Kyron calls out to me. I look back up at Jayden.

"Good luck in your battle, may the gods protect you" I whisper. He nods and pecks my lips one last time.

"Now go Avery" I nod and turn to my brother who had been standing there the whole time. I quickly pull him in for a hug.

"You didn't think i would forget you big brother, did you?" I ask giving him a small smile. He hugs me tighter but doesn't reply. After a minute, he pulls away.

"I love you sister, I'll see you tomorrow" he smiles as he uses my words. I smile

"I'll see you tomorrow Daniel. Good luck. I love you" I answer. I take one last look at both Daniel and Jayden, in fear I will never see them again. "Tell Tyson I will see him tomrrow to and I wish him my best!" I call as I run back to Kyron. Kyron looks at me sadly, I ignore his pity however.

When we walked into the house, Kyron raced upstairs and came back with a semi large back and a back pack. He chucked me the back pack and I slipped it on. "That contains, food, drinks and weapon. In this bag is a spare change of clothes for each of us, two blankets and a small tent that will hold both of us, barely" he explains.

I nod and we leave. We will only be gone for twenty four hours, so we don't need much.

I take one last look at the guest house as we depart. I wave good bye and then we head for the forest. We walk right, opposite to the battle field. After about thirty minutes of walking we had made the border. We cross it with out hesitation and there we go. We are officially no where near the battle. We walk further into the un explored woods and we come to a small camp site.

I see people from our pack setting up their tents. I spot Katy and Belle setting up at tent and beside them was Dylan. He was digging through a bag. I walk over. "Avery!" They yell and hug me. I laugh and hug them back. I raise my eye brow.

"So Katy has forgiven you then?" I ask smiling. Belle nods enthusiastically. "Good! But why... Why does your tent look smaller than the one Kyron brought?" I ask confused. I look over at Dylan and Kyron who have already started to set up their tent. Katy laughs.

"That's because our tent holds tree people, theirs only holds two!" She explains with a grin. I laugh and start helping them set up the tent. I grab my change of clothes out of Kyron's bag and I place them in Belles, just so I wouldn't have to wake in the morning and have to walk into the boys tent.

With in ten minutes, we had finished setting up. Katy grabs a third blanket and sleeping bag from her overly large bag. She passes them to me. I laugh and unroll the sleeping bag then lay the blanket out on top.

"Now we just have to wait" I say sitting down on a log out side. Katy and Kyron sat down on either side of me, Dylan and Belle sat on the opposite log.

"What's the time?" Katy asked a little anxious.

"11:58" we sit in silence a minute. "I can tune into the battle by using mind link?" Kyron offers. I nod quickly and his eyes start to go white. His first word of course, were: "It's started"

Vote? Comment? :)

Twenty four

A very

My legs were non stop shaking. Kyron was quiet for several minutes, his eyes were fully white which meant he was concentrating really hard. "Daniel has four rogues around him" Kyron says tilting his head slight. My breath hitches in my throat.

"Hey guys what you all doing?" I hear Clarise's chirpy voice. I hold I finger up to her to tell her to shush.

"Your boyfriend's on the edge of death here!" I hiss. She gasps and sits down beside Katy to listen.

"He's doing ok" Kyron finally says. I sigh in relief. "Tyson just killed two rogues that were about to pounce on Jayden from behind. They're all doing great" he explains, his eyes still white. For a second, his eyes flicker back to their normal colour, but then back to White again.

"What was that?" I whisper.

"He's weak. Doing this kind of thing, it drains him, fast." Dylan explains. "He might be able to hold up for another five minutes at the most but then he will need rest" Dylan sighs.

"Ok" I nod. "We'll give him a couple more minutes and we'll stop him before he loses all of his energy" I answer. They all nod.

"David has been killed" Kyron says, his voice is still emotionless. It's like his soul isn't here right now, but out in the battle field. Only his voice and body remain here.

I gasp at the news.

"No, not David!" I cry, Katy hugs me tightly from the side. I rest my head on her shoulder.

"Jayden has just found David's body. He is outraged. He starts attacking rogues randomly, with more speed, strength and agility-" Kyron's eyes flicker back to normal and he closes them completely. I gasp and catch him before he falls. He is unconscious, he is weak and tired but he is completely fine. His pulse and heart rate tell me so.

Dylan helps me carry him to their tent and we lay him down softly. We walk back out and sit back down on the log. Katy is hugging Clarise tightly whilst they both cry their hearts out.

"I guess all we really can do now.. Is wait" I whisper looking down at the ground.

.

.

.

.

.

A few hours later, I hear Kyron wake. I run over to his tent and go straight in. I sit on Dylan's bed, beside Kyron. Kyron groans and rubs his forehead. He opens his eyes and stares at me. His eyes go wide.

"Avery I'm sorry- I didn't know I would pass out that quick-" he appologised. I cut him off.

"It's fine, really" I smile. He nods in appreciation. "But do you think.. D-do you think you could take just one glance now? I mean just long enough to see if the battle is still going and everyone is ok? That should only take less than a minute-"

"Yeah sure Avery. But first, how long have I been out?" He asks.

"About three to four hours" I answer quickly. He nods and closes his eyes. When he opens them, they are white.

"Kyron? What do you see?" I ask him.

"The battle is still going. Jayden is fighting the Alpha, but he is surrounded by at least twenty other rogues. Tyson and Daniel have his back though" Kyron says. His eyes flicker back to normal for a second, and in fear of Kyron passing out from exhaustion again, I shake his shoulders.

"Alright Kyron stop, you're out doing yourself again" I demand. Kyron's eyes close and when they open they are back to normal. He has a worried expression on his face. My smile drops. "Kyron what's the matter?" I ask.

"I- I don't know. I didn't see. But something is wrong" he says looking up at me. Worry surges through me. "B-but don't panic Avery, I'm sure everything will turn out fine" he says reassuringly and he hugs me.

I wrap my arms around his shoulders and hug him back.

"What if someone dies out there Kyron?" I whisper, panic rises inside me.

"No one will die" he says calmly. I nod.

"I sure hope not" please Gods! Let everyone be ok!

Twenty five

A ^{very}

We waited impatiently for hours on end, wondering if the fight was over. I decided to let Kyron rest, for her would check again in the morning to see how the fight went, and who won. I tossed and turned in my sleeping bag and let out a sigh of annoyance when sleep wouldn't come.

"Can't sleep?" I hear Katy ask quietly. I role over to face her and shake my head sadly. I hadn't told her about Kyron looking a second time at the battle, and it was about that second glance I was so worried about.

"Katy, early this afternoon, when Kyron woke up.. He looked again through mind link to see how the battle was going. It was only for a few seconds so it didn't tire him out any further" I add. She nods.

"What did he see?" She whispers curiously.

"Nothing good" I answer. She nods and closes her eyes.

"I'll see you in the morning" she yawns "I'm actually really tired" she mumbles. Eventually my eyes started to droop and I welcomed the darkness.

.

.

.

.

"Avery! Wake up!" Katy, Clarise and Belle yell in my ear. I finch and my eyes snap open. They all had grins on their faces. I yawn and stretch my arms. Slowly sitting up, I look at each of them, they were practically jumping up and down on the spot.

"I'm guessing we won?" I ask, one of my eyes closed but the other opened, while I continued to stretch. I had the worst night sleep last night, the ground is so uncomfortable!

"Not only that, but we get to go home now!" Katy said with a grin. That got my attention. With in minutes I had gotten changed, packed my bag and took down the tent.

I then went around and helped everyone else with their tents, and finally we were all ready to head back. We started walking, Elder Brian led us slowly home.

I felt a tugging on the bottom of my shirt. I looked down to meet eyes with Finn. I smile at him, "it's over Finn. It's finally over" I smile happily.

"We won big sis" he grinned. I laughed at him.

"Yep."

The pace we walked at was far to slow and I was dying to see my beloved. Kyron noticed my anxiousness he walked over to me. "Want to run a head?"" He asks. I nod with a grin, Kyron leads me up to the Elder.

"Alpha has called us to come right away so we will run off a head of you and meet you all there" Kyron lies, not once stuttering, or breaking eye contact. Elder Brian nods and we run for our home.

The closer we get, the faster I run. I just wanted to feel safe again, I wanted to be in Jayden's arms, I wanted him to tell me everything was ok, and I wanted to tell him I loved him.

As we reached home we ran into the guest house to find it abandoned. We ran into every other guest house to see no one had returned from battle. "Let's go check the battle field" Kyron suggests. I nod and we run off.

A small gasp escapes my lips as we make our way to the large clearing. Dead bodies lay everywhere. Pools of blood stained the grass and what was worse is that only about thirty men and twenty women remained alive.

They stood in he middle of the field, all huddled together. I walked over slowly to them. They all snapped they're heads my way, fear evident in their eyes.

They sighed n relief when they saw it was me and they bowed their heads in respect. "Where's Jayden?" I ask loudly. Everyone clears and makes a path, I see Jayden squatted down holding someone in his arms.

A dark figure covered in blood stood beside him with his back to me so I couldn't make out who it was, and I most definitely could not see the body cradled in Jayden's arms. Worry and panic surged through me.

As I was about to run over there, Kyron gripped my wrist. "You don't want to see that" he whispered his voice cracking. I look up at him.

"Who is it?" My voice cracks too. Kyron was silent, but he never broke eye contact with me. "Kyron who is it!?" I cry.

"It's your brother" he barely gets out. W-what? No, I heard him wrong. It's not Daniel that lies dead in Jayden's arms. I look up at Kyron again to see tears starting to slip out of his eyes, and I know what I heard was correct.

And that's when I let it go. I screamed. I screamed loud enough to break glass. Tears streamed down my face. I tried to run over to Daniel but Kyron held me back.

He wrapped his arms around my waist and whispered soothing words into my ear, however I could not hear him, nor did I pay any attention. I continued to scream and cry until my throat was dry. I was numb with pain. I couldn't hear. I couldn't see, my eyes were so puffy, I couldn't feel and I knew I would pass out.

Nothing could describe the feelings that exploded inside me. I was swallowed by sadness, shock, pain, loss, grief, loneliness, worry, fear, but most of all, anger. And I was ready to seek vengeance. I continued to struggle weakly out of Kyron's grip, however I was no where near strong enough.

I knew he was keeping me back, knowing that if I saw the face of my dead brother, I would have night mares for a very long time. But I needed to say good bye. After what felt like a very long time, my struggles died down, my kicks became weak and my cries became small soundless sobs.

I see a blurry figure approach me. I couldn't make out the person, for my vision was way to blurry. "Daniel?" I murmur before passing out in Kyron's arms.

Vote? Comment?

Twenty six

A^{very}

"Avery" I hear Daniel call my name in a whisper. I giggle and run out from the old oak tree out the back of our house. I ran around the field in search of my brother. I see a flash of black and I stop running. I freeze and looks around.

The next moment I know, I am tackled to the ground, a big black wolf hovers above me. I laugh and push him off. He shifts back into his human form and chucks his clothes on. I walk over to the old oak tree and sat down on the wooden plank we use as a swing. I remember making this with Daniel when I was ten years old.

Daniel walked over to me and stood in front of me, his arms folded over his chest. His smile was now a frown and I saw the sorrow in his eyes. I look up at him confused, "Daniel what's wrong?" I ask slightly worried. He sighs deeply and closes his eyes for a moment. When he opened them, they started to glow. I gasp. "Daniel, what's going on?"

"Avery, I'm afraid to tell you that... After this, you will never see me again" he says quietly and very calm. My eyes almost pop out of my head.

"What do you mean? Of course I will! Are you moving back to our old home? We can always visit you-"

"No Avery. That is not it" he cuts me off. I frown

"Then what is it? What are you so afraid to tell me?" I plead him to answer. He sighs again and looks at the ground.

"I'm dead Avery" I gasp and tears cloud my vision. No, this isn't true.

"Daniel this isn't funny. Don't lie to me" I say sternly.

"I'm not kidding around Avery" he sighs in frustration. "I came to say good bye" he says looking back up to me. His sad eyes lock with mine, and I know he is telling the truth.

"Please don't leave me" I whisper, tears slides down my cheek. Pain crosses his face as he struggles to contain his posture.

"Avery, please tell Clarise I love her dearly and I will always be with her, watching over her... And tell her that I want her to look after my remaining pack.. And our son" I gasp.

"Sh-she- your son?" I ask confused.

"Well as you know last night, we completed the mating process... And when I came up here, the gods told me that she is pregnant. They also told me that Clarise will have no idea about this but by the time she finds out, it will be too late" he explains. I look at him confused.

"How so?" I ask.

"Well she is going to go through depression, out of losing her mate.. And the baby will die if she drifts to far away. The baby is the only thing that will keep her from going through all that. As soon as you wake up I need you to tell her about the baby, and that I love her very much" his voice sounds almost emotionless, I know Daniel is trying his hardest not to let them get the better of him.

"I will" I say standing up. I hug Daniel tightly, never wanting to let go.

"I will ALWAYS be watching over you, and Finn, and Clarise. And I want you to know that. Avery-" he pulls back a little, only far enough to look down at me. "I am so very proud of you. You make a great leader and a wonderful Luna. I wish you and Jayden the very best. Make sure to tell my nephews and niece about me!" He laughs, I can see the pride shining in his eyes.

I can't help but laugh at him. Tears of sadness continue to stream down my cheeks though.

"And don't forget to tell our parents of my death ok? When you see them next or even hear of their existence, deliver the message. I know they won't think much of it and they probably won't even come to say good bye, but they at least deserve to know. Take care of our baby brother, and take care of yourself too" he says cupping my cheek.

I squeeze my eyes shut, refusing to let any more tears escape. Daniel kisses the top of my head,

"I do have one more favour to ask of you" he adds. I look up at him.

"Anything" I answer. He gives me a small grateful smile

"Tell Kyron that 'I know it hurts now, but you can't block out love for the rest of your life'. Tell him that he needs to love. Tell him he needs to let him self fall, in order to pick himself up. Tell him, life's too short to waste time getting over something so small. Tell him that he should just get out there and live his life while he still can" he finishes with a small smile.

I sniff and nod with sad smile. "It is time for me to go now" he whispers. No it's too soon, don't leave!

"I love you Daniel" I whisper.

"I love you too Avery"

"I'll see you tomorrow?" I use my words from the battle. He chuckles and nods.

"See you tomorrow" he waves. He steps back and I watch as his body starts to fade. "Good bye Avery" he whispers.

....

My head pounded, it was as if I had fallen a thousand meters and my ears had exploded. The pain hurt everywhere, my muscles ached and my stomach and lower abdomen felt as if they were on fire. I forced my eyes to open and they opened very slowly indeed.

Jayden was the very first thing I saw. I smiled weakly. He smiled down at me. He mouthed words but I could not hear him. I look around the room. It is very bright, and the walls are white. I see a machine with a heart monitor to my left.

I am in a hospital.

I look down at my lower arms to see a couple needles in them with fluids flowing through them. I look back up to Jayden, my vision slightly blurry. "Why am I hear?" I groan. Jayden chuckled.

"You fainted, you must have really worked yourself up hard yesterday"

"How long was I out?"

"A mere twenty four hours" he shrugs.

"Where am I?" I ask looking around again.

"We're at the pack's doctors" he states with a small smile. I nod.

"When can I go home?" Right on cue, the doctor walks in. He bares a small smile my way. He walks over to the machine and checks it.

"Good morning Luna, I hear to took quite a fall" he chuckles. I nod and keep my eyes on him. He holds a small torch in his hand and holds out his index finger in front of my eyes, "Please look here" he holds it still. With his other hand he turns the tiny torch on and checks both my eyes.

"When can I go home?" I moaned.

"Well it seems here that you are perfectly fine, so.. Now I guess" he says with a smile. He unplugs the machine and takes out the needles.

"Thank you Doctor..." I trail off.

"Mewton" he smiled. I nod. Jayden and I walked out of the room and out of the large house. I walked over to Jayden's car. He opened the passengers door and I hopped in thanking him.

He shut the door and walked back around to the drivers seat and got in himself. The drive back home was short.

"What do you remember?" Jay asked glancing at me.

"Not a lot" I answer truthfully. I remember the moments right before I passed out, when I saw my brother dead. I remember before then how I was at the camp sight. The dream came flooding back to me.

However It felt more than just a dream. It felt real, like Daniel really was there talking to me, and perhaps he really was. Everything he said I know he actually said. It wasn't made up.

"Daniel visited me this morning" I finally say. Jayden raises an eyebrow. "I know he's dead, he told me himself. It's like he came to me in a dream" I explain. Jayden nods in realisation "but it was more than a dream. He told me important things, like Clarise is going to go into depression unless I see her right away to deliver her a message"

"Which is...?"

"Can't tell you sorry. It's a secret" I poke my tongue out at him and laughs when he pouts at me. "He also told me to talk to Kyron. He wants me to tell out parents of his death, and he says he'll always watch over us. He also says he wishes the best for us" I tell him. Jayden nods but doesn't say anything.

"Jay?" I ask softly

"Mm?"

"Did.. Did Daniel say anything to you? Before he died?" I ask. Jayden was silent. We pulled up into the drive way and as he turned the ignition off he turned to me. He looked at me with those sad brown eyes.

"Yes. He did" Jayden said quietly. I raise my eyebrow

"Please tell" I wave my hand. Jayden sighed. He scooped up both of my hands in his and held them tightly. He looked into my eyes.

"His last words were, Tell my sister, my brother and my precious mate that I love them. Take care of my sister. Treat her like the queen she is. Always let her know how beautiful she is. Be Kind to her. Be honest with her. Share with her. Talk to her. Love her" he finished in a whisper.

Aww I love you bro.

I feel tears spring at the back of my eyes and they threatened to spill. I squeezed my eyes shut and willed myself not to cry. I'm going to miss him so much. "We'll have his funeral in a few days once everything has sort of settled, ok?" Jayden asks as he pulls my in for a hug. I nod and let a few tears slip free.

.

.

.

.

I knocked on Clarise's door. "What?" She asked monotoned. I opened it and peaked my head through. "Hey... I just want to talk to you about something-" she cuts me off.

"You want to apologise?" She asks raising an eye brow. I look at her slightly confused,

"Well yeah I guess, sorry for your loss but listen-" I say stepping in to the room. She cuts me off again however.

"That's not what I mean" she says dead panned.

"That what do you mean?" I snap back. She looks slightly taken aback.

"I thought you of all people would be nice to me.. Anyway I thought you were going to apologise for sending Daniel to his death" she states clearly. So I say yes Daniel was telling the truth. She is going into depression.

"Ok first of all.. I think you are depressed. And I understand what you are going through," I place a hand on her shoulder. "I lost him too" I say softly. She shrugs me off.

"What ever" she mutters. My eyes soften as I see tears make their way down her cheek.

"Look... What I want to say is.. Don't let this bring you down. Daniel wouldn't want you to be this unhappy, he would want you to move on" I say sympathetically. She glares at me.

"My mate is dead! My soul mate! My other half! What am I to do with out him!? We were created for many reasons I believe, but we are not meant to be, with out our other half. They complete us!" She screams. I flinch and hold my hands up in surrender.

"Calm down, you'll kill the baby!" I yell throwing my hands up. I quickly slap a hand over my mouth. She looks at me confused and shocked,

"What do you mean baby?" She asks. I sigh and roll my eyes. I stand up and start to walk out the room.

"I suggest you take it easy, Daniel tells me that your are going to over stress, and let the depression get the better of you. By doing that you kill the baby" I mutter, my back to her.

"Baby.. Am I-"

"Yes you are pregnant. But not for long if you continue to act like this" I say quietly and leave the room.

"You said Daniel told you this!" She called out as I was walking out the door. I stopped and looked over my shoulder at her. "Did he.. Say anything else?" She asks quietly.

"Just that he loves you very much and he wants you to make sure the baby survives. He wants you to stay strong, and he says he will forever be watching over you" I answer quietly and walk out the room with out another word.

I walk down the stairs and out the back door. I walk straight into the woods to clear my head out. As soon as I entered the woods I punched the first tree in reach. I let out a scream, as that one person kept crossing my mind.

Daniel, if you loved me, why did you leave me?

Sadness and hurt erupted in side me. That sadness turned into anger. That anger boiled deep inside me.

It's not fair! Daniel was supposed to be here, he wasn't supposed to die! He wasn't supposed to leave me like this! He had a family and he just left us all! He is supposed to be there for my eighteenth birthday. He is supposed to be there for my wedding day. He is supposed to be there, the day I have children. He is supposed to be there to watch them grow up. Hs is supposed to be there for Finn. He is supposed to be there when Finn first shifts. He is supposed to help Finn through it. He is supposed to be there when his child is born. And he is supposed to be there to raise that child.

After hours on end of punching trees and kicking them down, I finally decide to head back home. My knuckles bled nonstop but I ignored the pain. They would heal over time. I walk upstairs and into my room. I lay down beside Jayden and try to get some sleep. I feel him pull me up into his chest.

"You feel any better?" He whispered. I nod tiredly.

"Just a little" I mumble. "Night"

"Good night sweet heart" he says guessing the top of my head.

"I don't know what's so good about it" I mutter.

Vote? Comment?

Twenty Seven

A^{very}

I look in the man sized mirror for the tenth time. A sad girl, dressed in a black knee, length dress, with laced fabric for the shoulders, stared back at me. It's been two weeks since the incident. Two long weeks of grieving and morning the death of my brother.

In fact.. I have to say, Clarise was surprisingly, the least upset. You could tell it was a struggle but she was trying hard for her baby. We've all finally pulled ourselves together and today was Daniel's funeral.

I see Jayden walk over to me. He has some sort of frown on his face, but he tries hard to not let his emotions get ahold over him, although I think that he secretly blames himself for the death of my brother.

A week and a bit ago, Jayden had told me that Daniel died saving his life. When Jayden's back was turned, an extremely large and very powerful rogue was about to pounce on him, however Daniel had jumped forward to defend Jay. When Jayden turned around to help Daniel out, it was too late.

Jayden's arm wraps around my waist and he draws me into himself. I rest my head on his shoulder and let out a long sigh. "I miss him" I say not taking my eyes away from the mirror. I glance at Jayden's reflection and he catches my eyes.

"I know you do baby" he murmurs. "I do too" he admits looking down at the ground. I sigh sadly.

"I guess we better go. They're waiting for us" I look over my shoulder at the empty hall way. Jayden nods and takes my hand in his. He entwines our fingers and together we walk out the room.

.

.

.

.

.

I take a seat beside Jayden and look up at the front. The grey clouds covered the sky above us. The cemetery looked pretty much the same as it did in the movies. Dull and gloomy.

Looking at the stand in front of all of us, the priest stands behind it. Behind him was the closed, shiny black coffin in which my brother lay. It was covered in bunches of white roses and multicoloured flowers of different types.

The man cleared his throat catching all our attention. I feel myself stiffen. Someone takes hold of my hand. I look to my left and trail my eyes up his arm and too his face.

I look into Kyron's dark, clouded eyes. He smiles sadly and rubs his thumb over my palm. I feel myself relax slightly. I return the sad smile and look back up to the man.

"Welcome. Today we come to morn the death of Daniel James Jedson" he looked around to see if anyone wanted to say anything. I stood up and walked straight over to him.

"May I say something please?" I whisper. He nods.

"Of course" he holds my hands in his. I nod a thank you and he steps away to the side. I take a shaky breath I step forward. I lower the microphone slightly and look around at everyone. They all stare back sadly, with sympathy in their eyes.

I take another breath and begin my speech. In case you're wondering, no I hadn't prepared myself for this. All the words that are about to come out of my mouth are completely from the mind.

"For those who don't know who Daniel Jedson was, for those who never had the time to meet him for he was only with us here a short time... He was my brother. He wasn't just an ordinary brother, he was someone extraordinary. He was someone who played different but equally special rolls in all of our lives. To me he was my brother. The big brother that was always their to save the day" I smile at all the memories I had shared with him.

"But he wasn't just a brother. He was more than that. Daniel was a very powerful Alpha, who cared deeply for his pack. He was a brother... And a son" I search the crowd for my parents but being the kind of parents they were, they hadn't come. "He was a best friend" I lock eyes with Mark and Brandon, they smile sadly and look down at their hands.

"He was a mate. One who had been searching his whole life for his one true love. Nothing could explain how happy I was for him when he found her.

And what a very special and lucky girl she was and still is." I say locking eyes with Clarise. She gives me a grateful smile filled with aw.

"He was also a father" I see lots of surprised faces. I look down at the wooden stand below me. I try to contain the tears that blurred my vision. I let a few slip. I sniff and wipe my tears. I look back up again, and continue

"Yes you heard me right. You may not know it yet, but on the last night of Daniel's life, he spent his time in heaven with Clarise. They had the time of their life" I chuckle lightly. I see her crack a small smile and she wipes her tears. "And now, she holds his child" I wave my hand at her with a small smile.

"Daniel was my hero" I let the tears spill again, "I remember one of the last things he had said to me, the night before he died" I close my eyes and recite "A wise man once said

'A mate is your equal. You will cherish them for who they are. You will forgive them no matter how many terrible things they have done. And if you love your mate and your mate loves you, your true family will except them no matter what, and they will always fight by your side'

What he meant by this.. Was that you can't choose who your mate is. But no matter who he is, how bad of a person he may be, you will always love him. And there is nothing you can do about it. And if your family love you, they will except your choices, and they will except your mate. And they will fight for you no matter what.

Daniel did exactly that. He stood by me, and my mate. He knew we were in trouble and under attack and he fought for us. What we didn't expect, was that he died fighting" I look up seeing sad faces everywhere. "But I'm sure Daniel would have rather died, fighting in honour of family and love instead of dying some other meaningless way" I let out a small chuckle. That made people smile.

"Daniel wouldn't have wanted this. He wouldn't want us to morn him this long. I believe that death is apart of life. Sometimes it happens all too soon, but all I know is that when someone dies, you morn them. You grieve and then you move on.

It might be hard but we will get through this. Today we won't remember how painful his death was or how sad it is that he has left us, but we will remember all the good this man has done through out his life, and what a wonderful man he was" I finish and bow my head.

Looking around I see people staring at me, their eyes filled with aw, admiration and pride. No one was crying, but they all looked deep in thought, few were smiling happily, probably thinking about some happy memory they had shared with my brother.

As I take a few steps back, I walk over to the coffin. I kiss the tips of my fingers and run them over the edge of the coffin. I stop at the end and sigh. "Rest in peace Daniel. I love you" I whisper. I then walk back over to my seat and sit down and listen to everyone else's speeches.

.

.

.

.

.

It's been a few weeks since the funeral now and it has started to settle down. Clarise is quite like her old self now, although she is just a little quieter. Finn is the only one that still remains sad for he still doesn't understand the full concept of death.

I took another bite out of the chocolate cake and rested my elbow on the kitchen bench. I looked over at Kyron and Tyson, then over to Katy. That little bump was starting to show on her belly. And of course, my stomach too had a small bump, slightly larger than Katy's.

Jayden sat down beside me and kissed my cheek. He looks down at my stomach and places his gentle hand on it. He rubs small circles on it and smiles.

"He's growing" he grins.

"They're" I correct him. He raises an eye brow.

"How do you know it's twins? We haven't had the scan yet, we're doing that tomorrow" he asks confused.

"How do you now it's a he? We haven't had the scan yet" I retort with a smirk. He frowns and takes a bite out of his apple.

"I crave strawberries" I say looking at him with a pleading look. He laughs and shakes his head,

"I'm not getting up. I just got comfy" he laughs. I look over at Kyron. He shakes his head no. I give him my puppy dog eyes. He sighs.

"Fine" he grumbles and stands up. I clap my hands excitedly. "I hate it when you do that" he mutters. I laugh quietly.

"Oh and some chocolate syrup would go nice with them!" I call with a grin. He rolls his eyes but the corners of his lips curve upwards.

"Kyron, please make that a double?" Katy smiles sweetly. Kyron bows

"Yes ma lady" he says sarcastically and grabs a box of strawberries out of the fridge. Tyson pulls Katy closer to him.

"My lady" he whispers possessively and pecks her lips. Dylan and Belle walk in the next minute hand in hand. Belle sits down next to me to my right and Dylan sits down on the other side of her. And right after Clarise joins the party. She sits down in the spare seat next to Katy and smiles nervously.

"Well look who decided to come out and join the fun" Tyson teases. She frowns then laughs. I look over at her.

"Has the lump started to show?" I ask. She shrugs.

"Not really. How long do we go through this whole thing for?" She asks tilting her head to the side.

"Four months for us Alpha's mates, I think" I answer, because of course.. Daniel was an alpha so it will only take her four months.

"Actually it will only take you three months" Jayden cuts in with a smirk. I smile, good only two months left for me then.

Kyron places a bowl of strawberries down in front of me with a small bowl of chocolate sauce next to it. He gives Katy the same. I grin up at him

"Thanks Kyron" I say then dunk a strawberry into the chocolate, then plop it into my mouth. I moan at the taste and shove the rest of the chocolate covered strawberries into my mouth.

"Easy there tiger" Dylan chuckles at me. I laugh and wipe my finger around the edge of the chocolate bowl scraping any left over chocolate, and then lick it off my finger. Gross I know... But yum!

"Avery, I was wondering if I could take you out tonight? Like on a date?" Jayden asks nervously. I smile

"Sure!" He breathes a sigh of relief and returns the smile. Well this ought to be good. I smile at the thought.

Twenty Eight

Only two more chapters including this one :(but there is definitely a sequel! It's called My Rogue, and it will be coming out as soon as I finish this book!

Anyways... Enjoy! :) sorry for any grammar/spelling errors.

Avery

I switch the TV channel again, trying to find something interesting to watch. Everyone had gone out to some pack thing, well except for Clarise, Kyron and me. I switch the channel again and sigh.

I switch the TV off and fall back into the couch. I close my eyes and relax my shoulders. I hear a small chuckle, and I feel the spot on the couch next to me, dip. I open up my left eye and look over at Kyron. My lips curve upwards.

I open my eyes and face myself to him. "Kyron, just the person I wanted to see!" I beam. He laughs

"Ok, what's up?"

"Well... I kind of have a message for you.. I was supposed to deliver it weeks ago but I just never got around to it I guess..." I trail off looking down. It still hurt to think about Daniel and I don't know if I'm ready to mention him again yet.

"Well ok, that's alright, what is it Avery?" He asks curiously.

"Ok.. When Daniel died, he came to me, in my dreams or what ever... And he told me things, he wanted me to tell you something.." I look up to meet Kyron's sad eyes.

"What did he say?" He asks looking down. I sigh.

"He said... 'Tell Kyron that I know it hurts now, but you can't block out love for the rest of your life. Tell him that he needs to love. Tell him he needs to let him self fall, in order to pick himself up. Tell him, life's too short. That he should just get out there and live it while he can' and Kyron he's right. You need to move on" I say placing a soft hand on his shoulder. He smiles sadly at me and his eyes start to water, but of course he holds the tears back.

"Thank you" he whispers, but I think it is directed for Daniel.

"Oh and Kyron there's something I need to ask you" I say quietly. Kyron raises an eye brow. I take a bit of a shaky breath, "Kyron Dauton, will you be my children's god father?" I ask clasping my hands together. Kyron grins and hugs me tightly.

"Really? You want me to be the god father?" He asks surprised. I nod and smile,

"Yep! And I want Katy to be the god mother" I say nodding. Kyron laughs.

"Thanks Avery, you've once again, made my day" he smiles in adoration.

.

.

.

.

.

"Clarise what do you think of this dress?" I ask walking into her room. She smiles up at me.

"I love it! It's so pretty!" She gushes. She stands up from her bed and walks over to me. I give her a small twirl. The red laced fabric at the ends of the skirt part, sways as I spin.

"I'm wearing it on my first date. Kyron has set up a dinner table at our spot and he wants us to have a romantic evening but that's all he's told me" I say with a laugh. Clarise nods and smiles.

"You really do look beautiful Avery, I hope your date goes well then" she grins.

.

.

.

.

"Ok we are almost there" Jayden whispers in the ear. Jayden had insisted on blind folding me on the way to our spot so I could be surprised by what ever he has done. At first I refused to walk through the forest blind folded but Jay then accused me of not trusting him so eventually I obliged.

I feel the blind fold being removed from my eyes. I gasp and cover my mouth with my hands. I looked at the beautiful sight before me, amazed by how simple he had set it up, but how spectacular and wonderful it looked.

We stood at the back of the lake on the thick but short cut grass. There was a small, brown coloured, round table set up in front of us. It had a cream coloured table cloth over it, and there were two dish trays on each side with a tray lid over the top of them.

Two silver candle holders with dimly lit candles were behind each plate and In the centre of the table was a bottle of champagne. He pulls back my chair and bows. I laugh and sit down. He then walks around and sits in his chair.

"Aww Jay, it's beautiful!" I gush. He smiles and pops the cork off the wine bottle.

"Thanks babe" he says with a laugh and looks us both a glass of wine.

"No thank you this must have taken ages to set up!"

"Oh a little while" he admits with a shrug.

Straight away we dug into the food, it was a lively roast chicken and neatly cut up salad. We talked about all sorts of things, like about names for the baby, well babies. I'm one hundred percent sure that I will be having twins.

Scott and Derek.

Jayden and I had agreed that if we ever had a girl, her name would be Jasmine. I wipe my mouth with my napkin and place it down on the empty plate. I stand up, and so does Jay. He looks extremely nervous for some odd reason. I look at him suspicious and I raise an eye brow.

He walks over to me and kneels down on one knee before me. I gasp and cover my mouth with my hands. Jayden pulls out a small, red, velvet box.

He opens it to present a small ring with a good sized diamond in the middle. He swallows the lump in his throat.

"Avery Michelle Jedson. Will you do me, the extraordinary honour, of become my wife?" He asks with a smile. I grin and give him my hand.

"Yes! Oh my gosh yes!" I squeal. He slips the ring on and stands up. I wrap my arms around his neck and give him a massive hug. He spins me around in a small circle and then puts me back down again. I pull back and then peck his lips.

"I love you Jayden" I smile.

"And I love you Avery" he grins and pecks my lips. I look down at the ring on my finger and a large smile spreads over my face. Oh it is beautiful! Jayden picks me up bridal style, and I squeal out of surprise.

"Put me down!" I yell as Jayden starts to run into the woods.

"No!" He laughs. Soon enough I see our house in the distance. Jayden carries me in and up the stairs, "Avery, I love you so much" he murmurs placing me down on the bed. I wrap my arms around his neck. Now I know what he wants, haha cheeky little bugger. I peck his lips.

"I love you too" I whisper. And that is how are night truly began.

I jump up and down nervously in the car. I couldn't contain my excitement. Today we were having the baby scans done and I just couldn't wait to get there and get them done.

Jayden pulls into Doctor Mewton's drive way and we hop out of the car. We walk up to the front door, and Jayden knocks loudly. A Middle Ages woman opens the door.

"Good day Alpha, how are you?" She chirps. Jayden smiles warmly at her.

"I'm fine thanks mrs Mewton. We're here for the baby scans" he announced. She smiled and blushed. She opened the door open wide and hurried us in.

"Oh of course you are. How silly of me, I must have thought that was next week!" She laughs. I just smile as she leads us through the house.

.

.

.

"If you look over here you will see the babies hand" doctor Mewton points at the screen. I nod. "And here is the other hand.... Oh look what we have here! Luna, I'm proud to say you are having a boy!" The doctor grins, however Jayden's grin is even larger. I laugh and point at the screen.

"I think you mean twin boys" I smirk. Jayden's jaw drops open.

"How did you know?" He asks surprised. Doctor Mewton looks confused. I laugh.

"He means the other day when we were talking about the baby, I told him we'd be having twin boys and he was surprised by how I knew" I answered the doctors unasked question.

"And how did you know, exactly?" He asks confused. I laugh

"Um.. I guess you could say it came to me in a dream" I say with a chuckle. Jayden looks at me strangely.

"What did they look like?" He asks.

"Um... Well.... All I will tell you, is that Scott definitely has your eyes" I smile. Jayden looks at me even more confused. "One green and one blue, and they are really pretty!" I gush. "Wait, is it strange I can see the future of my children?" I ask the doctor. He shakes his head and smiles.

"No it's completely normal for an alpha female" he said with a nod. I sigh in relief. Anyways... See I told you Jayden! Twins!

And today is where my story truly begins. It is where I start a new chapter, experience the unknown, and live my life! I will forever love all my friends:

Kyron

Katy

Dylan

Tyson

Clarise

Belle

I will always cherish my family:

Finn

Jayden

My future children

Clarise's future child

And alas, even my parents

I will never forget Daniel, my beloved brother, may he rest in peace.

And I will forever love my mate, Jayden Byson.

The End! Haha hope you enjoyed reading 'Mate? No Way!' :) I'll write an epilogue but yeah, that's the end. Please don't forget to vote and comment! Comment your for favourite character! Random yes but I'm curious, who's your favour character?

Epilogue

A^{very}

"Mama! Derek won't share his chocolate with me!" Scott whined. I laugh and bend down slightly to him. I ruffle his golden brown, silky hair.

"Well why don't you go get your own chocolate out of the fridge? I'm sure daddy won't notice if you steal some of his chocolate" I whisper. Scott's gorgeous multicoloured eyes lit up and he grinned from ear to ear. He hugged me tightly, although his small arms wouldn't quite fit around my large stomach.

"Thanks mummy" he sighed in content and then rushed off to the fridge.

A lot has happened in three years time. Yes it has been three years since I found out I was having twins, so long ago that was! Since then, Katy, Belle and Clarise and I have all given birth.

Katy gave birth to a beautiful girl whom she named Katherine. About a year after they gave birth to Katherine, she got pregnant again and Tyson couldn't be more thrilled.

They're second child was a son. He looks almost identical to Katherine. They called him Max. He's two now, and Katherine is three.

Clarise gave birth to a gorgeous baby girl, whom she called Denise. And as Denise grows, I start to see more and more of Daniel's features in her. Her smile, her eyes, however her hair is platinum blond and wavy like her mums colour but a different style. She really is pretty. As often as I can I try to spend time with her. Scott and Denise have started to bond too, although they are only three so...

And Belle, her and Dylan fully mated about a month after the twins were conceived. Belle had given birth to a girl too. They named her Shelby after Belle's mum. And my oh my were the children growing up so fast.

"hey baby, I'm home" Jayden smiles as he walks into the living room. This house that we lived in right now, Jayden had it be built right after our wedding. It's an old styled house, being three stories high but it is marvellous, and so beautiful.

I peck Jayden's lips. "Hi honey" I whisper. He grins and places a hand on my very fat stomach.

"She's growing, look how big she is!" Jayden exclaimed surprised. I'm due to give birth to Jasmine in less than two weeks from now, and honestly I am so excited I can barely sleep at night. "I got us all tickets to go see that new movie that's out at the cinemas" Jayden says grinning from ear to ear.

It's some action movie, but it's not to gruesome for children are allowed to see it. And my little boys have been nonstop begging to see this new movie and they will be thrilled to find out we get to see it on Friday.

You might be thinking, 'but they're only three! How do they know to think all this stuff? How do they speak exceptionally well?' Well being werewolves, our brains develop rather quickly and by the time we are two, we can talk and think as well as a normal ten year old human. Cool I know!

"Jayden did I ever tell you how much I love you?" I question raising an eyebrow. Jayden smiles and kisses the top of my head.

"All the time" he murmurs. Scott walks into the room with a large amount of chocolate in his hands, grinning from ear to ear. He freezes when he sees Jayden staring at him puzzled.

"Uh father... You're home early..." He smiles sheepishly and slowly hides the chocolate behind his back. Jayden raises an eyebrow.

"Is that.. MY chocolate?" He questions stalking his way over to Scott. Scott grins and runs out the room.

"Ahh! He's gonna take my chocolate! Runnnnn!" He yells. But being only the age of three, his running is like shuffling your feet. He doesn't get very far. Jayden picks him up and hoists him over his shoulder. Scott starts screaming and laughing. He takes another bite out of the chocolate and laughs again. Ahh my boys.. I smile at them.

"Put my brother down!" I hear Derek yell and he jumps out in front of them. The boys tackle Jayden but being how small they are, Jayden doesn't even budge. I laugh and sit down on the couch and start to read my newest book. Ah, life is sweet.

"Helloooo, guess who's hear!" Katy's voice rings through the house.

"Max!" Derek's head shoots up as he searches for his best friend.

"Katherine!" Scott shouts excitedly as he repeats Derek's actions. I laugh. Katy walks in with the kids and Tyson trailing behind her. Tyson carrying Max up high in the air.

He places Max down and the four kids run off out side to go play. Jayden and Tyson head outside to go watch them and Katy sits down beside me.

"Soo... Tell me everything" Katy says seriously and then laughs. I laugh too.

"Ok, where do I start?" I ask looking down at the book in my hands. I knew Katy would want me to tell her everything I read.

"From the very beginning" she orders. I laugh

"Ok.. So it all starts with..."

The End! This is the very end of the book! Thank you for reading!

www.ingramcontent.com/pod-product-compliance
Lightning Source LLC
Chambersburg PA
CBHW072013210726
48294CB00011B/515